DANCE WITH THE REAPER

A DCI MICHAEL YORKE THRILLER

WES MARKIN

ABOUT THE AUTHOR

Wes Markin is the bestselling author of the DCI Yorke crime novels set in Salisbury. His latest series, The Yorkshire Murders, stars the compassionate and relentless DCI Emma Gardner. He is also the author of the Jake Pettman thrillers set in New England. Wes lives in Harrogate with his wife and two children, close to the crime scenes in The Yorkshire Murders.

You can find out more at:

www.wesmarkinauthor.com

facebook.com/wesmarkinauthor

BY WES MARKIN

DCI Yorke Thrillers

One Last Prayer

The Repenting Serpent

The Silence of Severance

Rise of the Rays

Dance with the Reaper

Christmas with the Conduit

Better the Devil

A Lesson in Crime

Jake Pettman Thrillers

The Killing Pit

Fire in Bone

Blue Falls

The Rotten Core

Rock and a Hard Place

The Yorkshire Murders

The Viaduct Killings

The Lonely Lake Killings

The Cave Killings

Details of how to claim your **FREE** DCI Michael Yorke quick read, **A lesson in Crime**, can be found at the end of this book.

PRAISE FOR WES MARKIN

"An explosive and visceral debut with the most terrifying of killers. Wes Markin is a new name to watch out for in crime fiction, and I can't wait to see more of DCI Yorke." – **Stephen Booth, Bestselling Crime Author**

"A pool of blood, an abduction, swirling blizzards, a haunting mystery, yes, Wes Markin's One Last Prayer has all the makings of an absorbing thriller. I recommend that you give it a go." – **Alan Gibbons, Bestselling Author**

"Cracking start to an exciting new series. Twist and turns, thrills and kills. I loved it." – **Ross Greenwood, Bestselling Author**

"Markin stuns with his latest offering... Mind-bendingly dark and deep, you know it's not for the faint hearted from page one. Intricate plotting, devious twists and excellent characterisation take this tale to a whole new level. Any serious crime fan will love it!" – **Owen Mullen, Bestselling Author**

Text copyright © 2020 Wes Markin

First published 2020

ISBN: 9798848000528

Imprint: Dark Heart Publishing

Edited by Jay Reaperman Arscott and Katherine Middleton

Cover design by Cherie Foxley

For Ian and Eileen

1976

DOUGLAS FIRTH WATCHED his son's trickery with the football through the living room window. He smiled. Ian was really coming on with the football, and Douglas was glad. Poor lad had no one to practise with while he was away at work. And that was often. The curse of the travelling salesman.

Obviously, Ian's older sister had wanted nothing to do with a man's game.

'One day, it will be a woman's game too,' Jeanette had said, but their stubborn daughter did not believe her. Neither did Douglas for that matter.

While his five-year-old son continued to juggle the ball from foot to foot, Douglas flinched as a cold sliver of air found its way through a fracture in the single-paned glass. He reached out to touch it, taking care not to press too hard in case it should worsen, or cut him. He'd need to replace it as soon as possible. He wished he could afford double-glazing, but he merely sold the product, and didn't earn quite enough to purchase it for himself, even with the discount his employers offered.

Outside, the day darkened as a heavy cloud seized the day. Rain, and a storm that they'd been predicting for days, was about to make its long-awaited arrival. He tapped the window to alert his son, and then cursed out-loud for his thoughtlessness. He'd just worsened the crack.

Ian, distracted by his father beckoning him in, lost control of the ball and it bounced over the shallow garden wall.

Douglas watched the ball roll towards the main road, and watched his son break the rule to never leave the garden.

Yet, there he was. Already out of the gate, and onto the pavement.

Douglas banged the window again. No longer caring about breaking it. As his son ran out onto the road, he shouted his name.

'IAN!'

One second, *he* was there, the tiny person they'd nurtured, the next second there was the loud sound of brakes. Douglas saw a flash of red, heard a terrible sound, and his son vanished.

Douglas felt his daughter take his hand as the Ford Capri shrieked to a halt. There was a trail of blood on the road, and the realisation that Ian was underneath the car broke his world into pieces.

He snatched his hand away from his daughter and put his fist through the glass.

1978

B RADLEY WINKED AT Catherine, lined up the bean bag and attempted to take out the pyramid of tin cans. He clipped the top one. It clattered against the back of the metal stall and disappeared into the darkness. 'Shit!'

Beside him, Catherine laughed. Bradley turned to her. 'You distracted me.'

'How?'

'Your constant flirting.'

She hit him on the shoulder. 'You were the one winking!'

'Come on now, lovebirds,' the stall owner said, holding out the third, and final, beanbag. 'Some of us 'ave got to make a living around 'ere.' He was an elderly man with a chiselled face. 'And take a look be'ind you.'

Bradley turned and saw that the queue had swollen while he'd been fluffing his opening two shots. He turned back, nodded and reached out for the third beanbag. The weather-beaten old man handed it over, sneering. His few remaining teeth were discoloured.

'This one's for the biggest teddy you've got, Captain!'

Bradley looked at his girlfriend with the most heroic expression he could muster.

'They're all the same size, smartarse. Just throw your bloody bean bag before I charge you another twenty pence.'

Bradley took a deep breath. He let the sweet smell of candyfloss give him a boost. He let the thump, thump of the fairground music focus and steady him.

'Okay, let's end this, and get on *Hook a Duck*.' He pulled his hand back and lined up his third shot. He smiled. 'No wink this time, Catherine.'

As Bradley launched the beanbag, there was a loud bang, everything around them shook and the tin cans came crashing down. In dismay, he watched his beanbag sail through the exact spot where the cans had been standing a fraction of a second before.

'What was that?' Catherine said.

'Don't care,' Bradley said, 'I was on target, Captain, so pay up.'

'Kids kicking the back of my stall, I bet,' said the owner, heading to the back of the stall. 'Not the bloody first ... what the fuck?' He moved aside the stand for the cans and pointed at the beanbag that was stuck to the metal wall at the back of the stall.

Behind Bradley and Catherine, the Waltzers were in full flow. The music boomed, and the riders wailed. The young couple couldn't hear what the owner was saying. They didn't need to. The ride's multicoloured lights lit up the back wall of the stall. Blood streaked down the metal from the suspended bean bag.

As the stall owner reached out to touch the bean bag, Catherine moved in closer to Bradley.

Bradley held his breath and, when the owner withdrew his hand sharply as if he'd hurt himself, he flinched.

The owner went through a side door. It was clear he wasn't heading around the back to catch a couple of kids. This was more serious.

Due to the cacophony behind him, Bradley spoke straight into Catherine's ear. 'Stay here.'

'No, I'm coming with you.'

She clearly regretted this decision after they'd raced around the back of the stall to join the owner. Her hand flew to her mouth, and she turned to bury her face in Bradley's chest. Bradley wanted to turn away too, but he managed to keep up the pretence that he could take this obscenity on the chin.

A young man was pinned there. His mouth hung open, and the weapon which had speared him to the metal stall protruded from it.

'A socket bayonet,' the owner said loudly. 'I 'ad one just like it, back in '42. It was for using on the Fritz though. This is fucking blasphemy.'

Bradley held his girlfriend's head to his chest, so she didn't have to see.

The owner pointed at the glinting, metal rectangle emerging from the young man's mouth. 'That's the socket, see? That's where it fixes to your Lee-Enfield.'

Bradley shot the owner a confused look.

'A rifle! The socket also makes it easier to wield if it's not attached. Some psycho rammed this blade down the kid's throat and stuck him to my stall.'

Bradley had heard enough. Still clutching his crying girlfriend, he turned to one side and started to be sick.

'Jesus,' the owner said. 'You know who this is?'

Bradley was spitting out chunks of the hotdog he'd eaten minutes before and was unable to respond.

'It's that bloody lad ... the one in all the papers. He

mowed a poor kid down a few years back. Surely, you remember?'

'No,' Bradley managed to say.

'Yes ... it definitely is the little dickhead who got away with it.'

Bradley wanted to remark that he clearly hadn't gotten away with anything but vomited again instead.

1

THE WAITING ROOM was warmer than last time, and DCI Michael Yorke welcomed it. The weather this month had been particularly ruthless, and anybody who saw fit to crank up the heating was a hero in his books.

He looked at his wife, Patricia. She was engrossed in a newspaper article about the volcanic ash cloud which was currently turning their skies to the colour of mud and ridding their lands of the minuscule amount of sunlight late February usually allowed them.

'Planes are still grounded,' she said.

'Lasted six days last time, didn't it?' Yorke thumbed through a pile of magazines on the table beside him. Gossip magazines. He picked up *Heat* and considered selling his soul to this editor of trash talk to pass the time.

'Yes. Same volcano too. I won't even bother to try and pronounce it.'

'It's a good job we're not rolling in it, or our winter break to Dubai would have been in jeopardy.'

'Yes ... we won't have that problem getting to *Butlins*.'

'Be careful young lady.' Yorke grinned. 'That was the go-to holiday for most of my childhood.'

Patricia smiled and turned the page.

Yorke abandoned the unflattering pictures of celebrities and instead listened to *Sympathy for the Devil* by *The Rolling Stones* on the local radio which was playing through the waiting room speakers.

The song wasn't just a hit with Yorke; the young receptionist was also humming along. He looked up at Yorke with raised eyebrows. Yorke nodded his consent. The receptionist smiled and cranked the volume up a notch.

Yorke slumped back to consider the last couple of months, and how successful they'd been for his adopted son, Ewan.

Before his adoption, the fourteen-year-old boy had been through hell. Both his mother and father had been murdered by the same crazed lunatic who then went on to mutilate him just before Yorke and his team had managed to intervene.

The killer was no more, but that was not closure. Despite Patricia and Yorke offering him a loving home, he'd spiralled into depression and loneliness. Bullying at school had brought things to a head. As a family, they'd acted quickly, and come together to support one another. They'd also sought out private therapy, regardless of the costs. A weekly one-hour session was doing Ewan wonders. He'd also started dating. His girlfriend Lexi was lovely and very studious. She'd been helping Ewan with his maths - his weak spot, which was a huge bonus, Yorke thought, smiling, because it was saving him on obscene one-to-one tuition costs.

Yorke looked at his watch. The one-hour session with the child psychologist was about to come to an end, and then they were off to pick up their one-year-old daughter, Beatrice, from nursery.

Yorke started singing along to the next verse of the song. When Mick Jagger reached the lyrics suggesting that every cop was a criminal, Yorke felt an icy tingle in his bloodstream. He recalled a warning he was given several years earlier by the man who'd murdered his sister ...

Look at your own, pig. There's a bent bastard shitting in the same toilet as you.

'Are you okay?' Patricia rubbed his back. 'You look pale.'

'I'm fine.'

'Is it that overactive brain of yours again? That refusal to ever take a day off?'

Yorke gave her a wry smile. 'Just hungry.'

The door opened and Dr Helen Saunders and Ewan emerged. Both were smiling as if they'd just shared a joke. It was a good sign.

Jagger was bringing the song to a close in the background.

Yorke and Patricia rose to their feet to meet Helen and Ewan as they came across the waiting room. In the background, Yorke noticed that the female presenter on the radio sounded shaky. 'That was *Sympathy for the Devil* by *The Rolling Stones.*'

Yes. Her voice was definitely quaking.

'It was a request ...' the presenter broke off to take a gulp of air. *Was she crying?* 'A request from ...' Again, she broke off.

Ewan and Helen seemed oblivious to the radio presenter's distress and were still striding towards them. Yorke held up the palm of his hand. They stopped, and their smiles fell away.

'It was a request ... a request ... *okay, okay, I'll say it ... it was a request from the man with a gun to the back of my head.'*

Like most of Salisbury's residents, Yorke knew *Radio Exodus* well. It was based at the local hospital. If his fellow officers weren't already listening at the local police station, then their hotline would certainly be in meltdown from tuned-in anxious residents. Still, it was best to double check, so he delved into his inside pocket for his phone. He swore when he saw that his phone had no reception.

'The signal is bad in here.' The receptionist was now on his feet, pointing down at the phone on his desk. 'Do you want me to—'

The presenter had started to speak again, so Yorke silenced him with the palm of his hand.

'He has a question,' the presenter said. 'The man behind me ... the man with the gun ... he has a question.'

Yorke looked at Patricia. His wife was renowned for having the constitution of an ox; right now, she was ashen faced. He gripped her hand.

'He would like a listener to phone in the name of his favourite song. If they get it right, then ... then ...' Yorke flinched as she cried. 'Then ... I can live.'

'Jesus,' Yorke said.

'But he's only allowing twenty seconds for someone to phone ... please *somebody ... anybody.'*

'It's ridiculous,' Helen said, who'd enveloped Ewan and pulled him in close. 'What sort of question is that?'

Yorke nodded at the receptionist, who then picked up the phone and started dialling for the police.

The presenter said, 'Before he starts the timer, he wants to help ... he has a clue ... his favourite song is from the seventies. It is a song about the ...' She broke off again, spluttering on her tears. 'About the inevitability of death and ...' She groaned. '*Okay, okay, stop, stop! That hurts!* It's about the inevitability of death and the foolishness of fearing it. Please, I have twenty seconds, please help.'

Yorke felt the blood rush around his body. '*I know this, I bloody know this.*' He pointed at the receptionist. 'Look online for the number for Radio Exodus.'

Keeping the phone pressed to his ear, the receptionist looked stunned, and wasn't moving for the keyboard. Yorke read his name badge. 'Listen carefully Terry, *forget* the police. They'll *know.*' *Most of Salisbury will bloody know by now.* 'Just get the number for Radio Exodus – we can still help her.'

Terry heard Yorke, snapped out of it, parked the phone and typed on the keyboard.

'Yes, that's right.' Yorke could feel his every nerve-ending burn.

'*Please, I've ten seconds!*' The presenter said something else too, but it was muffled by her desperate tears.

Terry picked up the phone and dialled the number. Yorke counted down in his head. He gripped the side of the reception desk, feeling his heart threatening to burst from his chest.

Terry's eyes gave him the bad news before he had chance to tell him.

'On hold?' Yorke said.

Terry nodded.

Yorke smashed the palms of his hands into the reception desk. 'Shit, shit, SHIT!'

'*We have a caller!*' The presenter cried.

Yorke looked up at the speaker above the reception area. 'Thank God.'

'Nigel ... Nigel Hawkins ... hello ... *please give me the right answer.*'

Yorke took a deep breath. It was going to be alright. The correct answer was *Don't Fear the Reaper* by *The Blue Oyster Cult,* and Nigel was just about to unleash it.

'I hope this isn't real, Janice,' Nigel sounded distressed. *Who wouldn't be?* 'I hope it's some kind of joke ... the answer is ...'

Go on, save her life. For God's sake, save her life.

'... *Dancing with Mr D* by *the Rolling Stones.*'

There was a muffled thwap and a thud.

'Janice?' Nigel said. 'Janice?'

His question was answered with the steady hum of static.

'Are you okay?'

No, she's not ... you idiot. You just gave the wrong fucking answer.

Yorke felt his wife's hands on his shoulder. It was only when he opened his eyes, and looked up at her sad face, did he realise that he'd fallen to his knees.

2

WITH THE VOLCANIC ash cloud hanging heavy and low, there wasn't a moon and there certainly weren't any stars.

At the front of the hospital, the press were being fenced off. This had taken a police presence on an unprecedented level. There had been no keeping this one quiet. The murder had been broadcast for the world to hear – literally. Radio Exodus may have been local, but the web ensured it could be picked up in other countries. It would be hitting the international news in next to no time.

Martin Price, Public Relations Officer, and his team were among the media. Price was holding a large coffee from *Costa* as he attempted to calm the hordes. That would be the first of many caffeinated drinks. He'd a long night ahead of him fending off these vultures.

Yorke slowed his vehicle and flashed his ID out of the window at a police officer. The officer moved some cones and allowed Yorke to drive through into the hospital grounds. Yorke then followed the directions he'd been given from HQ.

The radio studio was tucked away around the back of the maternity ward. Its private carpark didn't accommodate many. It didn't need to. It was off-the-beaten track and little known. Yorke took the last space right beside the black major incident van.

Outside, a single, flickering bulb was the only source of lighting. Yorke also clocked that the CCTV camera was like something from the dark ages. *Getting in here undetected must have been the easiest thing in the world for the killer,* Yorke thought.

PC Sean Tyler was shielding the police incident tape which, in turn, shielded the crime scene. He already had his hand in the air to welcome him. He hopped from leg to leg as he scribbled Yorke's name in the logbook. He could have been cold, shaken up by events, or possibly both. He held out a sealed bag. *'Don't Fear the Reaper.* I knew the *bloody* answer to that question, sir. I was just too late.'

'Join the club, Sean.' Yorke took the over-suit and shoes.

'Bloody Nigel Hawkins. He beat us all to it. Too fast on the draw.'

Yorke ran his thumb and forefinger over his beard which was getting more unruly of late. 'A pub landlord too. The amount of quizzes he's hosted, and he couldn't get an obvious question right.'

'Strange though, isn't it?'

'Go on.' Yorke tore open the sealed bag and slipped on his over-suit.

'Well, if I'd have asked that question, I'd have *expected* the caller to get the question right. For him to get it wrong must have been quite a surprise ... yet, the killer sounded like he pulled the trigger without a second's thought.'

After Yorke slipped on the overshoes, he climbed over the blue-and-yellow tape and put a hand on Tyler's shoulder. 'Exactly right, Sean. He was *always* going to kill her. He was playing.'

'So, we shouldn't feel too bad about being too slow on the draw?'

'No, Sean, we need to feel *very* bad about it.' He squeezed his shoulder. 'And the worse we feel, the more likely we are to show this fool that he's chosen to play with the wrong people.'

Yorke entered the studio, patting his over-suit to check that his jacket underneath was zipped all the way up. As a university student, he'd discovered one of his best friends murdered. That day, he'd felt a cold start up in his neck, before spreading, relentlessly, all over his chest and torso. It'd felt like the talons of some demonic entity reaching around inside the trunk of his body. From that day forth, irrational as it seemed, he'd lived in fear of it happening again, and so always ensured that the base of his neck was hidden away when death was involved.

Additionally, with every crime scene, came a reawakening of Yorke's addiction to cigarettes. He could go months without a craving, but the presence of murder caused it to flare. He'd have to be extra disciplined today. His long-term colleague, DI Emma Gardner, was no longer with them, and it was her fierce stare that was always the main deterrent to a relapse.

Not that she didn't have her own vices. He smiled when he recalled her addiction to Tic Tacs. She couldn't go minutes without a crunch, especially when her stress levels were high. His smile quickly fell away. Without her here with him, he suddenly felt lonelier than ever.

The hospital hadn't been able to offer much space to the studio. If they were charging rent, Yorke hoped it was cheap; although in this age of austerity, he doubted it was.

Feeling the pinch, people were grabbing what they could while growing grumpier by the day. The white-suited Scenes of Crime Officers were hard at work in a narrow corridor. One knelt beside an open toilet door dusting the handle for prints. Another was inspecting the worn carpet, which was peeling away from the grippers at the edges. Slipping past the SOCOs in the corridor was difficult work. He received irritated stares, although he quickly wrote these off to his own paranoia. Without Gardner, he was feeling unusually vulnerable.

He bypassed a poky kitchen, where another couple of SOCOs appeared like they were engaged in a game of *Twister* to collect evidence. Then, he turned into the actual studio.

He'd never been into a radio studio before, but it was similar to how he'd envisioned it. Foam on the walls to soundproof. Two large desks separated by a glass partition. A mountain of mixing equipment, and a computer on the presenter's side. There were also trademark large microphones with bulbous foam heads.

However, it wasn't exactly the same as his vision. For starters, in his version, there hadn't been a young lady face down, dead in a pool of her own blood. Neither had there been a cameraman snapping close-up photographs of her ruined head.

Yorke recalled the muffled thwap, the thud, and the sound of static.

Lance Reynolds, Scientific Support Officer, looked less spritely than usual. He usually danced around his victim with the camera and had earned the nickname 'The Elf' as a result. Today, he seemed rather lethargic, ponderous even. It could have been the lack of space in the studio, but Yorke suspected that it was the event earlier which had him spooked. 'You were listening, weren't you?'

Reynolds nodded. 'He shot her in the back of the head.'

He was stating the obvious, but Yorke nodded his gratitude for the information. 'I didn't hear a gunshot on the radio show. Did he use a silencer?'

'Unfortunately, there're never any tell-tale signs of that on a gunshot wound, and it's unlikely ballistics will recover any markings on the bullet unless he used a homemade suppressor or a very old-fashioned one.'

'He executed her with a silencer,' Superintendent Joan Madden said from behind Yorke. 'That's how this man works. He's experienced and he's efficient.'

Yorke turned around. 'I agree. You don't play games like this unless you're confident.'

Madden was a firm woman with a firm figure. She sneered in the face of Body Mass Index recommendations and had opted to remove all traces of body fat by exercising in every available moment of her limited free time. She'd no family, and Yorke very much doubted that she'd any friends to socialise with.

'DCI Yorke, you look dishevelled,' Madden said.

Lost for words, Yorke's hand instinctively flew to his unruly beard again.

'Is this what being the father of a young child does to you? Press are in abundance over this one as I'm sure you've noticed. I need my SIO with his best face on.'

'I'll shave back at HQ before I meet my team.'

'Good. Where's Dr Wileman?'

'She had to go and pick up our daughter from nursery. We've another pathologist heading here from Southampton.'

Madden nodded, but looked disappointed. 'Always a shame when the best can't make it.'

She walked away from Yorke to talk to Reynolds.

Collette Willows stepped up to join him. She'd recently made the step up to Detective Sergeant. Deservedly so. She was a magnet for facts and information. Yes, she sometimes lacked emotional intelligence, but she was straight to the point and Yorke valued that in a team member.

Yorke also appreciated a familiar face in a world from which his closest colleagues seemed to be disappearing of late.

She flipped open a notebook. 'Sir. Vic's name is Janice Edwards. She's thirty-two years old and was born, and raised, in Salisbury. I feel for her on that one. She's been presenting on Radio Exodus once a week for the past two years. Her show is the most popular on this station, probably because it caters for the dusty middle-aged who want to relive their youth with nineties' indie classics.'

Yorke raised an eyebrow. 'Dusty?'

'Yep. Although she interviews authors which does suggest some sophistication in her audience.'

'Ah that's good.' Yorke offered a sardonic smile.

'And she had a guest tonight too,' Exhibits Officer Andrew Waites said from the side of the room. He held up a plastic bag. Inside was a blood-stained book. 'Matthew Peacock, Crime Writer. Writes about a detective called Phyllis Kemp. I'm a big fan actually. There's not a lot of violence in them, and they're more light-hearted than your average crime book. Gives me a break after all the shit *we* have to sieve through.'

'Cosy mysteries,' DC Lorraine Pemberton said. 'My partner loves them too. Keeps me up all night with her bloody reading light.'

Yorke was a fan of Pemberton. She'd emigrated down from Yorkshire and brought her deadpan humour with her.

'The bullet wound sprayed the book with blood,' Reynolds said. 'The killer then transferred her hand to the book post-mortem. We know this because the blood has transferred to her palm, and there is no blood spray on the back of her hand.'

'Matthew Peacock was a guest on this station at five o'clock,' Willows said. 'I've already arranged for someone to pick him up.'

'Good work, Collette,' Yorke said. 'CCTV?'

'Have you seen the camera, sir?' Pemberton said. 'Without someone cranking its handle, I doubt it was filming.'

Yorke smiled, but Willows didn't. 'Hospital security should be phoning us back at any moment.'

There was a series of flashes from Reynolds' camera and a sucking sound. Yorke looked over, squinting. A SOCO had lifted Janice's head slightly from the pool of blood. Her eyes were half-closed, and her mouth sloped at an unusual angle. There didn't seem to be an exit wound on her forehead.

The bullet from the killer's gun slept in her brain.

'Come over here, DCI Yorke,' Madden said.

'Yes, ma'am.'

Yorke stood alongside Madden and she pointed down at a SOCO crouched down underneath the table. 'Show me again what you just found, young man.'

With his gloved hand, the SOCO held up a sweet wrapper pinned between his tweezers. He dropped it into a plastic evidence bag. Reynolds knelt and took a photo of the floor before the SOCO swept up another wrapper.

Reynolds turned his head to look up at Yorke and Madden. He was smiling. '*Chewits*. I used to love *Chewits*.'

'How many wrappers?' Yorke said.

'Five,' the SOCO said.

'The victim's?' Reynolds said.

'Possibly. Probably.' Waites said, approaching them to collect the evidence.

'They could have been dropped *today* though. This place is probably cleaned daily. We can get confirmation on that,' Yorke said.

'So either Janice Edwards, or her killer, had a *Chewit* fetish,' Pemberton said. 'Good job it's not a chocolate fetish as that'd put me firmly in the frame.'

Willows raised an eyebrow. 'It'd put a huge amount of people in the frame. There'd be no statistical significance.'

Pemberton raised an eyebrow back at her.

Willows' phone rang. She answered it and offered it up to Yorke. He was given the details regarding the CCTV. He requested that the recordings be submitted to Wiltshire Police HQ, provided the details and hung up.

'CCTV footage is clear they reckon,' Yorke said. 'I remain dubious, but we will know soon enough when we watch it at HQ. Janice's writer guest, Matthew Peacock, left at 5:45 pm, and our killer, assuming it's our killer, arrived at 5:55 pm. I'm going to *assume* it's our killer though because he was wearing a balaclava. He arrived in a BMW. I've got the reg, but I'm betting any money that it's a fake plate. Not sure that our efficient killer will be making rookie errors like that. The killer left at 6:02 pm. Two minutes after the murder.'

'She still had an hour of airtime left,' Willows said. 'If her death hadn't been broadcast, she wouldn't have been discovered until 7pm when the next DJ, Ralph Simmonds, arrived for his shift. So, why did this madman bother to do it over the airwaves? He could've been far more covert. Gained himself more of a head start. What does he gain from a public execution?'

'Nothing to gain, but everything to enjoy,' Madden said.

Yorke nodded. 'His favourite song is *Don't Fear The Reaper*, remember? He wanted it known. It may've irritated the killer that Nigel Hawkins got that wrong, but he was going to execute this young woman regardless.'

Reynolds said, 'So the purpose of this whole charade was just to tell us the name of his favourite song?'

'And *potentially* what his favourite sweet was,' Pemberton said, pointing at the bag containing the *Chewit* wrappers.

'No,' Yorke said. 'The purpose of the whole charade was to tell us that *he's* the Reaper.'

3

OPERATION TAGLINE.

Yorke wasted no time in writing the randomly generated name at the top of the whiteboard in the assigned incident room at Wiltshire HQ. Tomorrow morning it would be full of core and non-core members but for now it was just his and all was still.

Rubbing his now-shaven cheeks, he looked out over the empty tables and chairs and recalled fevered moments in this place; times full of urgency, desperation and all too regularly, panic.

If anyone had asked him his state of mind during those chaotic moments, he'd have told them that he was in hell. If anyone asked him right now about those moments, he'd tell them that he'd loved every second of it.

And he genuinely had.

Yorke sighed. Even his recent promotion back to DCI had done little to ease the melancholy that was weighing him down of late.

He imagined DI Emma Gardner in one chair, crunching on Tic Tacs, admonishing him for not visiting his goddaughter, Anabelle, in over a month. On another chair, he saw DI Mark Topham using a compact mirror to check his expensive haircut was in order before briefing started. Patrolling the back wall was brooding DI Iain Brookes considering how best to frustrate his seniors and their meaningless orders.

Yorke looked at the empty chairs one by one.

He wandered over to the window and looked outside. He could see DS Jake Pettman in the carpark developing a nicotine addiction. Being thrown out of the family home had a nasty habit of causing that in some people. Jake was his best friend, or at least *had* been his best friend for many years. And was, right now, another reason that Yorke was feeling lonely. Since Jake's separation, which was almost certainly going to end in divorce, they'd grown apart. This wasn't Yorke's decision. He'd been trying. He really had. But Jake was starting to while away his time with characters that Yorke considered unsavoury. Most notably, the one he was currently smoking with.

DS Luke Parkinson.

In terms of policemen, Parkinson was as oppositional as they came. To have him in your incident room was akin to having a jagged stone in one of your running shoes during a marathon. However, he was highly thought of by Superintendent Joan Madden, and had over twenty years of experience on the job, so to moan about him brought more trouble than it was worth. Yorke had a history of conflict with Parkinson. On the night Yorke faced down his sister's murderer, William Proud, Parkinson took great pleasure in being part of the team that arrested Yorke, before taking even greater pleasure in his eventual demotion. And there was the big lug, Jake, his one-time best friend and former reliable colleague, cosying up with him.

The door opened and Willows came in. As usual, she skipped her greeting. She struggled with niceties. 'Our Cosy Mystery writer, Matthew Peacock, is talking to Pemberton and Tom in the interview room. And I got the intel on the victim.'

She ran through a potted history of Janice Edwards. 'It was only a year after Janice's father died that her mother emigrated to Greece to shack up with someone younger than her daughter. Did she have no shame? Janice's only employment up until two years ago was freelance cleaning. Not sure it was paying the bills because she ended up going to live in her uncle's house. Herbert Wheelhouse. Life got a bit brighter for her at that point, and she ended up taking a few courses, so she could pursue her ambition to be a radio broadcaster. She knocked the cleaning on the head.'

'Surely, once a week on the radio wasn't paying the bills?'

'No. Deciding to live with her uncle had been a masterstroke. He's loaded.'

'What does he do?'

'Did do.'

'Dead?'

'Not exactly. This is where it's going to get very interesting.'

'For someone who loves to get to the point regardless of the audience, you certainly revel in keeping me in suspense.'

'He's in prison.'

'What for?'

'Organised crime. He worked for the Youngs.'

Those familiar feelings he felt in an incident room - urgency, desperation and panic – suddenly came flooding back.

HMP Hancock was a large nineteenth-century building, and its decaying appearance was a perfect example of how austerity was hitting public services hard. It was a Category B prison, so prisoners did not need to be held in the highest security conditions. On appearance alone, that certainly looked the case; the average con could probably kick their way through those crumbling walls if they really wanted to.

Yorke preferred a good, old-fashioned Category A prison. Regardless of the nature of the crime, if someone had been deemed as a threat to the public, escape should *always* be impossible.

To have killers such as Christian Severance, and Lacey Ray, two serial killers Yorke and his team had caught, incarcerated in such a solid facility, eased Yorke's mind. To have people such as Herbert Wheelhouse imprisoned in this cost-cutting system didn't.

'Wheelhouse used to be in a Category A,' Yorke said while the prison gate opened for him. 'But I guess when you reach the grand old age of seventy, you become less of a risk.'

'Anyone who is capable of doing what *he* did will never be less of a risk,' Jake said.

Yorke nodded as he drove through the gate.

Back at HQ, Yorke had made a spur-of-the-moment decision to take Jake along with him and had grabbed him after that crafty cigarette with Luke Parkinson. Their relationship had been struggling for months but here was Yorke's olive branch. 'I want you on the team, Jake.'

Jake had jumped at the offer. He'd even smiled for the first time in God-knows-how-long. Yorke had felt momentarily euphoric and had even told him that he'd missed him.

But it'd not taken long for the reunion to sour.

Yorke's problems with Jake had begun when Jake had started an affair. Feeling responsible for Jake, like an older brother perhaps, Yorke had badgered Jake into ending it. Resentment toward Yorke and his incessant need to steer him in the right direction had grown. After Jake's new girlfriend had been murdered, and his wife, Sheila, had thrown him out of the house, Jake had turned his back on Yorke.

Immediately, in the car, these same problems resurfaced.

'Luke Parkinson?'

'What about him?'

'You know what he's like.'

'And what's he like then?'

'A pain in the arse. Untrustworthy. Caustic.'

'And? So?'

'Why're you knocking around with him?'

'A couple of fags in the carpark is hardly knocking around with someone!'

'It's been more than that, Jake. I've seen you two together around HQ on a number of occasions.'

'Good for you.'

The rest of the journey had passed in silence.

In the prison reception, they showed their IDs before being searched and led into a dingy, windowless room that stank of cigarettes. They were left alone. Still struggling to communicate, Jake and Yorke sat on stools that were fixed to the ground.

'How's the new place?' Yorke said.

'Fucking fantastic,' his best friend said.

Yorke drummed his fingers on the table.

Shit. It was in times like this that Yorke really, really missed his other best friend, Emma Gardner.

As they entered the interview suite together, DS Collette Willows did a quick calculation in her head of how long it had been since she'd last exchanged pleasantries with DC Lorraine Pemberton.

Five days.

Technically only four days if you crossed out the *actual* evening on which they'd kissed.

'Mr Peacock, why this jumper?' Willows pointed at his green jumper on which was a picture of a drunk Father Christmas throwing back ale.

'It's cold?' Peacock shrugged.

'An eccentric writer, Mr Peacock?' Pemberton smiled.

'No, just cold, as I said, and it's the only jumper I have. Welcome to the struggling lifestyle of a full-time author.'

Willows was proud that she'd managed to hold back on recommending a charity shop. On Yorke's advice, she was trying to think a lot more before blurting things out.

'I understand why I'm here,' Peacock said, 'I'm a crime writer, and there's been a crime.'

'It's not about your profession,' Willows said. 'It's about the fact that you were the last person to see Janice Edwards alive.'

'True, but there really isn't much to tell you, detective. I hardly knew Janice. She sent me an email a couple of months ago asking me to come on to the show.'

'Do you still have this email?' Pemberton said.

'Yes. I'll forward it to you.'

'How long was your guest slot?' Willows asked.

'Thirty minutes. I arrived early at about quarter to five.'

'And how'd Janice seem?'

'Fine. I guess. Polite, enthusiastic, gracious. All the things that you'd expect in a host really. She talked about how much she enjoyed *Phyllis Kemp*, gave me a cup of tea, and before I knew it, we were on air.'

'*Phyllis Kemp?*' Willows said.

'Mr Peacock's series. Think *Murder She Wrote,*' Pemberton said.

Stunned that Pemberton had spoken to her, and without an aggressive tone in her voice, Willows looked at her. Pemberton didn't look back.

Well ... baby steps.

'I don't really like that comparison,' Peacock said. 'For a start, my books are set in the UK, and Phyllis is much more reserved than Jessica Fletcher.'

'Ah, okay,' Pemberton said.

Willows watched her colleague pretending to take notes.

She's so sarcastic, Willows thought, looking back at Peacock. *Does he pick up on it? Am I starting to know her better than anyone?*

'So, the interview?' Willows said.

'Intense. Think your hardest job interview and then multiply it by infinity. Over the course of the interview, she only played one song, the rest of the time was me, and some bloody difficult questions.'

'What song was it?' Pemberton asked.

'It was one I'd chosen prior to the show. My favourite.'

'Jingle Bells?'

'Funny, detective!'

Pemberton and Peacock exchanged smiles. He'd taken it

in good humour; Pemberton seemed pretty adept at reading her audience. A skill Willows knew she didn't possess.

'It was a Radiohead song. *The Bends.*'

'You didn't strike me as the melancholic type.'

Peacock smiled again. 'It's the lyrics I like more than anything. Not a fan?'

'A big one actually.'

Were they flirting? Willows thought and then coughed to interrupt them. 'What questions did she ask you?'

'Many. There'll be a podcast ... you know ... at least, she said there'd be.' He paused. Willows watched him grow paler as some of the reality settled in. 'I guess you can still get the recording?'

'Already have done,' Willows said. 'And we will listen to it later.'

'You know, there was one question she asked which really threw me.'

'Go on,' Pemberton said.

'She asked me about a homosexual relationship in my book between two male officers. She spoke of one scene and its realism, and being that I was in a heterosexual marriage, she wondered how I'd so effectively captured the tenderness between them.'

Willows glanced at Pemberton again. This time, Pemberton *was* looking back, but she quickly turned away again.

'And what did you say,' Pemberton said.

'I just rambled on about how I'd asked a friend for some help, but now, in retrospect, I'd answer it differently. At the end of the day, what's the difference between a heterosexual relationship and a homosexual one? Surely, they're the same thing? Tenderness is born from two people regardless of gender or sexual orientation.'

Willows steered the conversation back to where it needed to be. 'And you noticed nothing about Janice which suggested she could be in danger? Was she perhaps nervous or anxious?'

'No. She was the perfect host.'

'And when the interview finished?'

'We took a couple of photos of me holding my latest book behind the mixing desk for her website ... I presented her with a signed copy ... we briefly chatted about doing another show when the next Phyllis book was out at the end of the year ... and then I was off ... ah ... hold on ...' He pulled out his mobile phone, fiddled with it, and pushed it over to Willows. 'I left at 5:44, you can see that I texted my wife to say I was on my way home. She wrote back to ask me to drive carefully because of the poor visibility. That ash cloud is relentless, isn't it?'

Willows nodded as she wrote the notes in her book. 'The CCTV camera told us the same thing, Mr Peacock.'

'So you'll have the assailant who shot her on CCTV?'

Willows looked up and saw the excitement in his eyes. *Crime writers*, she thought. *This is the real thing, you know! Nothing to get giddy about.*

'As a crime writer, you'll know we cannot discuss that with you, Mr Peacock,' Pemberton said.

He smiled. 'I really wish I could tell you more, detective. You have my DNA, fingerprints and I've nothing to hide. I don't think I'm a suspect, am I?'

Willows thought about mentioning his blood-spattered book clutched in Janice's hand, but decided against it. Pointless. He wasn't a suspect, and they'd already concluded that the killer had placed her hand on the book, post-mortem.

'One last question,' Willows said. 'Did you notice Janice eating anything?'

'Not that I recall. What exactly?'

'Sweets?'

Peacock shook his head.

'Did she offer you anything?'

'No, sorry.'

Willows made some notes and said, 'I'm sure you know the drill, Mr Peacock. Phone on you always and don't leave the area. We could be in touch at any point.'

'You can count on me.'

Willows chanced another look at Pemberton.

This time, nothing came back.

4

IT WAS A cold room. Dangerously so. How many lives a year were lost in HMP Hancock due to persistent underfunding?

Yorke didn't want the answer to that question.

The aging guard, who'd signed them both in, came into the visitor's room. He was accompanied by another elderly man. Jake, who had been leaning on the table, sitting upright on his stool. Yorke chose to rise to his feet. 'Good evening, Mr Wheelhouse. My name is DCI Yorke, and this is DS Pettman.'

The guard, a miserable man who was clearly desperate for retirement, rubbed his hands together. 'It's frigging cold in here. I'll rustle up a couple of hot drinks? Keep an eye on him though, would you?'

I get this isn't a high security facility, but isn't that just incompetence? Yorke thought.

'Tea, one sugar, please,' Jake said. 'And DCI Yorke will take a black coffee, no sugar.'

'Five minutes,' the guard said.

Stunned over Jake's encouragement of incompetence,

Yorke failed to stop the guard before he'd abandoned his charge and disappeared out of the door.

Yorke decided to make the elderly guard's wish for early retirement a reality by speaking to his superiors later, but for now, he had more pressing issues.

'Sit down please, Mr Wheelhouse.' Yorke gestured at the stool opposite both himself and Jake.

Wheelhouse moved slowly. His shoulders were hunched.

'And I'm sorry for your loss,' Yorke said.

Wheelhouse didn't respond as he lowered himself down on the stool. He kept his eyes down and was yet to make eye contact with either detective.

He was dressed in jeans, and a stripy jumper. These were his own clothes. This was getting more and more common in prisons such as these. Yorke didn't really know what to make of it. The fact that the guards were still forced to wear uniforms seemed to make it even more peculiar.

Finally, Wheelhouse ran both of his hands through his thinning white hair and lifted his eyes to the visitors. 'I'm much too old to be dealing with this kind of loss.'

Yorke could feel Jake squirming on the stool beside him. He'd be incensed by this man's self-pity. He'd been mixed up in crimes involving children.

Yorke shifted it on quickly. 'You were close then, Mr Wheelhouse?'

Wheelhouse nodded.

'Could you tell us a more about your relationship?'

'Not much to say really. She never really had anyone. Her father was never on the scene, and my parents died young. There was only me who gave a shit.'

'Her mother, Bridgett?'

Wheelhouse snorted. 'My sister? Don't go there. Don't

make an old man waste the final throes of his life dwelling on that stupid cow.'

'Doesn't sound like it ended well,' Jake said.

'We know Bridgett emigrated to Greece,' Yorke said. 'She's been contacted regarding her daughter's death, but I've yet to learn of her response. I assume she'll be back in the country shortly.'

'Don't count on it!' Wheelhouse snorted again.

'When was the last time you saw Janice?' Jake said.

'Last Friday. I saw her every Friday. We'd have a full hour together. It was the best hour of my week, and I'm sure it ranked pretty highly for her too.'

'Even considering your past crimes?' Jake said.

Yorke glanced at his colleague. *Not yet. You're charging in.*

'Even considering.'

Yorke had never seen Wheelhouse before, but he doubted that he usually looked this washed out. Grief was physically weighing on him. In a way, Yorke was glad. It meant that Jake would struggle to get a rise out of him, and they'd be able to unpick the man's value in this investigation in a more productive manner.

Yorke took his notebook out. 'A couple of things I'm interested in, Mr Wheelhouse, before I discuss more … sensitive issues. When looking at Janice's history, I noticed that she worked as a cleaner for many years. I also learned that she went into care when her mother abandoned her at fifteen. Why'd you allow her to struggle? You've not been short of money for many years, and certainly not in her lifetime.'

'Her mother's parting gift was to blacken my name. Janice chose to go into the system rather than come to me. Broke my heart at the time.'

'Blacken your name? *Come on!*' Jake said. 'I'm assuming the picture your sister painted was accurate?'

'Some of it, not *all* of it.'

'So, do you think if she'd only been privy to the actual *truth*, she'd have chosen you over the system?' Jake said.

'Probably not,' Wheelhouse said. 'Listen, I thought the world of that little girl. I never had my own children. She was, and still is, everything to me. I wrote to her from jail and told her I'd changed. Finally, she accepted me back into her life, and then accepted my financial support.'

'Your blood money?' Jake said.

Yorke coughed. 'Thank you DS Pettman. We appreciate everything you're telling us, Mr Wheelhouse. So, you financially supported her, allowed her to stay in your flat, which has been standing empty during your years in incarceration, and as a result, she has been able to pursue her ambition of being a radio presenter.'

'And a good one too! I listened to every show for two years.'

'Did you listen today?'

'Of course.' He stared at Yorke with a broken expression. 'I heard everything.'

Despite everything that this man had done, Yorke wanted to reach out and take his shoulder. He held back.

'Why do you think this has happened? Is there anything you can tell us? Who'd want to hurt her? Can you give us names of anyone she knew? Anyone she had problems with?'

Wheelhouse raised his eyebrows. 'I don't understand. I thought you already knew.'

'Knew what?'

'I assumed that was why you were here—'

'You're not making any sense,' Jake said. 'Get to the point.'

'She was killed because of me. I expected you lot here this evening for that very reason.'

'Come again,' Jake said.

'She was killed because of me.'

Yorke leaned forward on his stool. 'Okay, what makes you say that?'

'Because of the message I was sent by the killer.'

'Message? What message? Where is it?' Jake said.

'The message on the radio. His favourite song. Yes, the caller got it wrong, but that was all irrelevant. What is relevant is that *Don't Fear the Reaper* is *my* favourite song. The message came from *them*. The bastards I left behind. The bastards who won't let me retire.'

Yorke leaned back. *The notorious Young family were behind the death of Janice Edwards.*

FOLLOWING their interview with Matthew Peacock, Pemberton and Willows had filled pages with notes on *Young Properties*. This had been no easy task set by Yorke. This organised unit had their grubby paws on everything but were adept at keeping themselves insulated from any blowback. On paper, the Young family were dealers in real estate; whereas, according to the criminals who broke under police pressure, they were connected to prostitution, drug running, pornography, snuff movies and human trafficking. But every court case fell apart. The Youngs were so far removed from the people who were caught that any lawyer worth his salt could break the chain of connection. It was like holding a tattered old five-pound note in your hand and then trying to to track back to the very first person who spent it.

Even the murder of the CEO Simon Young at DS Jake Pettman's house last year had done little to chip away at this racket. His lawyers simply said that Young had found the whereabouts of his kidnapped child, Tobias, and had done what any father would've done. He'd gone to get him back. Sure, him and his closest colleague, David Hewitt, had been armed, but that didn't make them gangsters, did it? They'd just feared for their lives, and the lives of the young boy, from the fearsome Lacey Ray, and so had acquired guns illegally. Nobody else in the Young family had been aware of these events. Besides, both Young and Hewitt had been killed by Lacey Ray, leaving the remaining above-board Youngs to continue with the family business and pay high taxes in order to make Southampton a better place.

It was still frosty between Pemberton and Willows, but hot work like this was causing a much-needed thaw, and they were now communicating. At least on a professional level.

Pemberton put the phone down and laughed. 'Contacting Southampton over these past cases is certainly ruffling a few feathers. That one detective just spoke to me like my father did the time I borrowed his car after failing my driving test.'

'*You did what?*' Willows said.

'Don't worry. I wasn't caught. I guess that if I was, I wouldn't be sitting here now, would I? I was *so* pissed off that day. I spent a chunk of my driving exam in a traffic jam, and the examiner took offense at my language. Pretty sure everyone swears in a traffic jam. I could drive, and so the fail was bollocks.' Pemberton smiled. 'I shouldn't really be telling you this, should I?'

'That you've committed a crime? What do you reckon?'

Pemberton bit her bottom lip. 'Yes. Let's move on, shall we?'

'Good idea,' Willows said, and smiled.

And just like that, the tension finished melting.

At least *between them*. It only took twenty minutes for tension to rear its ugly head again, albeit for a whole different reason. 'My God, I don't believe it,' Willows said.

'Whenever you say that, something bad quickly follows.' Pemberton moved quickly over to Willows' desk.

Willows pointed at a picture of an elderly man on the screen. 'Douglas Firth.'

'Okay ... who is he?'

'Another old-timer that spent many years working in organised crime.'

'And?'

'Well, he's currently housed in HMP Hancock with Wheelhouse.'

'Is that such a problem?'

'Well, yes, after you see who he's related to ...'

'Go on ... who?'

'You might want to sit down for this.'

IT SEEMED Yorke had it figured out all wrong. The killer didn't want to be thought of as the Reaper. He'd been sending a message to Herbert Wheelhouse about the cost of betrayal.

Not that the nickname didn't fit. The grim animal had brought death to Janice Edwards. Not with a scythe, but with the same swiftness, and lack of emotion, as the original hooded monster.

The guard, who had earlier shown a complete disregard for security, was now sitting beside the door, nursing the hot drink he'd so desperately wanted. Jake drank his, but Yorke abstained. The only way he was picking his up was to throw it over the incompetent person who'd put it there.

Wheelhouse was avoiding Yorke's eyes. He was also squeezing his forehead so tightly that the already deeply furrowed skin threatened to split. Men from these kinds of occupations were masters at keeping emotion behind closed doors, but the death of the niece he so adored was threatening to smash down the shutters.

'How much did you steal from your employers?' Yorke said and stared.

Eventually, Wheelhouse relented and looked up. 'Technically, it wasn't stealing. I just took my retirement.'

'A retirement fund?' Jake said. 'Are you in the *Teamsters?*'

Wheelhouse managed a smile. 'No, it's very different. The Youngs don't allow retirement, and they certainly don't give out pensions.'

Yorke leaned forward. 'How much was it?'

'A couple of hundred grand skimmed over several years.'

'Where is it?'

'Gone. Every penny.'

Jake shook his head. 'Some retirement fund! What if you live to be ninety?'

'Unlikely. Short life span in my job.'

'And the chickens always come home to roost, don't they?' Jake said.

'When did they first approach you to ask for this money back?' Yorke said.

'They didn't.'

'Really? Not even a word of warning?'

'Janice was the word of warning.' Wheelhouse ran a hand through grey tufts of hair.

The Youngs were organised and efficient, but that didn't stop them being barbarians. Yorke knew a reasonable amount about this organisation. More than he cared to. Their previous leader had been killed in Jake's house last year by Lacey Ray. He looked over at Jake. He did look noticeably paler at this stage in the conversation.

Wheelhouse picked up his polystyrene cup. 'They'll kill my sister next, but the jokes on them with that one! I really couldn't care less if they did.'

Yorke made a note of this in his book. If she wasn't coming back to the UK, he would have to contact the embassy in Greece and get her some protection. 'How long ago did you steal this money?'

'Before I went to jail. Eight years ago.'

Jake snorted. 'And the Youngs have only just found out about it now?'

Wheelhouse nodded.

'Any ideas how?' Yorke said.

'I bet it was one of the younger lads I used to work with. For years, I gave them boys a cut of the skim. Caught red-handed I reckon, and had the truth tortured out of them. The Youngs are particularly good with torture. Anyone would have squealed. They'd have blamed me until they were blue in the face. It won't have helped them. If that was really what went down, those are some bodies that you'll never see again. Probably for the best. You wouldn't want to come across what's left of them.'

Jake sat up straight on the stool; his back cracked. 'I don't believe the money is all gone.'

'It is.'

'We only have your word for that,' Yorke said. 'It's not like it ever ended up in your savings account.'

Wheelhouse shrugged.

'Your niece's bank account perhaps?' Jake said.

'Check it.'

'We'll be doing more than that,' Yorke said. 'We will be searching your property too.'

'You're welcome to, detective. I doubt I'll ever be in it again anyway. I'll die in here.'

'That's pessimistic, but probably for the best ...' Jake rolled his head and his neck cracked this time. 'Do you ever feel guilty for what you did to those poor kids?'

For over two decades, Herbert Wheelhouse recruited children in smaller towns around Wiltshire on behalf of the Youngs. Having children run the drugs kept Wheelhouse and his employers firmly under the radar of law enforcement. In recent years, this operation had become known as *County Lines*. These young people were given mobile phones, known as *Deal Lines*, to take orders directly from drug users, who ordered heroin and crack. These young dealers were often forced to travel far and wide, putting themselves in all kinds of danger.

'Back then it wasn't the same,' Wheelhouse said. 'It's evolved into something I don't recognise. Something monstrous.'

'Bollocks,' Jake said. 'You were exploiting children too.'

'No,' Wheelhouse said. 'These children had nothing. They transported the drugs, and I made sure they earned solid money.'

'These were vulnerable children!' Jake rose his voice. 'Some ended up abused physically, and sexually. What possible justification is there?'

41

'Whenever anything happened to any of our runners, we dealt with whoever was responsible—'

'Dealt with them?' Jake was on his feet now. 'You were the ones who put them in harm's way in the first place! And what happened when you sent them to other towns far from home? How did you monitor it then?'

Yorke stood up and placed a hand on Jake's arm. 'DS Pettman?'

Jake turned his angry eyes up to Yorke; then, he turned to the guard. 'The toilet?'

The guard stood up. 'I'll take you.' He nodded in Wheelhouse's direction. 'You alright taking care of him?'

Yorke rose his eyebrows back. 'Are you actually going to wait for my answer this time?'

The guard sneered and then led Jake out the room.

No then, Yorke thought.

'Okay, detective, I regret it all. Is that what you want to hear?' Wheelhouse put his hands on his head and then closed them into fists; he looked as if he was going to tear those grey tufts of hair from his head. 'I thought it was a win-win at the time. The kids needed money. I needed money. It got worse. It became cancerous. When I started, we knew the runner, took care of them. It changed. *Massively*. That's why I took retirement.'

'Except, like you said before, nobody retires, do they?' Yorke said.

'You got that right.'

'If you were truly sorry, you'd give me everything you have on the Youngs,' Yorke said.

'I could, but it'd be useless. I'd never make it alive to a courtroom.'

'Well, we have to try. It may help me catch the man who did this to your niece.'

'Don't worry, detective, I'll tell you everything you want to know. That twisted family, the Youngs, made a mistake … I've nothing left to live for now. My sister means nothing to me, and I'd long given up on my own existence. But I warn you, it won't be much. It's all outdated for a start, and each part of the business was kept insulated from all the others. In fact, the whole bloody enterprise is filled with layer upon layer of insulation. But I'll tell you what I can.'

Yorke readied his pen.

'He was a nasty piece of work, Simon Young. I enjoyed reading about how he was killed by that woman who stole his child. She sounded like a right vicious creature. I'm so glad he met his match. But his father … the one who has stepped back up to run the business? He is far, far worse. I could tell you some stories about that man …'

JAKE PACED the prison bathroom like a caged animal. There may have been a door out of *this* enclosure, but there certainly wasn't one out of the hole he had dug himself into.

He leaned against the sink and stared at his pale face, then at his twitching eyelids, then at the red streaked whites of his eyes.

Inside those criss-crossed whites, he watched again the moments that defined who he now was.

He swung the back of the axe, missed the centre of Simon Young's head, and tore an ear loose instead … He watched Young stumbling towards him, before suddenly lurching towards Lacey … He ended Young's life by burying the axe in his back …

Jake took a deep breath through his nose and straightened himself.

Control yourself, man. Lacey has taken the blame. She's institutionalised. And rightly so ... she set the whole fucking thing up. Simon Young's father will not know what you have done. Just an innocent policeman and his family in the wrong place at the wrong time. Lacey's final gift to you. Sparing your life. Why? Maybe she wants to own you. Don't expect this to be the last you ever hear of her. But ...

Again, I say control yourself ... there is no immediate danger. Your family have left you. Good. They're safer because of it. Happier without you. You deserve this emptiness.

He took another deep breath and stepped away from the sink. He felt better. Empty ... but better. You could adjust to being empty. You could not adjust to living in terror.

This case has nothing to do with your situation ... nothing to do with who you've become ... what you're now defined as ... it is an assassination as a result of Wheelhouse's behaviour ... follow the case ... work with Mike ... be what you once were.

Pretend to be what you once were.

His phone rang in his pocket. He took it out and looked at the screen.

Luke Parkinson.

'And you can fucking wait,' Jake said.

5

FOLLOWING THE INTERVIEW with Wheelhouse, Yorke headed home to see if his family were okay. Their collective experience back in Dr Helen Saunders' waiting room had been particularly traumatic. After dropping the agitated Jake off at his bedsit with advice to get a good night's sleep, he'd phoned Helen to see if she was alright. She assured him she was and had cancelled all her appointments for the next day to spend some time with her husband. She thanked him for his concern and offered to spend a few sessions with Ewan next week free of charge. Yorke told her that was unnecessary.

Yorke drove well below the speed limit. The pincers of the demonic ash cloud were fixed tightly on Salisbury this evening, and his headlights wouldn't pry them open.

His infotainment screen indicated that there was a Voicemail message from Willows; he must have missed her while on the phone to Helen. Before he could hit the call-back button on the touchscreen, there was another incoming call. It was Madden.

She didn't bother with pleasantries. She rarely did, and

there was no chance when she'd already seen him today. 'Herbert Wheelhouse?'

'Receptive, ma'am,' Yorke said, and then filled her in on the most salient information.

'So, you were wrong about him considering himself the Reaper?'

'Yes, ma'am.' Yorke rolled his eyes.

'Don't worry about it, Michael. You can't be right every time, can you?'

'Of course not.'

'You need to know that the inevitable has happened. I just got off the phone to SEROCU. They are now on board.'

It had been a little while since Yorke had last had dealings with the South East Regional Organised Crime Unit, but he knew them well enough to know that this was no bad thing. They delivered specialist and niche capabilities to all the police in the South Eastern region. As soon as Janice Edward's uncle, Herbert, had been linked to the Youngs, the bane of SEROCU's existence, the alert had come out. Unsurprisingly, their response had been quick.

'When?' Yorke said.

'In the morning, Michael. Expect them at your 11 a.m. briefing. For now, though, it remains Operation Tagline. We could probably expect that to change, but until it does, it's still yours. I've sent them over preliminary crime scene reports, sequence of events, and all other relevant information. Have you heard anything from DS Willows?'

'Not since before my interview with Wheelhouse.'

'I saw her an hour ago. She doesn't fancy Peacock for the murder. She's documenting the interview for me. Can you also document your interview with Wheelhouse this evening and send?'

'Of course, ma'am. Shall I send the encryption code for the email to this phone number?'

'Yes, Michael. I know I can trust you to work well with them. Yes, they can ruffle feathers, especially if they think there's been sloppy work, but our relationship is strong, and they've helped us a lot in the past. Keep an eye on Luke. You know how he can be.'

So, why do you always protect him then?

'Yes, ma'am.'

Yorke pulled into his driveway.

'Get some rest, Michael. I suspect tomorrow will be a busy day.'

YORKE DECIDED to spend some time with Patricia, Ewan and Beatrice before writing up the report on his interview with Wheelhouse. He considered phoning Jake to ask him to do some of it, but that ground was shaky. Jake would probably think that Yorke was delegating to him because he didn't have any family to spend time with. It wasn't worth the risk. He needed to rebuild the foundations of their friendship, not chip away at them.

He found Patricia in the kitchen staring at a pan of boiling water. He approached from behind and slipped his arms around her waist.

'Eggs,' she said. 'Want some?'

'Always.'

'No soldiers, I'm afraid. Out of bread. We're having them with Ryvitas, unless you want to pop back out?'

'Nah. Crackers will be fine ... weird ... but fine.' Yorke kissed her neck.

'That's nice.' She leaned her head back. 'Again ...'

He obliged.

She sighed. 'The best part of the day.'

'The only good part of the day ... Ewan and Beatrice okay?'

'Beatrice went down easier than she's done in weeks. She obviously knew tonight wasn't the night to push Mummy.'

'Either that or the nursery wore her out. Ewan?'

'He looked stunned all the way home, so I deliberately gave him some quiet time. And then when we got back, he disappeared up the stairs to phone Lexi. He's been rattling on ever since! I hope you weren't expecting to see him anytime soon.'

'As long as he's dealing with what happened today.'

'I think he's letting his hormones deal with it. His phone bill next month will no doubt show us that.'

'Better than teenage pregnancy.'

She elbowed him.

'That hurt.'

'Good. The only person you should be having those types of conversations with is him. That's your job. Beatrice is mine. In about thirteen years.'

'Hmm ... thanks, I think,' Yorke said. 'And you? How are you coping with what happened today?'

The clock beeped. 'Six minutes.' Patricia took the pan off the stove.

'Too long for eggs, no matter how large. How many times do I have to tell you this?'

'And how many times do I have to tell you? No bacteria, no matter how insignificant and harmless, are surviving in my egg. Besides, it doesn't need to be runny. You can spread it like butter on your Ryvita.'

'Appetising.'

She turned around. Yorke saw that her eyes were puffy. They embraced. 'And to answer your question, Mike, no, I'm not fine, but neither are you, so we're not going to make this about you looking after me. Tonight, we look after each other. And, just for this one meal, we can abandon the *don't-talk-shop* rule because you know I'm desperate to hear what happened after you left us.'

Yorke's phone rang. 'Sorry, Pat.' He took a step back and pulled it out of his jacket pocket. 'It's Collette. She'll just be reporting back to me on Peacock, the writer Janice interviewed earlier tonight. Give me a second.'

Patricia nodded and Yorke took the phone call at the kitchen dining table.

'Sir, I need to talk to you,' Willows said.

'Of course, Collette. If it's about Peacock, Madden already contacted me to tell me it was a no-go.' He watched Patricia spoon the eggs from the boiling water. 'It was predictable—'

'Sir, it's not about Peacock. And Madden does not know about what I'm going to tell you. No one does. Well, apart from Pemberton. But she was there when I found—'

'Collette. You're doing it again. Keeping me in suspense.'

Patricia laid a plate in the middle of the table with a pack of Ryvitas on it. He smiled up at her.

'We came across the name of one of Wheelhouse's old associates. Someone he used to run with back in his youth ... someone called Douglas Firth.'

Patricia laid a plate in front of Yorke, complete with three boiled eggs in eggcups, a teaspoon, and a knob of butter to loosen up those Ryvitas a little first.

'Douglas Firth is currently in HMP Hancock *with Wheelhouse*,' Willows said.

'Okay, same area, similar crimes, identical prison? The point?'

'Some of his crimes are similar, but not all, and he certainly shouldn't be in a low-risk facility. It shows you how overcrowded the maximum-security facilities must be—'

'To the point, Collette, what did he do?'

Patricia smashed the top of her hard-boiled egg. 'He pinned someone's head to the back of a fairground stall with a bayonet.'

'Yes, that'll do it ... why?'

'Geoff Stirling, the victim, had killed Firth's son in a traffic accident a few years prior. The kid was five, and this Stirling, a young gangster, was showing off in his shiny new Capri and just ploughed right into him.'

Yorke took a deep breath. 'So, Stirling was a revenge killing ... HMP obviously don't think he's a risk to the public. Figures. How old is he?'

'Sixty-six.'

'Apparently less dangerous at retirement age ... anyway, I'm struggling to make the connection.'

Patricia smudged her egg yolk on her Ryvita and then smiled at him. He smiled back.

'Sir,' Willows said. 'This connection may not be what you want to hear.'

'Let me be the judge of that.'

'Okay ... I may not even be telling you something you don't already know, so ...'

'For pity's sake, Collette! Everyone else gets it acerbic from you, and with me, you are always dancing around a bloody tree—'

'Douglas Firth is Patricia's father.'

'*Who?*' Yorke said, only realising afterwards how ridiculous the question. '*My Patricia?*'

Patricia met his eyes.

'Yes sir.'

Borya Turgenev pressed the weight for the eighth time. His pectorals, deltoids and triceps all burned.

He lowered the barbell to chest level and went for a ninth repetition. This time he grunted as he breathed out. The bar moved slower this time, and his muscles trembled, but he maintained focus and the weight reached the summit.

His body was telling him to stop, and he was now in position to relinquish the bar; deposit it onto its rack. The bar *could* beat him if he went again. Probably *would* beat him.

He brought the bar to chest level again. It came faster this time. He was unable to slow it; his power was waning. He felt the pressure of the weight on his chest.

It *could* crush him. It *would* almost certainly do him some damage ... unless he maintained the tension in his muscles.

He could feel his body burn.

Was this what it felt like to be beaten?

He took a deep breath and felt the moment.

Everything was quiet. Still.

Peace.

He roared and thrust. The bar moved slowly and with control.

Perfectly.

He deposited the barbell on to its rack, sat up, took three

deep breaths and stood to look in a full-length mirror. His shimmering muscles were taut after the workout.

He ran a hand over his head, his face and then his genitalia. He felt the vile beginnings of hair. It was time for his second close shave of the day.

As he walked naked to his bathroom, he heard the ping of an email from his office. He looked at the clock on his landing wall. Never a minute before, or a minute too late. *Those* emails always came at the same time.

But before he found out what his next job was, Borya wanted to be as smooth as he could possibly be.

6

YORKE DIDN'T KNOW where to start. He opted to be confrontational. 'I always knew those skiing scars were lies. Are they from your father?'

Patricia looked up at him. 'You know I won't talk with you like this. There are reasons. Good reasons. And if you want to talk, we can, like adults.' She then continued to eat.

'Are you bloody serious? How've you got an appetite?'

'I don't, but it's either that or a conversation with you. I've given you my terms for that, and you're still not meeting them.'

'There is a woman dead, Pat. An innocent woman shot in the back of the head!'

Patricia put her Ryvita down. 'Now, I've definitely lost my appetite. Has my father anything to do with this murder?'

'How am I supposed to bloody know that without the truth? The truth you were concealing when we took our flipping vows! Herbert Wheelhouse, Janice Edward's uncle, is in the *same* jail as your father, Douglas Firth. I've just interviewed Wheelhouse and discovered that his niece's murder was a hit. A revenge killing for him turning his back on the Youngs and taking their money.'

'So, this probably has nothing to do with my father?'

'Bloody hell, Pat, you are being incorrigible! I don't know ... yet!'

'Precisely, so I'm going back to my eggs, until you calm down and agree to discuss this like adults—'

Ewan came into the kitchen. 'Someone stressed out?' He walked past the table and over to the fridge. He pulled out a bottle of milk. There wasn't much left, so he drank it straight from the bottle.

'It's been one of those days,' Yorke said. 'As you know.'

Patricia nodded. 'How are you, honey?'

Ewan placed the bottle in the sink. 'Lexi helped me come to terms with it. I was actually starting to feel better until I heard the raised voices. Takes me back to Mum and Dad ... you know ... before their divorce.'

Yorke stood up. 'Yes. Sorry Ewan. We should know better.' He looked at Patricia. '*I* should know better.'

'Yes, well,' Ewan said as he walked past Yorke and out of the kitchen, 'like you said, it has been one of those days.'

Yorke sat back down.

Patricia put down her spoon and offered him a smile. 'Calm and ready now?'

Yorke sighed. 'Calm, and most definitely ready.'

AFTER MAKING every inch of his lean, muscular body smooth, Borya replaced the razor in the bathroom cupboard and took a very long shower.

He liked to *feel* every part of his body as he washed. He

traced every defining line; massaged every swollen muscle; explored every orifice.

After the shower, he stood naked on his landing, and adjusted several canvases. To most eyes, they would appear straight. To his, they were anything but.

This was the way of the world, he knew. Everything subtly trying to exert power.

Borya saw it all. He took the power back. That was his greatest strength.

In his office, he sat before his computer screen and clicked the email from the company *'Power Protein.'* He opened a pad in front of him, picked up a pen, and starting with the words, 'Exclusive offer.' He counted twenty letters. R. Then, another fifteen. I. Another ten. V. Five. E. Back to the start of the sequence to count twenty. R.

Eventually, he'd written: RIVERSIDEPARKCAFE.

He then counted the testimonials from rabid consumers of Power Protein. There were thirteen, so he wrote down 13:00. Thirteen was also an odd number, so it meant tomorrow. An even number would have indicated the subsequent day.

He smiled. *He never touched protein shakes. Vile stuff.*

Protein Power may have been a fake company, but there were many real ones out there. Attempting to influence – attempting to make you *consume.* He deleted the email.

He felt the beginnings of an erection and looked at the clock on the computer screen.

The same time every day.

Like clockwork.

'AND WHEN I WAS SEVEN, while I held my father's hand, I watched my younger brother die.'

Yorke expected a tear, but Patricia remained stony-faced.

'The hit and run?'

She shook her head. 'Geoff Stirling didn't run. He got out of the car to plead his innocence because Ian had run out into the road for his football. It seemed speeding was a foreign concept for Stirling. It was for the courts as well – he never went to jail.'

Yorke reached over the table to hold her hand. She thanked him with a smile.

'Before I met you, Mike, I'd spent most of my life in turmoil over this. It took a lot of help, professionally and medically, to get to where I am today. I wanted to share it with you, I really did, but I was desperate for it not to interfere with what I'd found with you.'

'It *will* never interfere with what we've found.'

The first tear came. It rolled down her cheek. 'After the accident, my father smashed the living room window and marched out to Stirling with a shard of glass. Fortunately, some neighbours held him back before he could use it. I say fortunately, but it only really delayed the inevitable. He murdered Stirling two years later.'

'Collette gave me the details,' Yorke said. 'You don't have to go through them again.'

'The bayonet was my grandfather's.'

'So, they used that to get him for the murder?'

'No. The bayonet wasn't registered. I just remember my grandfather showing it to me when I was a little girl. He died before I was six. A small mercy for him perhaps? Never having to see what his son became.'

'Collette said he became mixed up in organised crime.'

Patricia nodded. 'My father was a good man, Mike ... before ... you must believe me on that. Even Mum will agree. But what we saw that day, with Ian, snapped something inside him.'

'As it would anyone, I'm sure.' Yorke squeezed her hand.

'Geoff Stirling was part of a British firm in Southampton connected to some of the crime families operating in London. Even though the police couldn't prove that my father murdered Stirling, this firm didn't need evidence. Normally, the murder of one of their own would have incited them, and on any other occasion my father would've been staring down the barrel of a shotgun. However, this firm had had a gutful of Stirling already. He was cocky and a liability. Driving around in a flash car that killed an innocent child was just one of the many incidents that irritated the firm and the connected bigwigs in London.' She paused to take a mouthful of water.

'So, they offered your father a job instead?' Yorke said.

Patricia sighed. 'He loved us dearly, and we were his everything. He got in with the wrong people because he thought he could better support us, *protect us*, and take us all into a life where nothing this tragic could possibly happen again. Be the top of the food chain, rather than the bottom. That kind of thinking. You've come across it before.'

Yorke nodded. 'What did they ask him to do?'

'They never asked. They *made* him do it. They said he owed them for taking out one of their men. Later, after he adjusted to this new life, he must have figured out he was better off. And as for what he did for them? I don't know absolutely everything, but it did involve murder. He went to jail in 1986.'

'The year DNA profiling was introduced,' Yorke said. 'Did they link him to a killing?'

'Yes. The Stirling crime eight years previous. He left DNA on the bayonet. So, he was given a life sentence and, while he was inside, they found DNA linking him to a firm-related murder too. So, he's now serving two back-to-back.'

'When was the last time you saw him, Pat?'

'Thirty years ago. The day he was arrested from our house. I was seventeen.'

'You must have been in contact since then?'

'Never contacted him, but I've heard from him. A lot. He writes to my mother's house every week. Two letters. One each.'

'And do you read them?'

'Every now and again. There are a lot, and once you've read one, you've read them all. They're all about how he regrets everything; how much he cares about us; Ian's death and what it did to him, and his desperate claim that he will never stop loving us. The same themes run through every letter. He's also become a big reader inside, so he liked to provide little book reviews to pad out his letters. I don't think he has a great deal more to write about. My mother keeps every letter. Mine and hers. Opened and unopened.'

'Does he ever try phoning?'

'He did. He's given up over the last couple of years. I can't have anything to do with a man who made those choices. I won't lie. There are times I have been tempted, and I remembered the times when he'd cuddle me all night because I'd relive Ian's death in my dreams over and over. He could be so tender, so adoring of me. I miss my father. I miss him so much. But, he made those choices, and by going back to him, I'd have to confront, again and again, what he's become. In some of the letters I have read, he seemed to understand this. Mike, my father is gone. I told you he was dead and, in a way, I didn't lie to you.'

'I'm so sorry, Patricia.'

'I know you are, and part of me feels so ashamed that I haven't told you. But I wanted to spare you, and as I said before, myself.'

'For better or worse, remember? Please never keep things from me again.'

She leaned forward and kissed his hand, which still lay on hers. 'I won't.'

'So the skiing accident?'

Patricia sighed and nodded. 'Yes, that's a lie.'

'What really happened then?'

'The worst thing you can imagine ... I died.'

NAKED, and fully erect, Borya checked the curtains in the living room. Satisfied that there were no spaces for intrusive eyes, he pulled the leather sofa out so he could access the small safe he concealed behind it.

He punched in the code, opened the safe door and took out the glass jar. After depositing it on the coffee table, he pushed the sofa back, and then sat on a wooden chair he'd brought in from the kitchen. Without clothes on, he felt every inch of the spindles. He ran his hands over the towel he'd draped over the arm of the chair.

He leaned forward in the chair and picked up the lighting control and pumped every bulb in the room up to 100%. Then, he reached for the second control and fired up the stereo.

Death Metal. The room was soundproofed, and the

windows as high as 95%, so he knew he could risk the volume. He jacked it up as loud as he could.

In such discomfort, how could anyone maintain sexual arousal? The spindles digging into his spine, the contents of the jar before him, the intense lighting that caused him to squint, and the band *Cannibal Corpse* eating up the quiet. He moved his thick tongue over his lips, dampening them as he stimulated himself.

The distractions *should* beat him. His erection *should* wane.

He stared at the jar, saw the body parts move in the formaldehyde, as if they were watching him, jarring with him. Up and down. Up and down.

He sensed the climax had moved closer, but it was evading him. His heart was thrashing too hard in his chest, and he felt rivulets of sweat racing down his body. He couldn't maintain this much longer. He would have to stop soon ... accept he was beaten ... or collapse with exhaustion, or worse still, with a heart attack.

He took a deep breath and felt the moment.

Everything was quiet. Still.

Peace.

He roared and found the height of pleasure.

Then, as he stared into his parents' eyes, he climaxed.

7

YORKE WAS NEVER going to sleep after the day he'd had. Neither was Patricia, but at least she was good at pretending. He just rolled around, fluffed a few pillows, and worked himself up into such a sweaty state that he was more geared up for a gym session than a rest.

When Patricia had defied the odds, and finally nodded off, Yorke lifted her vest and looked at the criss-crossing scars that she'd spent so many years passing off as the result of a skiing accident.

Then his mind wandered back to her revelations earlier about what had really caused them.

'He was doing all of this for us, remember? Good old Douglas Firth ... family man. At least that is what he had us all thinking. And he was probably right, to a certain extent, until he started drinking and taking cocaine, and then it became all about him.

'My father picked me up every day from school. He was very protective, and overly cautious, as a result of what'd happened to Ian. Sometimes, he may have had a beer or two, but he was never late, and was always sober.

'On the seventh anniversary of my brother's death, he broke this trend by being fifteen minutes late. Discovering that my father wasn't even driving, and that he was blind drunk and asleep in the passenger side made me panic. I was only fourteen at the time. After getting into the car, I started to cry. A young Irishman called Ryan, early twenties at the most, told me not to worry. My father had asked him to drive because he'd had too much to drink.

'Ryan started to tell me about where he was from in Northern Ireland. He told me about the troubles, and some of the things he'd seen and experienced. I remember thinking that my current situation was nothing in comparison, and I remember feeling quite guilty. No doubt this was his intention. A few times, he reached behind and patted my knee. I had a skirt on, and no tights, but tried not to read into him touching me at this point – my father was in the front, after all, and he just seemed very friendly. In fact, he'd started to make me feel better. But then ... sorry ... can I have some of your water?'

Yorke passed her his glass, and she took a large mouthful. 'Thanks. Jesus, Mike, why are the things that happened so long ago always the most overwhelming?'

Yorke kissed her on the forehead. 'Would you like to stop for a bit?'

'No ... I'll be okay.' She took a deep breath. 'Anyway ... Ryan's questions started to get *really* personal ... he asked me if I liked to drink. I told him I was only fourteen, and he claimed he was stunned by this. He'd thought I was sixteen. He said he'd started drinking when he was fourteen. He also pointed out that my father liked to drink. After I told him I didn't like the taste, he took the hint and moved on to talk about his ex-girlfriend in Ireland, who had been sixteen, and had looked quite like me ... I think you can see where this is going. I remember smiling but feeling very awkward. I also remember leaning over to shake my father but that did no good. He just slumped further down in his chair and started to snore.

'It got worse ... Ryan asked if I'd ever had a boyfriend, and again, I told him that I was *only* fourteen. And the weasel's response to this was to go for my knee again. Except this time, he left his hand there. I froze over. I *desperately* wanted to brush his hand away, but I was so young, embarrassed, and so, so scared. He was leering at me in his rear-view mirror and he must have been able to see how terrified and red-faced I was. Shit, I'm shaking even now, Mike, just give me a second ...'

Yorke squeezed her hand.

'Sorry ... I know it was so long ago ... but even now, over thirty years later, I see that face. I see his large smile and those yellowed, crooked teeth and sometimes, when the memories get particularly bad, I *feel* that hand on my leg again.

'I tried hard to keep myself calm. What could he do? He was driving me home ... I would be with my mother soon. And my father? Surely, the pervert must have known what my father would do to him if he kept his hand there for too much longer?

'But then he started to stroke my leg. All the time, watching me in the mirror. Telling me to calm down and that everything would be fine. Leering at me.'

She was crying now. Mike kissed her hand. 'Take a moment, Pat.'

'No ... no ... don't stop me now, Mike, I need to finish this. *I want to finish this.* Sometimes when I think back, I worry that I *allowed* him to do that. Ridiculous, I know. I was a fourteen-year-old girl.

'My memory gets a little hazy at this point, maybe because it was so close to the actual accident, or maybe because I was so emotional, but I'm sure I asked him to stop. He then moved his hand onto the inside of my thigh. I'm positive I told him enough was enough and that he should concentrate on the road. He only had one hand on the wheel. I'm sure I told him that my father would be unhappy with the way he was driving. I hope I did say all these things, but Mike, I'm not so sure I did ...'

'I'm positive you would have done.'

'Yes ... you say that Mike, but I genuinely can't remember. It all blurs. And sometimes I worry that I led him on to begin with. However, I'm absolutely certain the next thing happened. I mean, could anyone really imagine this level of fear? The bastard missed the turn off to our home.'

She pulled her hand away from Yorke's and looked him dead in the eyes. 'It snapped me into life – I remember that vividly too. I pushed Ryan's hand away and shouted at him to stop. I saw him glancing at my father. He was playing a dangerous game, and he knew it. I undid my seatbelt and told him to stop the car. I told him that I would walk home.

'He started to accelerate. He had both of his hands back on the wheel now which was something, but I had no idea what he planned to do and where he was taking me. I shouted as loudly as I could for him to stop, hoping it would wake my father up.

'When Ryan realised that this wasn't going to happen, he laughed. He started to take the piss by imitating me. He said he was going to take us somewhere quiet. He couldn't have meant it. If he did, he must have had a death wish. Unless he planned to kill us both perhaps? Was I really worth that amount of bother?

'He reached round again and grabbed my leg. Harder this time. I pounded his hand, but he kept a firm grip. I dug my nails in and drew blood. He was also looking around fully now and wasn't watching the road.

'He went through a red light ... and then ... well, that was it. For me, anyway, it was all over. I went out the front windscreen. As I was thrown, I must have caught Ryan, or the front seat because I was twisted around and went through the glass back first. It tore my skin to pieces and fractured my spine. I landed on the bonnet of the other car.'

Yorke took her hand again.

'The ambulance came, and despite having to resuscitate me three times, got me to hospital. I was placed in an induced coma. Not only did the doctors think it was a miracle I survived, they also thought it was a miracle I experienced no long-term damage apart from the scarring. Incredibly, my spinal cord remained intact. One doctor suggested that maybe the front windscreen was already cracked, so it had given out easier when I hit it.'

She took another mouthful of water.

'And Ryan?' Yorke said.

'Not so lucky. He broke his neck on the steering wheel. His death was instant. I didn't feel bad, not at the time anyway. He'd threatened me.'

'You shouldn't feel bad now.'

'Yes ... but over the years, my attitude has softened. Did he really mean what he said? Would he really have done those things? I'm not so sure. Was he just a silly boy making silly choices?'

'Probably, but they were *his* choices, not *yours.*'

'Yes, I agree, but still, it's hard not to feel some sympathy for him. Anyway, the accident *was* the only thing that managed to wake my pissed father ... and he was luckier than me ... he walked away with a mild concussion. And the people in the other car had cuts and bruises, but nothing serious.' She wiped away tears, took a deep breath and hugged Yorke. 'That's it ... I promise, Mike. That's the only thing I kept from you. My father's choices have caused so much damage. The fact that I am here, *alive*, is a miracle. I'm so sorry for never discussing these moments with you *before* but they've been so painful.'

After the revelation, they'd gone to bed to be as close as they could be. Without breaking their embrace, they'd taken it in turns to cry. The sense of relief Yorke felt over finally knowing the truth, coupled with the trauma his wife had suffered, was an emotional combination he'd never really experienced.

And now she was fast asleep ... and he was glad. He lowered her t-shirt, covering her scars again, and then remembered something important.

Shit!

With everything going on, he'd forgotten to email Madden his report on the interview with Wheelhouse. She'd have his bollocks for this!

He went downstairs to the kitchen. He eyed up the coffee maker but opted for one of Patricia's Chamomile teas. He needed to sleep tonight. He then typed up his report on Herbert Wheelhouse, omitting Jake's aggressive interviewing techniques. As he wrote the report, he made notes of reminders and questions he wanted to raise at tomorrow's briefing.

Janice's mother, Bridgett? Returning? British Embassy complied with protection request?

Couple of 100k skimmed by Wheelhouse? Consider all locations ... Bridgett? Janice? Property search ...?

Wheelhouse – eight years in jail. Why now? Would

SEROCU be aware of any missing 'soldiers' from Young Properties – possible confessors to Wheelhouse's skimming?

Request profile on Buddy Young from SEROCU. This original CEO of Young Properties emerged from retirement following murder of son, Simon Young, by Lacey Ray at Jake's home.

Yorke paused to scribble out 'Jake's home.' No one would be seeing these notes, but he didn't want to take any chances. He went over the words again, so they were completely obliterated.

In Yorke's report, there were lots of details about Wheelhouse's career as a modern-day Fagin. His use of vulnerable children as drug runners. The birth of County Lines if you will.

Just like Jake, it had also made Yorke angry that someone could claim that they were improving the lives of these people. The bottom line was that it was exploitation. Unlike Jake though, Yorke could keep his emotions in check when doing his job, and he detected some remorse in Wheelhouse, which always helped.

The report would probably offer very little to SEROCU. Wheelhouse was so far removed from those at the top. Wheelhouse had certainly been right when he'd warned Yorke of the 'layer upon layer of insulation.' In fact, Wheelhouse had only known one immediate superior, Johnny Ashman. Ashman had disappeared three years ago.

'At roughly the same time a new supermarket went up in his local area,' Wheelhouse had said with a smile. 'He's under those foundations, I bet.'

Yorke put this in his report but doubted anyone would be in a rush to dig up an entire supermarket on Wheelhouse's gut feeling.

The demise of Ashman was good for society, but bad for

this investigation. It meant that this layer of insulation which would have taken them to the next layer was gone.

He sent the report as an encrypted file and then texted the password to Madden. It was 1 a.m. but he wasn't surprised to receive a text back from the notorious workaholic.

Better late than never, Mike.

At 1 a.m. it was a longshot, but he called Special Visits at HMP Hancock. Predictably, he got the answerphone. He left a message warning that he would be visiting Douglas Firth first thing on police business. He would ring again in the morning to confirm.

Yorke grabbed a kitchen chair, so he could reach the top of the kitchen cupboard. He rooted around until his hand landed on the dusty packet.

It's been a tough day and the options are to have one of these or kiss any hope of relaxing goodbye.

Another option would be to phone Emma Gardner. Aside from Patricia, she was the only other person that really understood him. She'd know how to soothe his anxious mind. But she'd left the police force behind for many reasons. Nocturnal freak-outs were undoubtedly one of those. Would she appreciate Yorke sharing his with her while she was tucked up in bed? She had a new job as a security guard in M&S to think about after all.

So, nicotine, and thousands of other chemicals he couldn't name, was his only option.

It was late and cold, so he opted for Patricia's goose-down lined jacket. It was tight on him, but he managed to zip it up.

Outside, Yorke wondered if it was necessary to smoke. A deep breath of the smog currently dripping from

Iceland's ash cloud might have the same impact as a cigarette.

He heard a cat rustling in the bushes at the end of his garden, and then pound up the fence to flee the houseowner. Once it'd gone, silence descended. There were no lights from the other houses over the walls, at least none he could see through the low-hanging black shroud. He felt truly alone.

He looked at the cigarette in one hand, and the lighter in the other. He thought about the run he could possibly be doing instead, but that was out of the question, because he'd wake Patricia up getting his gear out the wardrobe. And if anyone needed sleep, she did. Retelling that story earlier would have drained her.

He lit his cigarette and took his first puff. The fact that it made him light-headed was a good sign. It showed that it had been a considerable length of time since the last one. His body wasn't used to the nicotine, and so he wasn't beholden to it.

Yorke recalled the first time his sister, Danielle, had caught him smoking at the age of sixteen. He smiled. She'd literally gone for him with a slipper! He doubted many sisters would have responded so aggressively, but she'd been more of a mother than a sister and despite smoking like a trooper herself, she wouldn't be suffering her younger brother killing himself on her watch.

'I'm glad you're dead, Proud,' Yorke said. He took another drag on his cigarette and blew it out into the volcanic spew.

The outside light was off; he'd ensured that before coming outside. It was disconcerting that his eyes were not adjusting to the darkness. It was as if tendrils had grown from the mass, and were continually wrapping themselves around everything, snuffing out its existence.

He thought of the tendrils from a dark world which had caught and squeezed his sister.

Addictions, sex, crime, despair.

Smothered by so many tendrils.

Drug dealer William Proud had raped Danielle Yorke while holding her face against a hot stove. She'd died from a heart attack. Proud had run, leaving Tom Davies, junkie boyfriend to carry the can. Yorke's best friend at the time, Harry Butler, had been threatened into framing Davies by someone in the force. Many years later, after Yorke had finally caught up with Proud, he was told by his sister's killer to *look at his own. That there was a bent bastard shitting in the same toilet as him.* Yorke still had no idea who this corrupt officer was, but it wasn't an enigma that went away. He thought about it daily. And sometimes, when his mind wasn't busy with work, it consumed most of his thoughts.

For many years, he'd turned his back on Harry Butler. There was a time he'd loved him like a brother. Harry had done this to protect them both. It wasn't until Harry's dying moments that the truth had come out and Yorke now dearly missed the man he'd rejected.

And now he was losing someone else close to him.

He took a last drag on the cigarette, threw it into the black, hoisted his phone out, and texted Jake to see if he was awake.

Less than a minute later, Jake called him. 'Did you want to read me a bedtime story?'

'The only stories I know are the ones that give you nightmares.'

Jake laughed. 'Already suffering from them.'

'Listen, I just wanted to check that you were okay? You seemed rather het up today.'

Yorke was pretending to be sympathetic; in reality, he was annoyed at Jake's unprofessional behaviour. But this was one relationship that needed healing. Desperately.

'Thanks. Yeah ... he just got to me. You know how I feel when it involves children. I just saw red.'

Yorke nodded. 'It's usually the way but we always need to try and keep them onside ...'

There was a pause. 'Is this a bollocking?'

Shit ... no! Get the hell out of boss mode, Mike! 'No ... just pointing out why I didn't lose it too, because he would try the patience of a saint.'

'So, you're a saint, and I'm a what? A hot-headed maniac?'

'No!' It was all going wrong again. Yorke sighed. 'That isn't what I meant! I just understand. That's all I'm saying, and I wanted to make sure you're okay before I turn in because ... because I know it's been very hard with you recently, but I need you to know that I'm there for you.'

There was a long pause. Yorke was already craving another cigarette.

'Yes. Thanks, sir.'

'Mike.'

'Yeah, sorry, Mike, been that long I forgot we did personal calls. Maybe, we should get together at *The Wyndham* this weekend, depending on how the case is going?'

'I'd bloody like that, Jake.'

'Sorry for being snappy. This sodding bedsit is getting on my wick. Radiator is on the blink. I'm sleeping in my coat under two fucking blankets!'

'Well, you know you can stay here anytime you want?'

'Thanks, but I have the plumber out tomorrow. It'll be fine. Okay, going to turn in.'

'Okay, goodnight, Jake. Sure you don't want that bedtime story?'

Jake laughed. 'I know all your bloody stories already. Night, Mike.'

After the call ended, Yorke stood there for a good while trying to work out if that went well or not.

AM I any different to Herbert Wheelhouse? To any of them?

Jake counted the twenty-pound notes again. It was exactly as promised. Not a penny less. They could have underpaid - what could he have done about it? Really? Maybe there was honour among those he'd spent a significant part of his life putting away.

He slipped the bundle underneath the bed.

And was this it? Am I now officially one of them? One of the bad guys?

Shivering, he slipped under the first duvet. Then, he reached down for the second which was on the floor beside him. It didn't help that they were five-tog duvets, built for summer rather than bitter weather.

He hugged himself until the shivering stopped, and then he reached over to the bedside table for the framed picture of his son. He looked at his five-year-old boy, Frank. He didn't need anyone else to tell him that they looked the image of each other.

They've been told. No children. My one condition. Nothing I do impacts on children.

He was so tired. He couldn't even remember the last

time he'd slept properly. And when he closed his eyes, he remembered why this was the case.

Lacey. Smiling at him. Simon Young dead on the floor. 'I always knew you had it in you,' she said.

He opened his eyes, sat up and asked himself the same question he asked himself every night. *Was she right? Had it always been inside me?*

Just like last night, and the night before that, he didn't want to lie back down. He propped the pillow behind his back, and prepared for a long night staring into space, waiting for exhaustion. It always came – a few hours before work usually.

He closed his eyes again, tried to force his issue.

Lacey prodded Simon Young's corpse with her foot. 'Your first?' she said.

He opened his eyes, hugged the picture of Frank to his chest, and cried.

This is who you are now, Jake. You are no different from all those monsters you put away.

Including Lacey Ray.

8

THE SKIES WERE no brighter the following morning, and neither was Yorke's mood. A quick phone call from Joan Madden did little to help.

'I want to see you *before* the briefing, Mike.'

The briefing was scheduled for 11 a.m. 'I'll try, ma'am, but I'm pressed for time.'

'Dropping the children off?'

'Yes ...' Yorke regretted the lie immediately.

Her silence suggested she'd seen through it.

'But I'll try my best,' Yorke said.

'*Before* the briefing, Mike. It's important.' And then she was gone.

She knows, Yorke thought. *She knows about Douglas Firth and knows that he may be connected to the case. She knows I have driven straight to HMP Hancock to rule him out of the investigation.*

She knows me.

Yorke knew that if he couldn't rule Douglas Firth out of the investigation, then he would be compromised. And the meeting she was demanding before briefing? It was to slice him off the operation like a large benign mole.

Just in case.

Yorke parked in the same spot as yesterday and stared up at the decrepit stone structure. The ash cloud hung low, and darkness dripped down the sides of the building.

Today, HMP Hancock looked swollen with malice.

IF THERE COULD BE A SAVING grace to being back in this stale chamber, it was a different guard, rather than the one who'd spent more time wandering the corridors looking for hot drinks than guarding. Feeling too agitated to sit, Yorke paced around the table and stools.

Just like Herbert Wheelhouse the previous day, Douglas Firth came through the door in his own clothes. He'd opted for a pair of tweed trousers, and a checked shirt buttoned right up to the collar in a similar way to how Yorke sometimes wore his.

The similarities stop there, Yorke thought.

On the journey here, he'd considered several ways to introduce himself to Firth. He'd opted for blunt. *I'm DCI Michael Yorke. I'm Patricia's husband, but I'm here to discuss an investigation that is unrelated.*

'DCI Michael Yorke, I believe.' Firth said, stepping right up to him. 'Patricia's husband. Here to discuss Herbert, presumably. It's savage what's happened. *Absolutely* savage.'

Firth had been allowed close enough for Yorke to smell the coffee on his breath. He glanced at the nonchalant guard, realising that ineptness was clearly a contagion, and that the HMP Hancock was in the throes of an epidemic.

'Right on all counts, Mr Firth,' Yorke said. 'Please come and sit.'

'It'd be my pleasure.'

After they'd sat on a stool opposite each other, Firth smiled at Yorke. It was a strong smile and creased most of his elderly face. It was also a smile that Yorke didn't understand. He chose not to return it.

'You're the first visitor I've had in quite a while,' Firth said.

'Mr Firth, I haven't got a great deal of time, so if we could?' Yorke pulled a notepad from his jacket pocket.

'How's my daughter?'

Yorke realised he'd have to offer him something to get the interview moving. 'Pat's okay. A little shaken up, as we all are, by what happened yesterday, but she's fine.'

He smiled again. 'And my granddaughter?'

Yorke took a deep breath.

'Beatrice, isn't it?'

'And how do you know about my daughter if you don't have visitors?' Yorke said.

'Come on now, Michael! It's okay to call you that, isn't it? We're family.'

Yorke didn't respond.

'My ex-wife and daughter may want nothing to do with me, but I'm not completely cut off from the outside world!'

'Mr Firth, you're in prison,' Yorke leaned forward. 'It's part of the package ... being cut off.'

Firth's smile fell away. He edged backwards on his stool and rubbed the white stubble on his chin. Yorke listened to the scratching sound. He wanted Firth to speak next and was prepared to wait. He didn't have to wait long. 'I write to them every week.'

Yorke nodded.

'And they never write back or come to see me.'

Yorke held back on asking him why he was surprised by this.

'Imagine if that was you, Michael.' He leaned forward again. 'Patricia ... Beatrice ...' He clicked his fingers. 'Gone in the blink of an eye.'

Yorke tapped his pad, offering the sharpest hint yet that he wanted to get on with this.

'And Ewan Brookes?' Firth said.

Yorke shook his head. 'You really have done your research ...'

'What do you expect? You married my only daughter.'

'Should I be worried?'

'I don't know. Should you?'

'Well, when a convicted murderer reveals my personal details to me, it's hard not to feel some concern.'

'But look where I am.' Firth held out his arms. 'What threat am I to you?'

Yorke glanced at the guard reading a newspaper. *More than you probably realise.*

'Do you know what that drugged-up wanker, Stirling, did to my son?'

'I do.'

'And you condemn me for killing him?'

'I'm not here to offer my views one way or another, Mr Firth, the courts did that. And it was your lifestyle following the murder which concerns me most.'

'Do you really think I had a choice in that?'

Yorke shrugged.

'I cared for and supported my family, Michael. That's all I ever wanted, and all I ever did. There's still money for them, if they ever need it. Not that they'll accept it. I've been trying for years. She's a feisty one that daughter of mine. She still blames me for that accident. I know she does. I don't blame her, but she needs to know I'm here for her. As long as she knows that, I'm happy.'

Yorke put his pen against the notepad. 'A Category B prison for someone who has committed two murders is unusual ...'

'I've been the model of good behaviour, Michael. I'm not the person you have me pegged down as. They transferred me when they knew I wasn't a danger. My life in the gang is long gone; the warden lets me run the prison library for pity's sake! When you haven't got family, reading is your everything ... and I can tell you that Herbert feels the same.'

Yorke's eyes widened. 'Good. Let's talk more about Herbert.'

'Okay,' Firth said. 'Because he's my friend, and because of the savagery committed by my old employers, I'm all yours.'

In describing how he made Wheelhouse's acquaintance back in the early eighties, Firth revealed a lot of his own connections to the Young family, long before they swelled into the goliath *Young Properties*. None of this outdated intel was relevant or interesting. Something Yorke was glad of. The connection between Wheelhouse and Firth seemed, at least on the surface, out-dated and irrelevant to the recent execution of Janice Edwards.

'We were good friends. Drinking buddies if you will. Similar ages, similar mindsets, similar interests.'

'Did you know he used children to sell drugs?' Yorke said.

'That was the only thing that we didn't see eye-to-eye on ...'

'A pretty big *thing* though, wouldn't you agree?'

Questioning his integrity was the conversation killer to end all conversation killers. Firth quickly brought the interview forward to the present day.

'When I was transferred here ... as a model prisoner I might add—'

'You already added that before.'

'Yes, well. I arrived here in 2012 and there he was in the library. It must have been over twenty-five bloody years since I'd seen him! A friendly face. Much better than I was used to back in the last prison.'

'The prison where you actually belonged?'

'Your tone is getting harsher, Michael.'

The conversation turned to the relationship between the two elderly men. Yorke steadily made notes. There was still nothing to suggest that there was any connection beyond reading and catching up on old times. Yorke could feel himself starting to calm. 'Did you know his niece, Janice?'

'No, although he talked about her a lot ... still does, of course.'

'Didn't you meet her when she visited him here?'

'You already know that I don't have visitors. The television is always free around that time, so I always make a beeline for that. Prefer to read to be honest, but it's nice to give the old brain a break every now and—'

'Has Herbert explained to you why Janice has been murdered? Or at least *why* he thinks she has been murdered?'

'Of course he has. Not that it takes a genius to work it all out. I know the same people he does, or at least did. There has been a lot of change, mind you. While I was part of it, it was all rather small fry; there was far less *insulation* as Herbert likes to call it. The way he describes it now makes it sound like a frigging empire rather than a couple of down-and-outs trying to make ends meet.'

'You were never down-and-outs,' Yorke said.

Firth smiled. 'Some of us weren't. You put the yards in back then, the rewards were great. From what Herbert has been saying, people these days are being handed it on a silver platter. It's becoming like the aristocracy – you must be born into it! I did hear Buddy Young was back on the scene since they put his son Simon in the ground. Now, there was someone who put in the yards ... but a yard with that man isn't good for your health.' He laughed. 'That's one man you never want to cross. He'd take pieces off you for it.'

Yorke tapped his notepad. 'So, you've no connection to Herbert, and this tragedy, other than friendship?'

'I've been a shoulder to cry on. Literally. The man's been an emotional wreck. It's not easy sharing a cell with him at the moment—'

'*Sorry...* you're cellmates?'

'Yes, for over a year.'

Yorke felt his heart beating faster. *Stay calm ... it means little ... he's out of the game ... he has no direct connection to this murder ...*

'Mr Firth, you—'

'For pity's sake, like me or loathe me, please just call me Doug.'

'Okay, Doug. You say that it is obvious what happened to Janice, could you tell me what you mean by that?'

'Herbert already told you. *Don't fear the Reaper.* Back in the day, when we used to catch-up, there was a small group of us that used to drink together regularly. He'd have that song on the jukebox two or three times a night! Wasn't long before he earned the nickname *Reaper.* To be fair, it's the most inappropriate name. He wouldn't hurt a fly.'

It's a good job Jake isn't here, Yorke thought, *he'd be wielding his stool in Firth's direction right now.*

'And the others in the group?' Yorke said. 'Who are they, and *where* are they?'

'They're all dead.'

'Nice,' Yorke said. 'Good job really, wouldn't want them on our radar ...'

'Seriously, they've all passed.'

'Even if it may weed out Janice's killer ...'

'I'm not lying to you, Michael. Besides, everyone in that group loved Herbert like a brother.'

'Romantic ... however, doesn't it stand to reason that they're connected? They knew the nickname. The nickname has been used to antagonise Herbert.'

'*Everyone* knew that nickname. And like I said before, insulation was not as thick back then, bosses would've talked to him, and they would've used that name.'

'Who were the bosses?'

'They're gone too, Michael. Seriously. People change like the weather in this game. There is one boss that remains though ... the top one. He would've known his nickname, and he'd every reason to put a hit out on someone Herbert loved.'

Yorke sighed. 'Let me guess. Buddy Young.'

'Yep. And good luck with that one. If you can get through his wall of lawyers to talk to him, you'll get nothing. He's a seasoned pro. I'm surprised he's back at it. Before this, I'd heard he was on his last legs and bedridden.'

'He must've recovered.'

Firth shrugged and smiled. 'Bet he has a relapse when you want to talk to him.'

Yorke chewed his lip and looked from Firth's smiling

face to the guard. He'd finished his newspaper and had his eyes closed.

He sighed again and looked back at Firth 'For someone who loves the Reaper like a brother, Doug, you're not that open.'

'I'll give you anything relevant, Michael, but I'm afraid I know very little.'

Well, at least I can tell Madden that you aren't involved.

'How about the money?' Yorke said. 'What has Herbert done with it all?'

'Didn't he tell you?' Firth said. 'Gone. All of it.'

'Come on,' Yorke said. 'Really? Hundreds of grand.'

Firth shrugged.

'And you. Your money?'

'Same. Spent ... enjoyed ... what can I say?'

'Did you skim?'

'Answering questions like that might get a relative killed. Being that we share family, do you really want to go down that avenue, Michael?'

'You're not taking this seriously, are you, Doug?'

'Try losing your freedom, your entire family, and then try being a serious man. It's difficult.'

'I don't believe it's all gone, Doug, and I'm prepared to check.'

'Obviously, I've *some* left. *Some*. For a rainy day, a pension maybe, if I ever get out.'

'And where is it?'

'With my accountant. A good man. He takes care of my financial affairs. He will show you if you see him, but like I said, there's nothing to get excited about. When I die, you and Patricia might get to pay off your mortgage, but that's about it really.'

'And Herbert, surely he squirrelled something away for a rainy day?'

Firth nodded. 'I guess I might as well tell you, you'll find out sooner or later anyway, and it's no biggie.'

Yorke's heart started to beat fast again. *Was this it? Was this the connection that compromised everything?*

Firth said, 'We share the same accountant.'

The same accountant.

Yorke felt a wave of nausea.

Money. Skimmed money. *Dirty* money.

He rubbed his throbbing forehead with the palms of his hands.

'Are you okay, Michael?' Firth asked.

Not really. Not now money was involved.

Money connected everything, and now he had to go and tell Madden that he was potentially compromised.

THE DIFFERENCE between me and you, Herbert, is that I don't do any of this for myself. People like you are bloodsuckers. Take, take, take.

After marching up the path to the house which was once his, after glancing at the garden gnomes his Frank loved to rearrange, after checking that the bundle of cash was still in his jacket pocket, and after he recalled killing someone in the living room here not so long ago, he knocked on the front door.

Sheila opened the door. She was in her dressing gown and her hair was dishevelled. She didn't look pleased to see him. Mind you, when he lived here, she'd never really looked pleased to see him.

'I'm busy,' she said.

'*Have you got someone with you?*'

Sheila smiled. '*Really?* That's the first thing you think of?'

Jake didn't respond.

'No, I haven't. I'm *just* busy. Look at the state of you.'

'I'm not sleeping well. The bedsit's freezing.'

'And that stops you going to the barbers, or having a shave? Why are you here Jake?'

'Thought I could maybe see Frank.'

'It's not your day.'

'That sounds like lawyer talk. I thought we'd agreed to make this amicable?'

'We have.'

Sheila had her hand on the edge of the door, waiting to close it. *Was she paranoid he might do something, or did she just want rid of him quick-smart?*

'He's young. He needs routine.'

'I'm his father. Seeing me should be routine. Five minutes won't hurt.'

'Not today, Jake.' She started to close the door.

'*You've got someone in there, haven't you?*'

'Precisely why it's *not* a good idea that you come in. You're completely paranoid.'

Jake reached into his pocket and thrust the wad of twenty-pound notes in her direction.

Her eyes widened. 'What the fuck is that?'

'Everything.' *I give. I do not take.*

'What do you mean *everything*?'

'Just take it Sheila. I love you, and I love Frank. Two certainties in this world. Two things that will never change. *Take it.*'

'Where did you get it?'

'Overtime. Nothing much else to do.'

84

'That's a lot of overtime. Those are twenty-pound notes! They've been cutting back on overtime for years and now they're throwing it at you?'

'Yes.'

'Why not just transfer it over.'

'Just take it Sheila.'

'I won't take it, not until I know where it's from.'

He heard crying in the background.

'Frank?'

'Goodbye Jake.' Sheila closed the door.

He looked across at the living room window.

Lacey prodded Simon Young's corpse with her foot. 'Your first?'

He looked down at the money in his hand.

'I always knew you had it in you,' Lacey said.

He thrust it through the letterbox.

This is not mine, Sheila, it's yours. I refuse to be the same as all the rest. I refuse to be the same as Herbert Wheelhouse, as Lacey Ray, as Luke Parkinson.

Take, take, take.

He turned from the door and headed back to his vehicle.

That's not me.

9

WILTSHIRE HQ GLARED.
Forget HMP Hancock, forget the brain-splattered radio studio, forget the ash cloud that looked like a pool of bloody phlegm, true anguish, for Yorke, could be found in an office on that third floor.

Superintendent Joan Madden was a stickler for the rules. A close relative of Patricia had become involved in the case. There was no way on God's green earth Madden was overlooking this one.

After parking his car, he showed his ID in reception, and took the stairs. Anything that slowed down this journey was particularly welcome. He was in no rush to be removed from *Operation Tagline*.

But the inevitable came very quickly, as it always seemed to do and, before he knew it, he was in the office, sitting before a spindly boss with cheekbones you could open bottles of beer with.

She got straight to the point; she knew about Douglas Firth. Yorke repeated back everything Firth had told him.

He then slumped back in the chair, preparing himself for a crippling blow.

'So you're compromised?' Madden said.

Yorke nodded. 'I guess so, but until we speak to George Johnson, the accountant, I guess we could stay openminded? Firth might have no connection with *Operation Tagline* whatsoever.'

'No connection?' Madden smiled. 'With money involved?'

'I'm still holding onto that chance.'

She stood up and went over to her window. She stared down at the carpark, where Yorke had been staring up from minutes ago. 'Every day I work out. Every *single* day. It might be a run, it could be a swim, it could be weights ... every single day. My heart beats below forty a minute - the same as an Olympian. My body fat's less than ten percent. I've a personal trainer, and I've read countless pieces of literature on fitness, and the evidence is overwhelming. To maintain this fitness level and weight, I don't need to exercise as much as I do. Not every day, and certainly not for the durations I go for. But even with all of this documented scientific proof, I'm not prepared to change it. And why? Because nothing can ever be an absolute certainly. *Nothing*. And no matter how small the chance. No matter how *minuscule*, I would never embrace it. Do you understand what I'm saying here, Michael?'

'Yes, ma'am, of course.' Yorke sighed. *I'm not a fool.* 'So, who're you thinking of handing it over to?'

'Luke.'

Yorke was back on his feet. *'Parkinson?* You're kidding! With all due respect, ma'am, do you want to find whoever did this?'

Madden smiled. 'Very much so. And in the process, I'd

like to kill two birds with one stone. Sit down, Michael, and I will explain. Don't be so tempestuous, it really doesn't suit you. I like you for all the opposite reasons. You are calm, collected and authoritative, you're not a wild animal.'

'Like Luke Parkinson?'

Madden smiled again. 'Like Luke Parkinson.'

'Okay ... so what's going on?'

'If I left you as SIO on this case, there'd be a few raised eyebrows in the station. You *could* be compromised. Probably are. Am I bothered? Not really. You're the best I've got, and you wouldn't let it interfere with your duty. But I need to be careful of those raised eyebrows. So, you're still on the case, just not in charge. At least not on the surface ...'

'Sorry, ma'am, but this really doesn't sound like you. Is something else going on here ...?'

'Come on, Michael. We all have pretence. How do you know this isn't the real me?' She smiled. 'So do you wish me to go on or would you rather I just took you off the case completely?'

'No, sorry, ma'am, please continue.'

'The outcome of this situation is inevitable. Luke is a loose cannon. In the limelight, he won't last a day running the investigation. With you watching him like a hawk, we can be certain of this. The first mistake, whether that be manhandling a witness, a racist comment, sexual misconduct or even forgetting to file his bloody paperwork, I'll haul him over the coals and have him on competency. Then, it's all a matter of time. We'll either get him transferred out of our station or, better still, out of the force.'

Yorke couldn't believe what he was hearing. He shook his head.

'Your thoughts?'

Yorke widened his eyes. 'My thoughts? I *thought* you really liked Parkinson!'

She wagged a finger at him. 'There's that *pretence* again.'

Yorke nodded. 'Keep your friends close and your—'

'*Precisely*. The best thing about all of this is that it becomes a win-win for you.'

'Go on.'

'In a day or two, when he's off the case, and you've hopefully proven that Firth is nothing to do with the death of Janice Edwards, I'll have to put you back in charge again.'

Yorke nodded. 'Are you sure this'll work?'

'Didn't you hear what I said about chance?'

'Yes, ma'am, but surely chance is involved here also?'

'Yes, on your part, Michael. Not on mine. If you want to stay on this case, you'll make it work. Now go and meet Assistant Chief Constable Robinson from SEROCU. He's sitting in your office. Then, after that, you can run the briefing. I'm not stupid enough to put Luke in charge until SEROCU have left the building.'

She turned to her keyboard and started typing an email. She didn't bother saying goodbye.

DOUGLAS FIRTH SAT NEXT to Herbert 'The Reaper' Wheelhouse on the bottom bunk. Firth had just run through his entire conversation with his son-in-law earlier.

'Mentioning George was a necessity, Herb. They're bound to look into the money now. Best to be open and up front. Like I told you years ago, George is the best. They'll find nothing out of order, and they'll leave us both alone.'

Wheelhouse didn't respond. He'd been crying hard and was only now getting his breath back.

The cell door opened. Gavin Harris stood there, chewing gum.

'We're busy,' Firth said. 'Go back to reading your newspaper.'

'Finished it. Hargreaves wants your section outside now for exercise.'

Firth stood up. 'Then I'll repeat what I just said. *We're busy.*'

'And I'll repeat what I *just* said,' Harris said. 'The warden wants you outside now.'

Firth took a step towards him. 'What do I pay you for exactly?'

'You pay me for what I *can* do. Arguing with my boss is something I *can't* do.'

Firth took another step forward, so he towered over the diminutive, younger man. He leaned over so he could speak into his ear. 'No such thing as *can't*. Didn't they teach you that at school, little man? Go and *learn* how to argue with the warden, or I will find someone who can.'

Harris took a step back, chewing with his mouth open. 'Ten minutes.'

He left the room.

'The youth have no fucking respect anymore,' Wheelhouse said.

'Like we used to have respect for anyone?' Firth said and smiled. 'We just did a better job of pretending.'

Firth took a moment to look at the framed photograph of Ian on the bedside table. His five-year-old boy was clutching a football to his chest. Yes, it reminded him of that day when he chased the ball out onto the street, but his son had loved the game, *adored* the game. It was an appropriate photograph, and one that brought back a lot of good memories rather than just tragic ones.

He reached down and picked up a copy of the play *Death of a Salesman* by Arthur Miller.

'I used to be a salesman way back,' Firth said.

'You still bloody well are,' Wheelhouse said, 'you could sell ice to an Eskimo.'

Firth smiled. 'That's probably why *Death of a Salesman* is my favourite read.'

'It's about a self-centred man, who does not understand that he isn't good enough at what he does.'

'*Precisely*,' Firth said. 'The tragedy of Willy Loman. What better warning is there?'

'Indeed. It's a warning we should've heeded long before now, I guess.'

'We always got it, Herb. We always knew we weren't good enough, and we were never self-centred.'

'It's a shame our families would disagree with us on that one.'

Firth waved his hand and laughed. 'Ah, what do they know?'

'All I ever wanted to do was protect them, and I've failed ... I've *fucking* failed.' He started to cry again.

Not again, Firth thought. *We will be outside in five minutes. Weakness is not something you want to parade around anywhere, especially in prison.*

Wheelhouse looked up at him. His face was red. 'I need your help.'

Firth shook his head. 'No ... you *just* need time—'

'*No!* I need help. If roles were reversed, you'd be asking for the same thing.'

'Which is what exactly?'

'You know what Doug.'

'It's not a good idea. Everything has a cost. You know that as much as anyone.'

'I'll pay you whatever you want.'

Firth sat down beside him and put his arm around his old colleague's shoulders. 'It's not about the money. It's never about the money. Most'd disagree but remember we're better than Willy Loman.'

Wheelhouse looked him in the eyes. 'If not money, then what'll it cost me?'

Firth raised his eyebrows. 'Well, what did revenge cost me ... eventually? *Everything.* My freedom, my family ...'

'But I've lost all of that already.'

Firth shook his head. 'You've never truly lost everything.'

'Ah come on, Doug, cut out the philosophy. I'm in my twilight years, and I'm in jail. If I walk out of here, which I probably won't, it'll be using a fucking Zimmer frame.'

Firth reached around to the back of Wheelhouse's head and pulled him close to him. Their foreheads touched. 'Whatever you want then, Herb. Whatever you want.'

'Make it happen, Doug. George can sort out the money.'

With their foreheads touching, Firth was forced to lift his eyes to meet Wheelhouse's again. 'Please don't say I didn't warn you. I don't know the *true* cost of your revenge yet, but I do know this ... if it's against Buddy Young, the cost will be high ...'

Despite Assistant Chief Constable Riley Robinson's slight build, his handshake was one of the firmest Yorke had ever experienced. 'Thank you for having me, Detective Chief Inspector.'

'Thank you for your support, sir, please make yourself comfortable.'

Robinson undid a button on his suit and sat down on a sofa chair at the side of Yorke's office. Yorke wheeled over his office chair and sat opposite him.

'Support is something we all need to be calling on in these trying times, DCI.'

'Please call me, Mike, and yes, I really hope we can support you in turn.'

'I was bringing someone with me today. Louise … a capable Inspector. Unfortunately, the ash cloud is causing her problems.' He touched his chest. 'Asthma.'

Wendy, the Management Support Assistant, interrupted them with coffee. It was a welcome refreshment for Yorke after a long night prowling the garden, and it was a welcome duty for Wendy due to the high praise she received. 'Coffee doesn't taste this good where I'm coming from, I can tell you,' Robinson said.

Wendy smiled. 'It's all in the quantity of ground coffee, and the timing. And *never* from a machine. Always a cafetière.'

'If you *ever* fancy a change of scenery …'

Wendy laughed and nodded at Yorke. 'And leave this one? Whatever would he do?'

'I wouldn't last a week,' Yorke said and smiled.

After Wendy had left, Robinson continued. 'I spoke to your Superintendent at length this morning, and she wanted me to take you through everything again. That's quite a compliment – she thinks very highly of you.'

Yorke smiled. Life was certainly full of surprises.

Robinson swallowed a mouthful of coffee, and then said, 'Have you heard of *Article SE?*'

Yorke nodded. 'It's the name given by your department to an organised crime syndicate based in the South East.'

'Organised crime has been evolving for years, but in my career, I have never seen anything quite like this. *Article SE* have a hand in everything. And I mean everything. Not just the obvious stuff either like human trafficking, drugs and prostitution. We've found an arm of the organisation illegally importing foods such as pufferfish, and shark fins. Last year, we closed a record number of sweatshops full of illegal immigrants. And last month, we moved on a racket that were using prostitutes to breed children for sale. Identifying the top of this organisation has been impossible. We know the epicentre is in the South-East, but it is growing at a remarkable rate.'

'Could *Young Properties* be the top of the organisation?'

Robinson shook his head. 'You have it the wrong way around. *Article SE* have absorbed *Young Properties*. This is down to the last CEO, Simon Young. A ruthless, ambitious individual. After growing their dirty company to remarkable heights, Young was happy to let it metamorphose into one of the cancerous lumps growing from the malignant mass which is *Article SE*.'

'If you can't beat them, join them?' Yorke said.

Robinson nodded. 'And make more money in the process. Since Simon's death, his father Buddy Young, a very old-school racketeer, has come out of retirement, and from what we can find out, which is very little, it seems he isn't best pleased with the more modern approach in which all these facets of corruption work in synergy and he's not the leading figure.'

'You say you can't get to the top, but surely, with all the current surveillance technology at your disposal, you should be all over them ...'

'That's what you'd think,' Robinson said. 'But, alas, *this* technology you speak of is a better weapon for them than it is for us. Genuinely, I've been doing this for almost twenty years, and I've never known criminals to be so evasive. You move in and sever an arm off this outfit, and another arm grows somewhere else. It doesn't matter who you catch red-handed, and burn in an interrogation room, they take you nowhere. They always know *so* little, if anything at all. There are layers and layers of ignorance and diversions. Last month, we followed one trail which had us all excited, and it led us right to a priest ...'

Yorke shrugged. 'Priests aren't always innocent.'

'This one was, he'd been dead for 60 years.'

'Ah,' Yorke said. 'Slippery bastards.'

'They'd actually have to be there to be slippery. It's more like mist. You can see the arseholes moving, but that's all you're allowed. And if you walk into the mist, you just get lost.'

'Or possibly worse?' Yorke said.

'Yes ... unfortunately, there have been some incidents like that.' Robinson looked away and sighed. 'The worst thing is the Russian involvement. There're a lot of Russians, who know very little English. They're also quite mercenary. They work for money with no real knowledge of what they're doing. Great soldiers, poor informants. Which leads me to why I'm here.'

Robinson lifted a briefcase up onto his knee and reached in for a brown folder and handed it to Yorke. He withdrew a handful of photographs.

On the first photograph, a man lay sprawled on the floor. The entire bottom half of his face was red with blood, and he had a bullet hole in the centre of his head. Yorke shuffled to the next photograph. Snap. A man with a bloody face executed with a headshot. Yorke only had to see two more murders to get the Modus Operandi.

'Carry on,' Robinson said. 'To the close-ups.'

Yorke did so. When he reached the first of them, he flinched.

Someone had sliced and diced one of the victim's mouths. His lips were in tatters; some pieces hung loose while other pieces were completely missing. Yorke could see the victim's bloody teeth through the gaps. The killer had also sliced from the corners of his mouth to the top of his cheeks, spreading the bloody mutilation further up his face.

Yorke looked up at Robinson. 'You're going to tell me these monstrosities are linked to our case, aren't you?'

'I hope we're wrong, but yes, I think they are,' Robinson said, reaching into his briefcase for another brown envelope. This time Robinson took the photograph out himself and handed it over to Yorke.

Yorke looked down at a mugshot of a tall well-built man with a shaved head and a long aquiline face. The wall he stood in front of, and the jail jumpsuit, were white. The only colours on the photograph were his eyes and his red mouth. The rest of his skin was pale and barren and smouldered with the surrounding whiteness.

'The cutter, I assume?' Yorke said.

'A more appropriate name for this beast, I agree, but no, he's the *The Dancer*.'

Yorke creased his brow. '*The Dancer?*'

'That's what they call him. *The Dancer*. Back when he was in Russia, before he worked for *Article SE*, he was a Russian ballet dancer. His real name is Borya Turgenev. It may interest you to know that his name translates to *Energetic Fighter*.'

'It doesn't interest me,' Yorke said. 'It just worries me.'

'You need to be worried, I'm afraid. Borya is *Article SE's* most prolific hitman.'

'So, if you know who he is, why don't you have him yet?'

'The man is a shadow, Mike. He's been caught on camera once. Two years ago, leaving a vic's residence, he passed a local park. A fourteen-year-old boy, truanting from school, was taking selfies of him and his girlfriend. Borya showed up on one of these photographs. The boy's mother, who had sneaked a peek at her brat's phone after confiscating it, alerted us to the photograph when we put the feelers out for information regarding suspicious behaviour in the area. Borya was behind the young couple, staring at them with those same dead eyes you just saw on the mugshot. I haven't got the photograph to hand, but he did look truly sinister. What compelled him to stop and look I have no idea, but we had our first image of him. Then, we found a match to a passport he used to enter the country five years ago. We've got some history of the man from the Russians but not as much as we'd like or need. That mugshot is of him serving a short spell inside. Apparently, he had a disagreement with someone he was dancing and performing with. We've struggled to get a reason why. Who knows, maybe he trod on his toes during the dance routine? Anyway, the disagreement led to a near-death experience for the victim, and Borya did a spell inside for GBH. This is a real monster here, Mike. There have been a lot of hits in the South East in the last five years. Every single one of them has been male, and every single one of them has had his face mutilated. We suspect he's ruining their mouths to send out a message from his employees. Something along the lines of: if you talk, we will take your mouth to pieces too.'

'Nice,' Yorke said.

'Just a theory,' Robinson said. 'He could just be doing it because he enjoys it.'

'Don't,' Yorke said. 'I've met some people like that before. Not pretty.'

'And now you're wondering how we know that all the murders were committed by Borya? After all, anyone can cut a face to ribbons.'

'Not sure I could,' Yorke said with a grimace. 'But go on.'

'The hitman uses a pistol called a Para Ordnance P-18 with a suppressor. An interesting weapon based on a vintage pistol from 1911. Ballistics have matched all of the bullets from the thirty-eight hits.'

'Bloody hell ... thirty-eight.' Yorke said. 'His press nickname, *The Reaper*, just got a lot more fitting.'

'Actually, Mike, it's now thirty-nine hits.'

Yorke signed. He knew what was coming.

'I hope you don't mind, but we fast-tracked ballistics on your behalf.'

'He killed Janice Edwards, didn't he?'

Robinson nodded. 'She's the first woman he's killed.'

Yorke sighed.

'Small mercies that he didn't ruin her face, and just shot her from behind.'

Yorke sighed. 'I guess *The Reaper* is a gentleman.'

———

THE BRIGHT RED BILL FLASHED, and the bread disappeared.

With a gloved hand, Borya threw a handful of breadcrumbs to the other swan; a black-feathered female with a much shorter bill. It crooned, appreciating the gesture. Borya glanced back at the male, who now held its neck erect with its feathers raised in an aggressive display.

Borya showed the empty bag to the male and smiled.

'*Please* Mummy, look, he's feeding the swans!'

Borya turned to his right to look at a young boy pointing at him. He was holding his mother's hand.

The mother frowned at Borya and then nodded over at the *Don't feed the Swans* sign.

Borya stared at the mother. Not with any intent, or anger. Just with curiosity. He wasn't too sure what the correct response to her challenge was.

Like he'd done with the swan, he showed her the empty bag. She shrugged. She was unrelenting. He *felt* her challenge but did not understand it.

'I'm sorry,' he said.

She shrugged again. 'It's not good for them.'

She would not be pacified. She would not be controlled. She would not be beaten.

He took a deep breath and felt the moment.

Everything was quiet. Still.

Peace.

He spat on the floor at her feet and walked away.

BORYA WATCHED the man sit down. He moved with no grace. No elegance. He could never be a dancer.

He was also timid and shaky. His glasses didn't fit him properly and continually slid down his nose.

'Are you ordering a coffee?' he said.

Borya shook his head. He unwrapped another Chewit, slipped it into his mouth, and rolled the wrapper into a tight little ball. He laid the wrapper beside another one on the table.

'They're calling you *The Reaper*.'

Borya looked at the tiny, squirming man and chewed.

'Maybe you should try to be more ... more inconspicuous.'

Borya swallowed. 'I do not know that word.'

The man coughed and his glasses slid right to the tip of his nose. He pushed them back. 'More subtle.'

'Again, I do not know your vocabulary. I deliver messages. I delivered. Next?' He held out his gloved hand.

'Yes ...' The man rustled in his backpack and handed over a file.

Borya looked through the file. He noticed the mother and child from the river earlier come into the café. She glared at him.

He respected her for her fight but ignored her. He looked at the picture of the man again; then, he put the file down.

'A policeman?'

The man shrugged. 'I don't know. Like you, I just deliver.'

'Hmm,' Borya said and started to unwrap another Chewit. 'Not inconspicuous or subtle, is it?'

The man's eyes widened.

'When?' Borya put the Chewit in his mouth.

'Tonight.'

'That soon?'

'Yes.'

'Hmm.' Borya chewed.

'I just deliver the message.'

'You said,' Borya nodded, stood, picked up the file and walked away.

10

THE INCIDENT ROOM was its usual swollen self.

It was inevitable that the person Yorke's eyes settled on first was Luke Parkinson; it was equally inevitable that he had a smirk plastered across his face.

So, he's aware that this is my swansong and that he'll be stepping up to the fore later in the day.

Yorke was tempted to smirk back but resisted the urge. This man was deserving of a big surprise. The bigger the better.

At the back of the room, Joan Madden entertained their special guest from SEROCU. Yorke, himself, couldn't recall a single time she'd been entertaining. Yet, here was Robinson smiling away. Yorke was in awe of Madden's ability to turn it on with other VIPs. There was no end to his boss's talents.

Yorke's hand settled on Jeremy Dawson's shoulder. An operative for the Home Office Major Enquiry System that had been with them through thick and thin. Yorke leaned over. 'Congratulations on getting married.'

'Thanks, sir, it was great.'

'I saw the photographs that were pinged out last week. That cake in the shape of a laptop was a nice touch.'

Dawson patted his laptop. 'Based on this very one. It's how we met.'

Jeremy had married another HOLMES 2 operative he'd met on the Christian Severance case.

'I know, Jeremy, I was there.' Yorke smiled.

As Yorke backed away towards the whiteboard on which *Operation Tagline* was scrawled in black, jagged letters, Yorke swung his eyes around the room for friendly faces, as he always did before a briefing. Following an initial pang of sorrow at the absences of Topham and Gardner, he offered a smile to Jake, and then to both Willows, and Pemberton. The two detectives who'd really stepped up to the plate in recent months and offered him solid sanctuary for his trust. Yorke had observed that they hadn't been getting on too well of late but was pleased to see that they were deep in conversation and looked to be getting over whatever had been bothering them. Pemberton's dry humour was often a good antidote to Willows' extreme acerbic tendencies, so having them on the same page could only be beneficial.

Yorke started the briefing, introduced Robinson, and then weaved from image to image on the whiteboard recapping the previous day's events. As he did this, he thought of Borya Turgenev, and his nickname, *the Dancer,* and a strange thought settled in his mind. *We all dance, don't we? Every day. We dance.*

To raised eyebrows, he filled his team in on Patricia's father's connection to Operation Tagline, laying the foundations for Parkinson's later step up. Even with this groundwork, Parkinson's elevation would still come as a surprise to everyone in the room, even those who *actually* liked the idiot. There were far more colleagues worthy of promotion. But this was Madden's masterplan, and who was he to question it?

'The accountant, George Johnson, is where both myself and DS Willows will be heading next. He handles Firth and Wheelhouse's money. And we all know, from experience, that where money is involved, the answers aren't too far away.'

He watched Parkinson grin. On every other day, a comment would be forthcoming. Something along the lines of: *Does it not worry you that your wife's father is connected to this murder?*

That's why Madden will have warned him of doing this *before* the briefing. If he so much as breathed a controversial word in this meet, he could kiss goodbye to the biggest step up of his career. She'd bought his silence.

Yorke gave Willows the opportunity to feedback on her interview with author, Matthew Peacock, before briefly discussing the media circus that was growing around their new headline-spinner, *The Reaper*.

'Are we going to tell them that *The Reaper* is *actually* Herbert Wheelhouse's nickname?' Jake asked.

'We could do,' Yorke said, 'But I doubt that it'd make a difference. A killer called *The Reaper* is excellent clickbait for their news outlets, I hardly think they'll be in a rush to change it.'

It was now time to introduce SEROCU's involvement. 'We're no longer just relying on Herbert Wheelhouse's say-so that organised crime is behind the murder of his niece, Janice. SEROCU today have bought us more conclusive evidence. I'm going to let Assistant Chief Constable Robinson introduce this evidence to you. He will also introduce a new suspect.'

There were mutterings around the room as Robinson approached the front. It took him about ten minutes to cover everything he'd discussed with Yorke before in his office including the shadowy umbrella organisation *Article SE*, and their most trusted hitman, Borya Turgenev. He opted not to unleash those photographs of Borya's crimes but didn't omit any necessary details from his brief. After he'd finished, Yorke handed out copies of the mugshot of Borya.

'The fucking Dancer,' Yorke overheard Parkinson whispering to one of his cronies, 'he sounds like a fag.'

Robinson continued by giving everyone information on Borya's background. 'He had a privileged upbringing. By privileged, I refer only to wealth. His late father was part of a Russian syndicate and had links with running prostitutes from the Ukraine over to Russia. So, nothing privileged about being raised in a morally bankrupt family. We've pushed for more information regarding his family – the Turgenevs, and their history but most of the information is classified by the Russians. His sheltered upbringing led him to great opportunities. Dancing being one of them. By his mid-twenties, he was quite a well-known ballet dancer. He had a leading role in the famous ballet, *The Nutcracker,* which was a consistent sell-out in Moscow. He was quite the big name – could've gone somewhere with his life. Instead, he opted for a fight with another dancer and ended up spending the latter half of his twenties in jail – that is where that mugshot just handed out comes from. According to our sources in Russia, when he was released from jail, over ten years ago, he disappeared. The next available information we have is a record of him landing in Heathrow on a visa. It was five years ago, so the visa has since expired.'

Willows' hand was in the air. Robinson nodded at her.

'How did a man with a criminal record, and known ties to organised crime, get a visa?'

'A question we've asked our embassy in Russia more than once. The person who granted the visa is long gone. And I mean *long gone*. A year after granting this visa, he disappeared. It's a lead we have pursued, relentlessly, to no avail.'

'So, Borya could have changed his identity?' Jake said.

'A certainty,' Robinson said. 'There's more too. But first, can I add that anything that we mention in this room is strictly confidential? This operation will remain with Wiltshire HQ as long as we have unfettered access to the investigation, and you remain receptive to our instruction and support. With the manpower, and knowledge of the area you have available, we can really help each other. But you must be warned. If information relayed in this room starts to find its way into the press, or the political aspect of this investigation begins to heat up, which it may very well do so, we'll have to take complete control of the case. I like to be transparent. We want to work with you, and we do not want to condescend, but as you can see, we are dealing with a very sensitive situation.'

There was collective nodding from the dozen occupants of the room, and murmurings of agreement.

'We believe that Borya is being supported by Russia. We're not basing this assumption on the lack of support in obtaining a profile of him because that reluctance to help is common enough with Russia. We're basing our belief on the fact that Borya has assassinated four former GRU officers.'

'Ex-Russian spies?' Willows said without putting her hand up.

Robinson nodded. 'The sanctuary and protection we

offered them in the United Kingdom didn't pan out for them.'

Yorke had heard the story back in his office, but he found himself thinking the same thing he had before. *It seems no amount of sanctuary and protection can hold off Borya.*

Jake put up his hand. Robinson nodded in his direction. 'So, he doesn't just work as a leading hitman for this *Article SE*, but he also works for the Russian Government silencing double-crossing spies?'

Robinson raised his eyebrows.

Yorke interjected at this point. 'As farfetched as some of this may sound to us, you must all remember that Assistant Chief Constable Robinson lives these scenarios daily. The evidence he has presented for us today is compelling.'

Robinson nodded. 'And you can all now understand the need for everything to remain strictly confidential.'

All eyes swung to Yorke. He could see the same question in every face. *What now then?*

Knowing that this would be the last time he'd be issuing orders in a while, Yorke delivered his plan of action with extra vigour. He again danced around the whiteboard, pointing out salient information, including the fact that Borya Turgenev executed Janice Edwards in a more humane manner than his other victims – if there *could* be any humanity in murder. Rather than point out the jobs attached to the whiteboard, he went through every officer, individually, personalising their task.

'At the end of the day, it doesn't matter who he is or where he comes from. Borya Turgenev executed an innocent woman in cold blood. He must face justice. And to do that, we must do what we do best. We must catch him.'

EVERYONE LEFT the incident room apart from Yorke and Robinson.

'Seemed to go well,' Yorke said.

'As well as anything can go when dealing with the great British cynicism.'

'Yes, I apologise, there can be a lot of that in this room.'

'There can be a lot of it in any room, including the room I come from.' He smiled. 'You quickly grow a thick skin in my job. Funny thing is, when you read about spies and whatnot in a daily rag everyone laps it up as fact, but when you present it with cold hard evidence everyone raises an eyebrow.'

Yorke wanted to make himself scarce before it became public knowledge that he was being asked to step down as SIO of *Operation Tagline*. 'I'm meeting one of my officers in the carpark, we're going to check out Wheelhouse and Firth's accountant, George Johnson. You are welcome to tag along if you want?'

'I'm due back at HQ for a meeting regarding a potential *Article SE* informant. Before you get your hopes up, I've had many of these meetings before and they rarely come to much, but I must be vigilant. One day something will come off. Besides, I've had a gutful of George Johnson. He does the accounts for many of these bastards. Before I leave though Mike, I want to talk to you about something else ...'

'Sure, sir.'

'There's more to Borya Turgenev than what I've already told you. Not knowing my audience, I didn't want to go in too strong. I wanted to leave this final piece for yourself so you can decide how best to utilise the information.'

Yorke nodded. 'My team ... they've been through a lot in the past. I don't think they'd be easily rattled.'

'Still. I thought it would be prudent to mention it to you first and we didn't get time to discuss it in our meeting before.'

'Okay, sir, I'm all ears.'

'Borya Turgenev's the worst I've come across, and not just because his thirty-nine hits or his sadistic behaviours towards his victims. I told you before that the Turgenevs were a prominent crime family. *Were*. Before Borya left Russia, he wiped them out. Every last one of them. He shot his parents and mutilated them - cut out their eyes I believe. He shot his three brothers, their wives, his three-year old nephew and his eight-year-old niece. He also paid a visit to his two uncles. Both of whom were also prominent in the syndicate. They'd have welcomed Borya with open arms, and it will have been the last thing they ever did. Reports suggest *more* facial mutilation. It seems Borya was experimenting, refining his tastes, and developing. Because he'd been reasonably famous in the past for his ballet dancing, the Russian media nicknamed him *The Dancer*.' Robinson sighed. '*The Reaper* in the UK, and *The Dancer* in Russia. Which do you prefer?'

'Both fill me with dread,' Yorke said. 'How the hell did this monster get out of his country and into ours?'

'Good question. The Russians claim that he'd left before the bodies were discovered. Eight bodies? Nonsense. We suspect they let him leave. If I was a gambling man, I would wager that he was tasked with removing his own family, and then allowed to relocate to the UK to pick off ex-GRU agents. *Article SE* clearly has ties to the Russians. They have offered Borya a good home and have gained a loyal soldier in return.'

'And the conspiracy grows.'

'Yes. Welcome to my world. Listen Mike, you need to stay in constant contact with me. If, for any reason, you cannot get in touch, you should contact my office. I have faith in your investigative abilities, and your team, and that is why we are allowing this to continue. Killing Janice Edwards will be his undoing. I think you can get closer to Borya than anyone has done before, but he is dangerous, *incredibly* dangerous so keep your updates coming. I should be back here early evening anyway.'

Yorke shook Robinson's hand, went to the toilet, stopped for a glass of water at the cooler, descended in the elevator and joined Willows in the carpark to go and hunt a Russian hitman.

THERE WAS a bench in the target's back garden. Borya decided to sit a while. The property was detached and the fences high, so he did not worry about being seen.

The target lived alone and would be out for the rest of the day, if not most of the evening. His job for the Wiltshire police demanded such commitment. But, if the officer did make it home early, for whatever reason, Borya would not be at a disadvantage.

He stroked the outline of his pistol through his leather jacket. He was never at a disadvantage.

He felt droplets of rain and looked up at the dark skies. Could this be the bout of turbulent weather many were wishing for? An end to the ash cloud? No one was wishing harder for this than those losing money from the grounded aviation industry. Not that turbulent weather was a guarantee of clear skies. The volcano in Iceland was still erupting, and there had been cases in the past where volcanos had spent over twelve months in flow. If it continued, north-westerly winds would continue to bring the darkness this way.

Borya let his head loll backwards and allowed the sky to spit in his face.

He didn't want the fury ever to end. It was a symbol of strength and power.

The fiery beast's volcanic fissures lay under a thick slab of glacial ice. Lava, at over 1000 degrees C, was riddled with pressurised gases. It formed an explosive interaction with the ice. The ash and smoke shot 30,000ft in the air.

It would not be pacified. It would not be controlled.

It would not be beaten.

Borya took a deep breath and felt the moment.

Everything was quiet. Still.

Peace.

Borya stood up. It was time to enter the house.

He always liked to get to know his victim before he silenced them forever.

11

G EORGE JOHNSON'S PREMISES weren't what you'd expect from an accountant on the payroll of the wealthy and the corrupt. Yorke guessed that his ability to keep a profile so low that it was practically non-existent was what made him so employable.

His office was above an off-licence. It had a clearance sale notice in the window.

'I don't think I've ever seen a clearance sale on alcohol before,' Willows said.

'Me neither,' Yorke said, turning the car engine off.

Willows pointed at the looming housing estate. 'You'd expect it to shift pretty quickly around here.'

'To be honest, it'd probably shift quicker if it was beside HQ.' Yorke killed the engine.

'Yep, there's a lot of stress in that place.'

Yorke nodded. 'And I'd be first in line ... well, at least you and Lorraine seem to have buried the hatchet.'

Willows flushed.

'Sorry,' Yorke said. 'I just noticed that you'd fallen out

over something ... just tell me to shut up if I've overstepped the mark—'

'We kissed.'

It was Yorke's turn to flush. 'Ah ... okay, sorry, I'm getting involved in something that I really—'

'*Just kissed.* Meant nothing. To her, anyway. Over now.'

Yorke nodded. 'Always difficult when you work together. I can give you real-life examples of that—'

'She has a partner. I should've known better. We'd just had a few drinks and it was one of those impulse things. You know?'

Yorke nodded again. 'Yes, impulse things. Know all about them.'

'Shall we go in then?'

Yorke opened the car door. Before getting out, he looked back. 'You okay?'

'Good. Over now, remember?'

'If you ever want to talk about it ...'

'We just did.'

'Yes, right.' Yorke stepped out of the car. He felt the first drops of rain. He held out the palm of his hand. 'Do you reckon it'll clear the cloud?'

Willows shrugged.

Before they'd had chance to knock, George Johnson opened the door beside the failing off-licence. They'd rung ahead, and he'd been waiting at the bottom of his stairs, obviously keen to lead them up. Common practise amongst dodgy accountants and lawyers. He wouldn't want to give law enforcement a second's freedom in his premises. From the moment they crossed his threshold, everything would be on his terms. Unless Yorke got a warrant. But Johnson would be keen to avoid that. Yorke prepared himself for a schmooze fest.

Johnson was unshaven, needed a haircut and his suit had seen better days. Yorke wanted to remark that trying so hard to keep *this* low a profile may actually arouse suspicion, but he left it alone.

Johnson led them up a set of badly carpeted stairs and took them into his dishevelled office. There were mountains of paperwork everywhere.

After they sat down, Willows couldn't help herself. 'How do you woo potential clients here?'

Yorke looked down, forcing back a smile.

'You mean the disorganisation?' Johnson spoke quickly. He lifted a pile of papers from one of the office chairs so Yorke could sit down.

'Among other things,' Willows said, looking him up and down before raising an eyebrow.

'Have you ever heard the expression that one man's disorganisation is another man's organisation?' He raised an eyebrow back at her.

'No, I haven't.'

'That's because I made it up. True though.'

'Debatable.'

Yorke put a hand on Willows' arm. If it wasn't Jake, it was Willows. Both knew how to rile an interviewee. Again, he panged for Gardner. 'Let's get on with this. I'm sure Mr Johnson is very busy.'

'I've always got time for important matters such as these.'

Yorke and Willows sat down.

'Tea? Coffee?' Johnson said.

'No thank you,' Yorke said. 'I'd just like to talk to you about the two men I phoned ahead about.'

'Herbert and Douglas?'

'Yes.'

'They've been my clients for years.' He stood behind his office swivel chair with his hands on the back of it.

'We're aware of that,' Yorke said. 'We were hoping you could share some information.'

'Of course. I'm an open book.' He swivelled his chair.

'Could you sit down, please, Mr Johnson?' Willows said.

'I can, but I fidget. I've got a diagnosis of ADHD. I took my Ritalin ten minutes ago, but it can take a bit to kick in. Shame cocaine is illegal. Believe it or not, a burst of that really settles down the hyperactivity.'

Yorke didn't really know how to respond to this, so he didn't. 'Just talk me through your duties to Herbert and Douglas.'

'What you'd expect,' Johnson said, slipping into his seat. 'Accounts and tax returns. They have me monitor spending, and budgets.'

'How does that work when they're in prison?' Yorke said.

'Their income now comes from interest on one or two investments, and several pension schemes. Balancing their books is a lot easier than it used to be.'

'How so?'

'Well, they used to earn from multiple investments. And I mean, multiple.'

'And you have records of all these investments?'

'Of course. I wouldn't be doing my job very well if I didn't.' Johnson was tapping his fingers on his desk as he spoke.

'Can you prepare a list of all these sources?' Yorke said.

'Of course, but it's all available to you at HMRC anyway. Whatever I provide to you will match up identically with their records. I'm not a lawyer. There is no confidentiality agreement in place. I offer full disclosure to the tax office, and I offer full disclosure to you. It'll be with you by the end of the day.'

Yorke looked at Johnson's tapping fingers. The hyperactive accountant took the hint and stopped.

'Whet my appetite,' Yorke said. 'Tell me about some of these multiple investments.'

'Off the top of my head, *Riley's Running Shoes, Prior's Electricians, Luigi's Pizza, Prime Lighting* ... there're more. Many more.'

'And when these companies grew, Herbert and Douglas declared their income to you?' Willows said.

'Yes. It's my duty to report tax evasion, so I ensured that they were very thorough.'

'Were *Young Properties* one of their sources?' Yorke said.

Johnson laughed. 'I don't think they'd be using my services if they had shares in that company! No, all of their investments were from small businesses.'

Yorke could hear the tapping of the accountant's feet. When were those meds going to kick in?

'The next couple of questions are really important, Mr Johnson, do I have your complete attention?'

Johnson smiled. 'Contrary to belief, detective, ADHD is not about the lack of attention, it's about the difficulties in regulating attention. If I'm interested, you have my complete attention. And believe me, I'm interested in *this* conversation.' He moved his affirmation in time with his tapping feet.

'Did Herbert and Douglas ever invest in the *same* company?'

Tap-tap. 'Not that I recall, but as I said, you'll have that list of all of their investments by the end of the day.'

'Herbert and Douglas must've had a lot of money in order to invest in *all* of these companies – where did it come from?'

Tap-tap. 'They'd already made their money long before they came to me. You'd have to track further back, I'm afraid.'

'You handle all of their expenditure now. What are they spending it on?'

Tap-tap. 'Not much. Maintenance of their properties. Herbert had been giving money to Janice before ... the tragedy.'

'Is there much money?

Tap-tap. 'It's not to be sniffed at. We'd all like to be on the receiving end of that inheritance.'

I might be, Yorke thought. 'How would you feel if I told you that we suspected Douglas and Herbert of being involved in organised crime?'

Tap-tap. 'Not much.'

'Even if I told you that we suspect that Janice Edwards was murdered by Herbert's employers for skimming money?'

Johnson stopped tapping. 'It sounds very far-fetched.'

'You stopped tapping,' Willows said.

'Sorry?'

'You stopped tapping your feet.'

'The Ritalin must have finally worked its magic.'

Yorke sensed blood. 'Does it in anyway concern you, Mr Johnson, that Herbert's employers might come here to look for the skimmed money?'

Johnson leaned back in his chair. His expression darkened. 'Do I need a lawyer?'

'I don't know what you need, Mr Johnson, that's the

problem. And without more information, I'm no closer to figuring out what.'

Johnson ran a hand through his dishevelled hair. 'I don't really know what to tell you.'

'Well, let's see if this helps, Mr Johnson. Have you heard of *The Dancer?*'

Johnson went pale. 'A myth ... he doesn't exist.'

'Oh he exists alright,' Yorke said. 'He's wanted in connection with the murder of Janice Edwards.'

Johnson looked like he was about to throw up.

———

On the way back to HQ, Yorke checked in by phone with Robinson at SEROCU.

'George Johnson, wow,' Yorke said, 'not sure they get any dirtier than that.'

'Oh they do, believe me.'

'Is that ADHD thing for real? He doesn't sit still.'

'He played that card, did he? Not sure. We think he spins in circles to hypnotise his interviewer into thinking everything is fine.'

'It didn't work. And everything is certainly not fine. There's been a lot of dirty money laundered through small businesses over the last couple of decades.'

'Multiply that by thousands and you get an idea of the scale we have to deal with.'

'Don't envy you your job.'

'Love it or hate it. Marmite. As you can see, a head for numbers comes in handy. So, did you get anything useful?'

'He's panicked about *The Dancer*. He's pleading ignorant to knowing that anything untoward was going on with his clients.'

'*Despite* their obvious connection to the most corrupt outfit since the *Corleone family*. It's laughable.'

'He's sending over a list of all the businesses Wheelhouse and Firth have *invested* in. When that arrives, I'll see what I can draw up.'

'Forward it to me too. Might be an idea for me to conduct a second interview *especially* now he's rattled. We can serve up all kinds of pressure.'

'Sounds like a plan, but he shut up shop. He thinks he's on the hitlist. He's run to his mother's house.'

'Even better. We could try and get him to deal. You've done well, Mike.'

'No one has done well until Borya is off the street.'

'A matter of time. We're working on a few things here which I'll catch up with you about later.'

After hanging up, Yorke turned the wipers up higher. The rain was coming harder now; the ash cloud was getting its first serious test. He looked at Willows. She was gazing out the window, deep in thought.

Yorke wondered if she was thinking about George Johnson, the corrosive accountant, or that kiss she'd shared with Lorraine Pemberton.

WITH SURGICAL GLOVES ON, Borya thumbed through a copy of *QX* he'd found on his target's bed.

He had no sexual interest in the naked men but was curious to observe their toned bodies. He preferred definition, rather than bulk, so he flicked through until he found a picture of a blond man spread-eagled on the bonnet of a sports car. Borya estimated 5% body fat. The man was lean.

He looked through other images, avoiding anything too sexual, and then cast the magazine aside. Most of the men were shaved, but not shaved *enough* for his liking. He wouldn't trade in his own body for any of theirs.

Beside his target's bed was a framed photograph of his family. He stood alongside his wife and his twin daughters in front of the Sydney Opera House. From reading his target's profile, Borya knew that one of his twin daughters had died from meningitis four years ago. He also knew that the tragedy had destroyed the marriage. His remaining daughter, and wife, had emigrated to Sydney, Australia where her family had originated from.

Leaving Borya's target in a great deal of pain.

He felt the beginnings of an erection, so he turned the photograph face down. Now was the time for focus, rather than distraction.

He spent some more time exploring the house, adjusting to his kill zone, and learning more about his target. He learned that the condemned man had asthma, enjoyed cycling, loved action movies (probably the muscular heroes), was a member of a gay hook-up site, read comic books and once had a terrier.

He also discovered that he was on high doses of antidepressants.

Pain. Lots of it.

Ignoring another sudden rush of arousal, Borya instead reached for a glass bulb that the target had left beside the living room lamp. He held it up and had an idea. An idea that would teach his target to throw his rubbish away and keep a clean home.

One last lesson before the man in pain died. Yes, that sounded good.

Borya put the glass bulb down and started to undress.

12

O N THE CORRIDOR leading to his office, Yorke bumped into Parkinson. 'Are you waiting for me?'

'No, Mike, but I'd like an update on the accountant.'

'You may be overseeing *Tagline* now, Luke, but could you still address me correctly?'

'Could I get an update on the account please, *sir?*'

'Of course.' Yorke filled him in.

'How soon could you have the report typed up, sir?' Parkinson said.

'Probably by the end of the day.'

'No sooner?'

'I was hoping to catch up with Wheelhouse again before the accountant sends his data over.'

'No need,' Parkinson said, 'I've assigned Moss and Blanks. Could you type up the report please? You can present it at briefing tomorrow morning. I'm shooting early. I've got something to follow up on before I head home.'

'What exactly?'

'I'd like to keep this one quiet until it pans out.'

'Interesting leadership style.'

'Come again?'

'Well, the best leaders act with transparency.'

'Says who?'

'Says me. This department has a successful track record.'

Parkinson did his best to look bored. 'I'll let you know, sir, if the lead comes to anything. The report, please?' He smiled and strolled off down the corridor.

Piss off, your days are well and truly numbered.

⸻

THERE WAS a file on Yorke's desk which hadn't been there earlier. When he opened it, and looked inside, his hands began to shake.

It was a signed statement from the late Tom Davies – the man wrongly convicted of murdering Yorke's sister, Danielle. Yorke had never seen the statement before.

He felt the room sway. He took deep breaths to try and steady himself.

In the statement, Davies admitted that the drug overdose had been forced on him by the real killer, William Proud. Proud had meant to kill Davies to make the frame-up easier. Proud had not expected his scapegoat to recover.

Yorke collapsed in his chair.

This statement had never been officially logged, but someone had kept a copy. Who? Was it the same person who'd left it on his desk?

However, figuring that out was the least of Yorke's problems. The most pressing issue was the signature of the interviewing officer at the bottom of the statement.

Yorke put his head in his hands.

Parkinson was connected to the death of his sister.

YORKE TAILED PARKINSON.

In movies, Yorke always wondered how the pursued never cottoned onto the pursuer. Knowing this, Yorke was prepared to confront Parkinson out in the open if he was spotted. Still, if possible, it'd be better to find out where this vile little man was going.

As they entered Tidworth, Yorke conceded that there must be some truth to the tailing he'd seen in movies, because Parkinson was yet to notice him despite their thirty-odd minutes on the road.

They passed the *Rising Sun*, a notorious pub riddled with drugs and prostitution. He doubted they pulled a good pint of *Summer Lightning* in there. He doubted they pulled a good pint of anything.

Parkinson turned off down a dingy street that was familiar to Yorke. It was filled with a row of Edwardian houses. Some of which were squats, housing up to seven or eight people. The last time Yorke had been here, it'd been during the Christian Severance case, and they'd been interviewing sex-workers.

What you up to Parkinson?

Ahead, Parkinson pulled up alongside a boarded-up house. Yorke drove past, turning his head away as he did, so as not to be caught out. In his rear-view mirror, Yorke watched Parkinson bypass the boarded-up house, and then opt for the property next door.

Yorke parked, and then looked in his wingmirror. A young lady welcomed Parkinson, and then admitted him.

Are you seeing prostitutes Parkinson?

If that was the case, Madden's assignment to get him out

of the force was going to be quicker, and easier, than they'd first anticipated.

Yorke readied his phone to take photographs when Parkinson emerged. He didn't know how he could use the photographs exactly but presenting them to Joan Madden would be as good a place as any to start.

Parkinson was only in there for five minutes. Technically, long enough for sex, but Yorke doubted it. He was the type of guy who'd want to get his money's worth when exploiting someone.

Yorke took a burst of photographs through his wingmirror, before switching camera setting to film him driving past. He could easily have been rumbled at this point, but it was worth the risk. This footage was solid gold.

After Parkinson was out of sight, Yorke exited his vehicle. The rains from earlier had stopped, but the sky was still overcast from the ash cloud, and the darkness of evening wasn't far away. He felt like he was wading through gloom as he approached the house. Here was a place of exploitation, and tragedy. He'd visited it once before, and he hoped that the revelations hidden behind that door weren't as disturbing as they'd been back then.

The same young lady who'd admitted Parkinson answered the door. She was heavily made up and chewed gum. 'Can I help you?'

He showed his ID. 'DCI Yorke, ma'am. Can we talk?'

She chewed harder. 'I don't understand. I just saw the other one.'

'Sorry, what don't you understand?'

'You know?' She raised her eyebrows. 'Why it takes two of you?'

'Two of us to do what?'

She stopped chewing. 'Why did you say you were here?'

'Just to talk.'

She stood aside and let him in. Last time he'd been to one of these brothel-squats he'd expected squalor before discovering tidiness and order. This time was different in only one way. It came with the tang of citrus air-freshener.

'What's your name?' Yorke said.

'Helen.' They came into the lounge. 'Listen ... I do what I'm told.'

'By whom?'

She pulled a tissue out of her pocket and spat the chewing gum into it. 'I really don't want to talk to you. I think you should come back another time.'

These brothels were a long-standing project of Vice. Vice worked with a charity called *Second Chance* to help the workers. This industry was being managed and contained, rather than being torn to pieces. Yorke would not be flavour-of-the-month if he became destructive here.

'Ma'am, I don't want to bother you. I know what happens here, and I'm not here to create any problems for you, or whoever you work for. All I want you to tell me is why my colleague was here moments ago.'

She walked over to a bin in the corner of her room and dropped in the tissue-wrapped chewing gum. 'For money. That's all I know. My boss gives it to me, and I give it to your friend when he comes.'

He's not my friend. 'How often does he come?'

'Once a week. Either him, or another fella.'

Yorke felt his heart up-tempo. 'Describe this other fella to me.'

'Big. Strong-looking. A lot nicer than this one. Polite with me, you know?'

There were plenty of polite, strong-looking men in the police.

'A shaved head. Talks to me sometimes. Been having marriage problems.'

Yorke felt sweat crawling down his back.

He took a deep breath. He couldn't bear to entertain these thoughts. Not with everything else going on. Not right now. 'What is the money for?'

'I really don't know. *Honestly*. I'm told to pay. That's all.'

'How much?'

'Again, I don't know. I don't look in the envelope.'

'I'm going to need the name of your boss.'

She went pale. 'You promised.'

'I know. And I promise that I'm not going to go after him.'

'My boss is a woman.'

Yorke raised his eyebrows. 'Her name?'

'Shit ... Amy.'

'Surname?'

'I honestly don't know. She comes here. Calls herself Amy.'

Shit.

'When does she come?'

'Most mornings.'

Yorke realised he'd have to get in touch with Vice to identify and find the pimp known as Amy. Then, he could get full clarification of what he thought he knew already.

Parkinson was on the payroll of organised crime.

Article SE?

Nothing would surprise Yorke at this moment in time.

Leaning down from his sofa, Parkinson put his bottle of beer on the floor. He then counted out the money three times. There could be no margin of error. Lives, most importantly his own, depended on it.

Amy had skimmed two thousand from the reported profits. This envelope was exactly one thousand pounds heavier; his fifty-percent share. As per usual, their employers, hiding away in their greasy offices, would be none the wiser.

He counted off his thousand pounds in fifty-pound notes and laid it to one side. He then pushed the remainder of his employer's money into an envelope and sealed it.

He picked up his bottle from the floor, tilted his head back, closed his eyes, and drained the remainder in four gulps.

He took a deep breath and opened his eyes.

There was a naked man standing in his room.

Yorke knew he should have phoned it in immediately. No one would have been more eager to hear of these developments than Madden.

But there were a couple of questions he wanted answering first before giving Luke Parkinson over to an internal investigation; most importantly, who had employed him to play such a pivotal role in framing Tom Davies with Danielle's murder?

He parked up outside Parkinson's house and killed the engine.

He closed his eyes and remembered Proud's warning the night Yorke had confronted him at the brewery.

There's a bent bastard shitting in the same toilet as you.

Unbelievable. He'd been talking about Parkinson. No wonder the slimy dickhead had been one of the first attenders to the scene that night. He must have breathed an inward sigh of relief when he'd learned of Proud lying dead at the bottom of a ladder with a broken neck.

Yorke knew that he couldn't allow his confrontation with Parkinson to play out in the same way it had with Proud. Career wise, he wouldn't come back from it again.

But he had to know. Look him in the eyes, just once, and get the truth, before the worm disappeared into the system forever.

Another thing was bothering him too.

A big, strong-looking man. Marriage problems. Polite.

It couldn't be Jake. It *just* couldn't be. Parkinson could at least put his mind at ease on that one.

He looked at the house. The front room light was on.

Yorke opened the car door.

PARKINSON'S HEART beat his ribcage.

If he stood, he'd be dead before he was at full stretch. A silenced gun was pointing down at him from barely a metre away.

And while Parkinson shook, Borya 'The Dancer' Turgenev was as steady as a rock.

The man from that mugshot handed out earlier by Robinson was unmistakable. The demon's eyes leached the colour from everything around him.

He didn't have a hair on his body. He chewed slowly on something.

'Why are you here?' Parkinson said.

Borya took a step forward, so he was now only half-a-metre away. He cracked his neck and swallowed whatever he'd been eating.

A Chewit, Parkinson thought, recalling the crime scene at *Radio Exodus. The killer eats Chewits.*

'Have you finished your count?' Borya said. His Russian accent was strong.

'Yes,' Parkinson said, trying to keep the fear from his voice. 'It's all there. You can take it in with you if you want.'

'I will do,' Borya said, raising his other hand. He was holding a lightbulb. 'After.'

'I think there's been a mistake. I've been loyal—'

'No mistake. Only certainty.'

'Seriously, I've done nothing wrong.' He reached for the envelope. 'Look count the money. There's your certainty.'

Borya shook his head. 'Certainty like your dead child. Certainty like the wife that hates you.'

Parkinson narrowed his eyes. He felt a surge of anger but swallowed it back. 'Whatever you think you know—'

'Or you can think of me as certainty. I stand before you, hiding nothing. My intentions are clear.' He held the lightbulb out. 'I want you to put this in your mouth.'

Parkinson gulped and then slowly shook his head.

'Take it and put it into your mouth.'

'I don't understand—'

'I will count to three.'

Parkinson shook his head again.

'One ... two ...'

'*Okay!*' Parkinson took the bulb. His hand shook as he turned it, so the bayonet cap was facing towards him; then, he slipped it into his mouth.

'*No,*' Borya said. 'Put it in the other way.'

Parkinson withdrew the bayonet cap. '*How?* I can't squeeze the bulb in ... that's—'

'I can help you if you want.'

That *certainly* wasn't an option. Shaking hard, Parkinson turned the bulb towards his mouth and started to push. Part way in, he raised his eyebrows to suggest that this was the best he could do. When Borya stepped forward, Parkinson did better. He hammered the bayonet cap several times with the palm of his hand, and the bulb slid home.

Stretched wide, the corners of his mouth burned. They would soon split and sting for days. He stared up at Borya. He must have looked ridiculous. Like a fucking blowfish. The Russian's expression didn't change. If he was finding Parkinson's humiliation amusing, he was doing a great job of hiding it.

What now?

Borya took another step forward, until he was within touching distance. Parkinson noticed that Borya had the beginnings of an erection. He was well endowed, and the lack of pubic hair accentuated the size further.

Was he expecting a blowjob? Impossible with a bulb in his mouth. But it was an interesting idea nonetheless … could he buy his way out of this situation with sex? It was a powerful currency. He wasn't averse to the idea either. The large Russian had a wonderfully toned physique, and the lack of any hair, including eyebrows, made him look smoother, and shinier, than any person he'd ever seen before.

He could feel Borya's gun lying flat against the crown of his head. Pinned there by a wide hand.

By not keeping the gun aimed at him, Parkinson wondered if Borya had sacrificed his initiative. The policeman could strike for his genitalia and bring the assassin down. It could be his only chance.

Parkinson instead went for the other option and

reached up. He moved his hand down over the jagged abdominal muscles and watched the Russian close his eyes and take a deep breath. He continued his journey, stroking his smooth, *shiny*, crotch and then caressed the shaft of his semi-erect penis.

Parkinson felt his own erection growing, and if it wasn't for the bulb forced into his mouth, he would be chewing his bottom lip in anticipation.

His heart was still thrashing in his chest, but his adrenaline now came from arousal rather than fear.

He'd beaten the Dancer, the feared assassin, with sex.

Parkinson reached up with his other hand to extract the bulb, so he could place his manipulated, new lover into his mouth.

Borya's empty hand darted out and closed on Parkinson's wrist before he could reach the bulb. His grip was tight. The policeman winced.

The killer's eyes opened. His face suddenly seemed so full of colour, and life, while everything else around him seemed barren, and lost.

Parkinson tried to pull away, but the strong man strengthened his grip. He moaned. The assassin started to press downwards on the crown of his head. Parkinson felt the steel of the gun digging into his scalp. His neck began to burn as the sheer pressure soaked into his bones. He was being crushed to death.

Watching the serrated muscles rise from the giant's body, Parkinson desperately wanted to scream at this monster, but his mouth was plugged.

He was certain his spine was starting to splinter.

Borya's knee jerked upward. Parkinson felt the impact on his chin, and a popping sensation between his tongue and his hard palate.

His mouth was no longer stretched, but it was suddenly full of glass. He was just about to spit it all out when the knee came again.

And again.

The pain in his mouth was truly sickening. It was a deep burning sensation.

Borya released Parkinson's wrist and seized him by the bottom of his jaw, so he had his head sandwiched between his two large hands. He started to squeeze like a vice.

Parkinson couldn't believe he was still alive. The monster was on the verge of bursting his skull.

Now, Borya was manipulating the policeman's lower jaw from side-to-side, grinding shards of glass deeper into the soft warm flesh of his tongue, cheek and gums.

Parkinson's mouth felt like it was full of rocks.

Borya stepped away.

Parkinson spat the glass, the blood, and the remains of his mouth onto the floor.

AFTER YORKE HAD EXITED the car, his phone started to ring. It was Patricia, so he climbed back in and answered. 'Hi Pat ... everything okay?'

'Of course. Just wanted to check what time you were back.'

'Got side-tracked by something, and it might delay me, but I'm not going back to HQ, so I'll head home straight after, okay?'

'You don't have to ask my permission.'

'It's been a tough couple of days, and I want you to know I'll be back with you soon.'

'Nothing I'd like more. I went to see my mother today.'

'How is Jeanette?'

'Not great after I told her about Dad.'

Yorke sighed. 'Well, there's no confirmation that he's involved yet. I'm still trying to rule him out.' He considered telling her about being relieved of the SIO post for Parkinson but opted against it. It was a long story and would inevitably lead to Parkinson's role in his sister's death. He just wanted to get into his house and have it out with him. 'Did you tell her not to worry?'

'Have you ever tried telling my mum not to worry about something?'

'Good point. Beatrice and Ewan okay?'

'Bea seems a little bit under the weather. In fact, she came out with a new word. *Calpol.*'

Yorke snorted. 'So, she can say *Mama* and *Ewan* and now she can ask for painkillers. Should I be offended that she doesn't say *Dada?*'

'Painkillers are important ...'

'True.'

'Ewan has been upstairs with Lexi for a couple of hours.'

'Door open?'

'Not this time.'

'Pat ...'

'Don't worry, Mike, they're not having sex.'

'How could you *possibly* know that?'

'I just know. Mother's intuition. But one day they will have sex ...'

'Not now,' Yorke said. 'My brain already feels waterlogged.'

'Well, as long as that conversation is on the radar ...'

'It is.' Yorke wondered if he possessed such a radar. 'But I've got to shoot.'

'For the secret mission that side-tracked you?'

'Yep. I'm looking forward to seeing you.'

'Me too.'

'Oh ... and go and open that door!'

'Yessir.'

Yorke hung up and left the car again.

BORYA WATCHED his target writhing on the floor in a puddle of his own blood and flesh. He was moaning, crying and dying of blood loss at the same time. A perfect symphony.

Before this final stage, his targets *usually* fought with the belief that they couldn't be beaten. And they *always* failed spectacularly.

This target had been more challenging though. He'd tried instead to seduce him with flesh and, for the briefest of moments, he'd almost succeeded.

Almost.

He reached behind the lamp beside the sofa, picked up a boxcutter he'd concealed there earlier, and pushed out the blade. Then, he knelt, and stilled the target by pressing down hard on his forehead.

'First, the message I am paid to deliver. You took from someone you should not have taken from.'

His target tried to plead with him, but his tongue was practically destroyed, and his useless words bubbled out with bloody saliva.

'Next, my message.'

Borya placed the blade of the boxcutter against the corner of his mouth and drew it up his face close to his ear. His cheek split open.

He listened to the deep guttural moan, before carving open the other side.

Borya leaned back, punched his target in the stomach, and watched his target's whole face open when he gasped for air.

As a child, Borya had been fascinated by dot-to-dots. He'd adored the way that everything came together with patience and control. His pen brought order and organisation to the chaos of the dots.

When he looked down at the mouth of a target, he saw again those dot-to-dots. The disorder, the disorganisation, the chaos.

So, he put the blade to Luke Parkinson's top lip and, with patience and control, joined the dots.

***

YORKE EXTENDED AN UMBRELLA AND, as he walked over the road, he realised he was going to have to work hard to control his temper. Nothing would give him greater pleasure than swinging for Parkinson and grilling the idiot afterwards while he was nursing a bloody nose. But Yorke had acted on impulse and passion once before in the past; it had almost cost him his job, and his sanity. It was better to approach more formally. He had the evidence, after all. He had the signed statement back at HQ, and a video of Parkinson coming out of the brothel-squat. He also had the name of a pimp who would probably give him up with little pressure. Parkinson's days were numbered. He simply had to tell him this, and then force the bent copper to give him some closure on what'd happened to Danielle all those years ago.

At the beginning of the path leading to Parkinson's

house, the front door opened, the light flared, and someone stepped out onto the porch.

It wasn't Parkinson.

Yorke stopped and reached into his inside jacket pocket for his ID. The man, who was even taller than Jake, stepped off the porch and onto the path. He then started to move with purpose. Yorke felt adrenaline whip through his guts. He held up his ID. 'DCI Yorke. I'm here to see Luke Parkinson. Who are you please?'

The man marched onwards. Quickly. A gust of rain-filled wind sent his open leather jacket flapping up around him like a cape.

'STOP THERE! I'M AN OFFICER!' The words died in his throat when he recognised the killer from the mugshot Robinson had shown him earlier.

Yorke felt the blow to the side of his head. A hard, crushing punch which came from an incredibly well-conditioned human being. Everything flashed, and his legs buckled, but as he went down to his knees, Yorke let go of the umbrella and managed to deliver a firm shot to his assailant's stomach. It was like hitting a brick wall. He didn't have to wait long to find out that his blow had little impact. Borya reached down, seized the front of Yorke's jacket and threw him into the garden. He landed on his arm, which immediately went numb. All the air was knocked from his body. He rolled onto his back, gulping for oxygen, and saw the assassin standing over him with a boot raised in the air, planning on crushing his skull.

Yorke thrust his own booted foot into the bastard's knee. There wasn't a reassuring crack, but it had more impact than his previous effort, and the killer went down on his other knee.

Yorke scurried backwards on the muddy garden, brushing rain from his eyes.

Borya was coming again, moving gracefully and elegantly like a swooping eagle, rather than a lumbering heavy. Yorke knew he was embroiled in a fight that he was very unlikely to win.

Expecting the killer's boot again, Yorke shielded his face, but Borya instead knelt as he charged, and threw an arching roundhouse punch. Yorke managed to adjust his lying position as the strike came, so it struck his shoulder rather than his head. It burned, and a numbness now descended on his right arm too.

'Stop, Borya! It's over. There're more officers coming. You don't want to make—'

Borya's next blow struck home. There was an exploding sensation in his cheek. He was sucked into the inevitable flash but managed to open his eyes just in time to watch the second, fiercer, shot descend.

He was thankful for the soft soil which his head sank into. Solid ground would have fractured his skull.

When Yorke opened his eyes, he expected a descending fist again, but simply saw Borya looking down at him, glimmering under a slicing sheet of rain.

The weather made it difficult to see what Borya was doing. Yorke cleared his eyes with his sleeve, and then felt his internal organs melt.

The psychopath was holding a boxcutter.

Yorke kicked out, and managed, for a second time, to catch the assassin. Where, he couldn't be sure, as the rain and the heavy blows had turned his vision to mush. It had impact though. The big man came down on top of him, boxcutter first.

Luck, more than skill, allowed Yorke to catch the killer's

wrist and soften the impact of the extended blade. But his luck only went so far. The boxcutter sank into his face.

With both hands, Yorke pushed Borya's wrist, but the man was too strong, and the blade remained buried in his cheek.

If he succumbed to the pressure, Borya would cut his face to ribbons. He held on with everything he had left, but he was already starting to tire. So, he took the only option available to him. It was terrifying option, but preferable to having his face removed.

He released Borya's wrist and snapped his head left. Caught off guard, the Russian slumped forward. The blade burned as it ran across his cheek, potentially carving it open, before it left his face, and sank beside him in the soil. Screaming in agony, Yorke managed his first real punch and hit him hard in the nose.

Yorke was not a fighter, and didn't enjoy it, but he was proud of that blow. He threw another. This time, he caught the fucker's throat.

Borya reached up to his neck with both hands, and fell backwards, gagging.

Knowing he'd only seconds before Borya recovered and came again, Yorke ignored the gnawing pain in his face, and rolled onto his side. He then managed to work his way onto his knees, and then to his feet. All the time, he could hear *The Dancer* gasping for air behind him.

On his feet, Yorke turned and sprinted for the garden wall. It was stone, waist height and only several metres away. Vaulting it would take him out onto the lamplit street. Someone then would call emergency services. He shuddered over the final part of the plan: turning back and holding off the Russian demon until they arrived.

Where luck had partially come to his rescue moments

before, it completely abandoned him now. As Yorke reached the wall, he slipped on a patch of mud, and went over it face-first. His hand was already up at his face to brush away rain-sodden hair, so the concrete didn't connect directly with his nose. It still hurt like hell though. As did the other injuries Borya had already inflicted on him. He tried to turn himself over—

There came a shattering blow to his ribs.

Yorke lifted his head from the concrete and started to cough. He was directly under a streetlight, so he could see the blood dripping from his mouth. He prayed that it was coming from the gash on his cheek, rather than the result of an internal injury.

The next blow to his ribs landed with a crunch, and it was potent enough to flip him over onto his back. He looked up at the towering Russian kicking him.

Yorke didn't have long left. His vision wasn't swimming because of the rain anymore but was down to the catastrophic damage being inflicted on him by this monster. There was a pocket of emptiness looming up inside his consciousness; it was so appealing, but if he went to it, it surely would be the end of him—

Everything glowed. Tyres crunched. The kicking stopped.

Yorke laboured to breathe and nearly every part of his body was burning, but he forced his eyes open, and let his head loll to the side so he could see who had interrupted *The Dancer.*

Yorke saw an elderly man with a shock of white hair plastered to his head by rain. He was coming this way.

'*No ... no ... Get back!*' Yorke wanted to shout but struggled to even get the words out.

The man, who must have been in his seventies, was

dressed smartly in a suit. He had a worried expression on his face. 'Do you need any help? Is he okay?'

Yorke tried to warn him again. *'Run ... get the police ...'* Again, his words failed to make it through the downpour.

'Help us,' Borya said. 'He's been hit by a car.'

The man was fit and agile. He ran to Borya.

'No ... go back to your car!'

Borya had his arms behind his back. Yorke could see the boxcutter in his hands. He must have retrieved it from the ground before.

He'd primed the triangular blade.

The good Samaritan reached Borya and looked up at him. 'Have you phoned an ambulance?'

'Yes. They said a couple of minutes. Should be any time now.'

'Please ...' Yorke said. *'Get away ...'*

'What's he saying?' The man stepped around Borya and approached Yorke. 'Help is coming, young man, don't you worry.'

'Get ... away ...'

The man knelt. 'My ears aren't what they once were. My name's Alfie ... wait ...' Yorke watched his eyes widen. 'Your face ...'

Alfie turned his head and looked back up at Borya, who had also turned so the boxcutter remained concealed behind his back. 'What happened to him?'

'A car ... I told you.'

'Really? What's his name?'

'I don't know him. I just found him like this.'

'This wasn't a car, son. His face. He's been badly beaten.'

'Run ... run ...'

Still kneeling, Alfie turned his head back. 'Run, did you say? Why? Stay calm, young man. We're here to help you.'

'*It's him.*'

Yorke watched the realisation dawn on Alfie's kind face. The elderly man stood up, and Yorke prayed he would now take the advice he'd desperately been trying to give him.

Alfie turned and marched past Borya. Yorke looked up at the killer and saw him smile.

The blade flashed and opened a deep gash from Alfie's right shoulder down to his left hip. Screaming, the elderly man arched his back and staggered forward.

'NO!' Fighting the pain, Yorke gritted his teeth, and forced himself into a sitting position. He looked up and saw the monster smile again before smashing his boot into Yorke's already-broken face, sending him onto his back again.

When Yorke opened his eyes, Alfie had turned back towards them both. He was swaying on his feet, staring up at the big Russian. '*Please ...*'

Yorke reached out to grab the killer's leg, but his hand closed on empty air. '*Stop ....*'

Borya sank the blade into the side of Alfie's neck. When he yanked it free, blood spurted everywhere. The old man's hand flew to his neck. Blood spewed out between his knuckles.

Borya continued to stab the dying man.

It's a fucking performance.

Yorke threw his hand out and clutched empty air again. He felt tears in his eyes, and a searing white pain ripping through his badly damaged body.

The Russian plunged the blade into the bottom of Alfie's stomach, just above his groin. On the verge of death, the poor man leaned into the weapon and looked up at his killer through half-closed eyes.

Borya slashed upwards, right to Alfie's chin, splitting him.

Alfie collapsed to the ground beside Yorke. His eyes were still half-open. Yorke could feel his ragged breath on his face. He was still alive.

'I'm sorry ...' Yorke said.

Alfie closed his eyes.

Yorke looked up at Borya, who was slipping the retracted boxcutter into the inside pocket of his leather jacket. He reached behind himself and pulled his pistol from where he'd tucked it into his belt.

It was Yorke's turn to die.

Yorke tried, and failed, to sit up. He could barely breathe, and he wouldn't be surprised if his ribs were broken and had torn through his lungs.

The Russian leaned over him and pressed the silenced weapon against his forehead.

Yorke closed his eyes. He'd rarely given the manner of his own death much thought, but on the few occasions when he had done, this hadn't featured highly on the list of possibilities.

He closed his eyes and waited for the emptiness ...

When it didn't come, he opened his eyes. Borya looked down at him, still smiling. Then, he turned and walked away.

Yorke closed his eyes again—

'*Hey Mike ...*'

Yorke tried to force them back open, but it was hard.

'*Mike ... come on fella!*'

He opened them slightly, light swelled in.

'Imagine the *Summer Lightning,* fella, that'll bring you round!' The accent was thick Irish.

Yorke opened his eyes fully and focused in on Kenny's familiar face. A seventy-plus hardened drinker, who would have a memorial erected outside every public house in Salisbury when he finally passed on.

For a moment, Yorke hoped he'd dreamt everything that'd just happened. But when he let his head fall to the right, he saw Alfie's body, and the headlights of his still-running car.

No sign of Borya though.

Thankfully.

'It's a good job I've changed my drinking-hole, or I wouldn't have been coming this way. *The Cloisters* just hiked their prices.' Kenny said.

Yorke wanted to reply but didn't have the energy. *You change drinking establishments more times than you have hot dinners, Kenny.*

'You'll appreciate this one. Going for an old classic tonight, Mike. *Deacons.* And before you worry, I phoned an ambulance.' Kenny held his phone in the air. 'I may be an old fella, but I can use technology like the best of them.'

Kenny knelt beside Yorke and took his hand. 'You've been roughed up pretty bad tonight, buddy, but most things are fixable.'

Yorke took a deep breath. It was agonising and his chest rattled, but he wanted to speak, and he was able to send out a single word with his broken breath. '*Alfie ...*'

'Not fixable, I'm afraid.' Kenny tightened his grip on Yorke's hand.

Yorke could see the tears in Kenny's eyes. It stood to reason that he knew Alfie. Kenny knew everyone.

'Hard to believe it now when you look at a frail old

142

thing like me, fella, but when I was a young man in the late sixties, I took a few beatings when the troubles began in Ireland.' With the hand holding the phone, he pounded his chest. 'And every time, I got back up stronger. Nothing holds people like us back, Mike. Now, look at me. Still going. Fit as a fiddle.'

You drink like a fish, Kenny ... Yorke tried to smile but his face burned too much.

Yorke heard the ambulance.

'And when you get back up, Mike, you'll be stronger for it.'

Yorke felt the darkness laying claim to him again.

'And God help the monster who did this to you.'

13

DOUGLAS FIRTH PRESSED *enter* on his keyboard and then stamped the new book.

PROPERTY OF HMP HANCOCK LIBRARY. DATE:

He scribbled in the date, added his initials, closed the cover and sat back in his chair.

'All done?' Wheelhouse said.

'Yep. Three months of hard negotiation with the warden, and voila, one hundred and two new books, logged, and ready to read.' He gestured down at the pile on the trolley. 'And now it's over to you. The shelves await.'

'Why do I always get the shit job?'

'It's called being second-in-charge. An honourable position.'

Wheelhouse laughed. 'Fair enough. I was never that high up on the outside.'

'Precisely,' Firth said. 'I've *empowered* you.'

Wheelhouse picked up a book and stood there a moment longer.

'So, what are you waiting for?' Firth said.

Wheelhouse looked up at him; his expression had morphed into a serious one.

'It's in hand.'

'It's been two days, Doug, I've given you space. Not mentioned it.'

'Doesn't crying yourself to sleep every night count as a mention?'

Wheelhouse looked away.

'Sorry, Herb.'

'They stepped out of line, Doug. We never behaved like this. We never moved on families. Those that paid were those that deserved to pay. She was innocent.'

Firth sighed and stood up. He placed his hands on Wheelhouse's shoulders. 'It's sorted. Maybe today, maybe tomorrow, maybe the day after. Payback is coming. It can't be rushed. There is a natural order to these things – you more than anyone know that.'

'There was nothing natural about what happened to Janice.'

Firth nodded but didn't respond. He gestured down at the books again. 'Let's just get these on the shelves, old friend.'

Prison guard Gavin Harris walked into the library.

'Never figured *you* for much of a reader,' Wheelhouse said.

'Maybe he's come to learn?' Firth said.

Harris marched over to them, chewing gum with his mouth open.

'I'll get to work, while you give this man some culture,' Wheelhouse said, turning and taking the trolley handles. He chuckled to himself as he pushed it down the first of three aisles.

Firth sat down in his chair, leaned back, and looked up

at the pissed-off guard. 'Easy does it tiger, just a little banter.'

'The services you pay me for Firth don't include ridicule.'

Firth shook his head. 'You did get out of the bed the wrong side this morning, didn't you? Can I help you, Harris?'

'*Help me?* That's an interesting reversal of roles.'

'Look, Harris, I'm not in the mood right now.' He picked up an old copy of Robinson Crusoe, located the ribbon bookmark that was attached to the spine, and opened it to the page he was on. 'He's just about to tame his goats. Apart from the ones he's going to kill and eat of course.' He looked down at his book.

'George has disappeared,' Harris said.

Firth wound the ribbon bookmark around a finger. 'He's probably gone to his mother's.'

'Not what I heard. I heard that your flea-infested accountant disappeared into the wind.'

'He'll be back.' Firth picked up a pair of blunt scissors from his stationery box. 'He always comes back.'

'And if he doesn't, who'll pay me?' Harris had stopped chewing and loomed over Firth trying to look menacing.

'He'll return.' Firth cut off the ribbon bookmark.

There was a clatter. Harris looked round to see what it was. Firth didn't bother. He knew. Clumsy Wheelhouse had dropped a pile of the new books.

When Harris looked back round, Firth had the ribbon bookmark stretched out between two clenched fists. 'They don't make them like they used to. Strong these. Like garotte wire.'

Harris took a step back. 'Is that a threat?'

Firth opened his hands and let the ribbon flutter down

to the table. He then returned to his book. 'George will be back, Harris. Now leave me in peace before I decide to stop paying you anyway.'

'So, WOW, IT KEEPS HAPPENING,' Willows said.

'Yes,' Pemberton said from the other side of the bed, 'and the snog that had us all in a tizzy the other night suddenly seems like much ado about nothing.'

'Well, I'm not going to get stressed out about that … I *fucking* loved it.'

'Appropriate word,' Pemberton said, turning onto her side so she could run her fingertips over Willows' breasts. 'But there is a problem here.'

Willows nodded, but she was too busy enjoying the physical contact to speak.

'For me,' Pemberton said, moving her hand to Willows' hair now.

'We're in this together.'

'But I'm the one with the other half, remember?'

'I know …'

Pemberton sighed. 'It'd be easy for me to lie. To say that what happened to Mike has really shaken us up, left us vulnerable, and this is a coping mechanism. But I'm sick of not telling the truth.'

'Which is?' Willows' heart beat faster for the answer.

'That we like each other …'

'How much?' Willows raised an eyebrow.

Pemberton chewed her bottom lip. 'A lot.'

Yorke looked out of the hospital window.

The ash cloud continued to overstay its welcome. It didn't seem as dark as it'd done prior to the rainfall, but it was still there, *lingering,* and it was going to take more heavy rain to clear it any further. There was some forecast for the next day.

He closed his eyes and again saw the moment that the smiling killer walked away from him.

Sparing him.

Why? Did he want him to feel beaten?

Tick. He did.

Did he want him to feel devastated about being unable to stop Alfie's murder?

Another tick.

He caught sight of his reflection in the hospital window. His eyes were puffy and bruised, and a large bandage covered the right side of his face, just under his eye. The cut had been deep and would leave a significant scar. But it could have been a lot worse.

'Borya really does have a thing for faces.' Yorke tried not to move his mouth too much as he spoke. Not only was it incredibly painful, but it threatened to jar loose the stitches. Consequently, his words came out as a mumble. But they'd be doing that for a while yet, so anyone listening to him would have to get used to it.

He turned back towards Madden and Robinson who were sitting by his hospital bed.

The SEROCU bigwig nodded. 'What did the doctor say?'

'That my future grandchildren will think it's cool.'

Robinson smiled.

'It's just a shame that most people will be staring in horror at it,' Yorke said.

'People like us pick up war wounds,' Madden said, 'it's par for the course. The fact that you're alive is a miracle, are you really going to dwell on a scar?'

That was Madden. Pragmatic and straight to the point.

'I guess not ma'am. The best-case scenario is slight nerve damage. More than likely, my speech should return to normal, and the scar will fade over time.'

'Glad to hear it,' Madden said. 'Unfortunately, Parkinson's wounds won't fade over time … I decided not to bring the photographs of him with me, Mike. People always say it's ten times worse if you leave it to your imagination, but in this instance, that's simply not true. Your imagination isn't capable of creating anything worse than this.'

'I saw the photographs of Borya's last victims.'

Robinson sighed. '*The Dancer* is becoming more ambitious. Enjoying himself more.'

'He's unrecognisable,' Madden said.

Yorke felt an itch under the bandage on his face. He reached up to scratch it but checked himself at the last moment. 'Depraved animal. Was Parkinson definitely shot *afterwards*?'

'Definitely after,' Madden said.

Yorke sighed. There'd been no love lost between him and Parkinson, and he was bent as they come, but the manner of his death was knocking him sick. 'I need to get back up and at it.'

'Look at the state of you, Mike,' Madden said. No smile, no sympathy, just a statement of fact.

'It looks worse than it is …' He winced as he climbed back into bed. He realised he wasn't helping his argument.

'You've broken some ribs,' Madden said.

'Cracked. Not broken. Internal organs are in no danger from jagged edges. I'm good to go.'

'You're being ridiculous,' Robinson said. 'I did that to my ribs playing Rugby years ago - you're going to be in pain for months. And that's just the physical damage. God knows what witnessing that murder will have done to you.'

'Yes,' Madden said, 'You're going home, Mike. I've already signed you off. I didn't come here today to bring you grapes, I came to tell you that *Operation Tagline* is no more - we've passed the investigation completely off to SEROCU.'

Robinson nodded.

Yorke scowled.

'We're more than capable you know!' Robinson said.

'I understand that,' Yorke said. 'It's just ...'

'You'd like to finish what you started?'

'Yep.'

'I get that one, fella. But, listen. Janice's death is connected to *Article SE*. We let you continue running it, not just out of courtesy, but because you were in prime position to potentially accelerate the investigation. Unfortunately, that acceleration has now led to the death of a police officer, it would be negligent to let this go on.'

'Luke brought *his* own death on. It was nothing to do with Janice Edwards.' Yorke winced again. Both his ribs and face were conducting an orchestra of pain. He was going to have to try harder to keep emotion out of his voice.

'It was *everything* to do with *Article SE* though.' Robinson sighed and leaned forward. 'I'm going to level with you.' He paused. His Adam's apple nodded as he gulped. He clearly didn't want to do any levelling. 'We've known about Luke Parkinson for a long time.'

Despite the pain, Yorke let his body tense over. 'How long?'

'A long time,' Madden interrupted. 'You're getting

details but you're going to have to accept that they have to remain confidential.'

'*So you knew too?*' Yorke said. He winced again.

Madden nodded.

'That he was involved with the death of Danielle? My sister?'

Both Madden and Robinson looked at each other.

'*Jesus!*' Yorke crossed his arms. He immediately regretted it. The sudden movement made his battered chest feel like it was going to implode.

'Understand it from our point of view, Mike,' Robinson said, 'What would you have done if we'd told you that Luke Parkinson was a long-term employee of the Young family?'

'Arrested him?'

'*Precisely*,' Robinson said. 'And often, in these situations, that's not the best course of action. We usually stand to gain more by monitoring a dirty police officer than simply taking them out the game.'

'Doesn't seem right,' Yorke said.

'No, it doesn't, which is why it's down to us to make those judgement calls. Keeping Parkinson loose has got us more bang for our buck. He wasn't the most careful of bent officers. We've shut down countless rackets as a result of his incautious behaviours. He's the lesser of two evils.'

'There's nothing lesser about my sister not getting the justice she deserved. And there's nothing lesser about the conviction of an innocent man who then went on to commit suicide in jail.'

'I'm sorry, Michael, I really am, but it's over now, and if it makes you feel any better, we identified Parkinson years after the incident with your sister.'

'But you realised that he'd been involved?'

There was a pause while Robinson and Madden looked at each other again.

'We did,' Robinson said. 'We also knew about William Proud. He was a valuable asset in the Young's drug-dealing arm. Parkinson facilitated Proud's exoneration and the framing of Tom Davies.'

'And he used Harry, my best friend, to help him do this.'

'Yes. Butler was an accomplice. But I believe you found this out already?'

'Yes, after years of blaming him for letting the real killer get away, he told me, right before he died, that he'd been threatened into doing it. He didn't tell me it was Parkinson though.'

'I'm sorry for these experiences, Mike, I really am. He probably threatened Butler with the Young family. That would've put anyone under a lot of pressure.'

Yorke sighed and thought of his sister's smiling face.

Was this closure then? After all these years of pain, had it finally arrived? And if it truly was closure, and not another false alarm, how was he supposed to feel right now?

It certainly wasn't relief.

'It seems Parkinson underestimated the Young family,' Yorke said.

'The Youngs are only a small part of it. Since *Article SE*, organised crime has grown at a remarkable rate. Parkinson wasn't alone; most of this country are underestimating this entity.'

'Well, after meeting their go-to assassin, I'm certainly not going to underestimate them anymore. Have you got any closer to catching Borya since I've been laid out in here?'

'He's more shadowy than his bloody employers,'

Robinson said. 'He emerges, kills and vanishes without a trace.'

'There's always a trace,' Yorke said.

'I agree with you. And we'll find it. And this is one person that we won't monitor. We'll stop him. Stop him dead, if necessary.'

'From what I've learned of him,' Yorke said. 'I think that'll be your only option.'

'There's one more thing, Mike, before we leave you to your family,' Madden said. 'I haven't been totally truthful with you about the reason Parkinson was elevated. We weren't simply exposing his weaknesses. SEROCU believed that by increasing his profile, by putting him at the centre of the investigation and therefore, the media, he would become more valuable to *Article SE*. These bastards are drawn to power.'

'Do you really think that would have worked?'

'Yes,' Robinson said. 'People higher up in Article SE would have exposed themselves and we'd have been there to round them up. But Parkinson's habits of skimming money, and a visit from Borya, killed that plan before it had even got started.'

'I watched that lunatic split an innocent old man in half,' Yorke said.

'I'm sorry for you, Mike,' Robinson said. 'And I'm sorry for Alfie Marshall and his family. But we will get him.'

'So, that's it then?' Yorke said. 'Case closed?'

'There will be justice for Janice, Alfie Marshall, and Parkinson, even if he's rather undeserving, but your role in all of this is over. I want you to take a month, possibly longer, to heal. And then I want my best police officer back at HQ. Do you understand?'

Yorke nodded. 'Not really, ma'am, but what choice do I have?'

'None,' Madden said. 'And if experience has taught me anything over the years, Mike, it's far better to not have the choice. It's just so much simpler that way.'

BORYA OPTED for a weight that was beyond him.

And then he owned it.

Every individual repetition was smooth, every burn was controlled, and every roar was restrained.

After dropping the barbell onto the rack and catching his breath, he swung his legs off the bench, sprang to his feet, and beheld himself in the mirror.

His body rippled.

Then, his eyes wandered down to the single blemish.

Just beneath his left knee. An oval bruise. Administered by DCI Yorke. A bruise that had caused him to limp for the last two days.

In the heat of battle, Borya had been aware of the blow administered by the officer but hadn't been aware of the damage caused by it.

He would have still let the officer live to feel the defeat. As an opponent, he'd been the best he'd encountered in this country. Most of them succumbed, quickly. DCI Yorke had continued to fight and would have fought to the death if necessary.

Borya believed that honest fighters deserved to live through their defeats as well as their successes. They were entitled to feel the pain of failure, as well as the joys of achievement. Borya could think of nothing else in this world that was more appropriate.

Still, Borya did not appreciate the damage to his leg.

Not at all.

He felt sullied. Any damage to himself. Any mark. Must come only from him.

He looked at his right hand. It was already wrapped in a *Kumpur*, a strip of cloth used by boxers. Suitable protection.

He took a deep breath and felt the moment.

Everything was quiet. Still.

Peace.

He roared and drove his fist into the glass mirror. A spider-web exploded out from the point of contact.

No blood. Just pain in his knuckles.

Perfect.

14

THIS WASN'T THE first time Yorke had seen Jake since his near-death experience, but it was the first time he'd seen him without a head full of painkillers.

Jake was eyeing up the colourful flowers on his bedside table while Yorke finished off his final hospital lunch. Patricia and Ewan were due to collect him within the hour.

'The flowers from Madden?' Jake said.

Yorke smiled. 'She told me how she spent an age selecting the most interesting flowers. She delivered them with the vow to brighten up my dark days as best she could.'

'Shit ... I was joking.'

'So was I, they're from Emma.'

Jake laughed. 'Well, she's obviously got more time on her hands these days if she's managed to put together a bouquet like that.'

'Everyone has more time on their hands than us, Jake.'

Jake sat and they talked as if they hadn't spoken in a long while.

In truth, Yorke considered, they hadn't. Not properly anyway. Not like best friends.

Yorke filled Jake in on his experiences as a new father, while Jake told Yorke about a woman he'd met on Tinder and shared two dates with.

They were like two estranged childhood buddies desperate to fill each other in on life's journey as quickly as possible lest they were suddenly separated by life's obligations again.

And all this with a shadow as thick as the ash cloud hanging over both of their heads.

A big, strong-looking man. Marriage problems. Polite.

The words of the young woman in the brothel-squat. The sex-worker who delivered envelopes of money to bent police officers.

Bent police officers who ended up dead.

'Jake ... I'm worried.'

Jake reached over and let his large hand settle on his shoulder carefully, so as not to put too much weight on his fragile friend. 'These are turbulent times, Mike. But SEROCU has taken the case now. We did our best, and now we just need to take a deep breath and let it go.'

Yorke looked down and took that deep breath for different reasons. 'I'm not worried about the case; I'm worried about you.'

Jake withdrew his hand and sat back in his chair. 'This again? You don't have to—'

'It's not just *this* again, Jake. It's more now. Much, much more.'

'You've lost me—'

'What *are* you mixed up in?' Yorke looked back up at his best friend.

Jake looked away. 'I don't know what you're talking about.'

'Parkinson ... Do you know *why* he was killed?'

'Of course ... doesn't everyone? I mean it's not really information they can keep squirrelled away when *Article SE* and their infamous hitman is involved.'

'You and Parkinson were close.'

'Didn't we discuss this already? We were colleagues. We both smoked—'

'People will have noticed how close you've been ... not just me.'

'People notice a lot of things which don't mean a great deal.'

Yorke turned from Jake and gazed over to the window; outside, the day remained dark.

'The prostitute who'd been handing envelopes to Parkinson, she told me there was another officer.' He resisted looking back at Jake. He didn't want to see his reaction. He was desperate for this not to be true. 'She mentioned someone who was big and strong. And polite.'

'Could be a million people.'

'With marriage problems, she said.'

There was a moment of silence. 'That still doesn't narrow it down significantly.'

But the silence, although momentary, had been there, and Yorke now *knew*.

Yorke turned back to look into his eyes. 'Jake, I want to help you. I'm asking you now, as a best friend, and not an officer, are you mixed up in this?'

'No ...'

'I can't keep asking you. At some point, I'll have to do my job.'

Jake sighed and took a moment to think. Eventually, he said, 'It's over. Anything that may have happened, has happened. And it's done. I can assure you.'

'You *need* to talk to me.'

'Who do you think put that file on your desk?'

Yorke felt his stomach lurch; he'd not seen that coming.

'I will always be on your side, Mike. *Always.*'

'Jake, I need to know how involved you are. How deep this goes for you. I can't protect you otherwise.'

Jake rose to his feet. 'It's done, Mike. You have to trust me.'

'It's not enough, Jake. You have to—'

The door opened, and a smiling nurse came into the room. 'Sorry to interrupt, but this gentleman needs his medicine.'

'I was just going, ma'am,' Jake said. He put his hand on Yorke's shoulder again. 'I'll see you later, buddy.'

'Jake, stay. We need to finish this.'

But Jake didn't listen. He turned and left.

VANESSA NOTICED a young man smiling at her from the end of the *Sports and Games* aisle.

She was used to male attention. She knew that she was way above average and then some.

But she also knew young male students were like dogs with two dicks, so the attention didn't make her feel special. If any of her fellow female students were here today, they'd be getting the same stares.

Despite this, her interest had been piqued more than usual this afternoon.

Not because the lingering stare came at her in the *Southampton Public Library*, because when did that ever stop men? A library, or a bar? Both were meat markets as far as *they* were concerned. No, what made her curious was that she didn't recognise him at all.

She was a third-year English major, and had notable celebrity due to her wealth and connection to a large business empire. She knew *everyone*. She made it her business to know everyone. Janice, her bezzie, often referred to her as Southampton's most prominent socialite. The West Country's answer to Kim Kardashian.

Yet, here was a young man, a very attractive one she might add, who she simply didn't recognise. Yes, some people did slip through her social net, but never ones as good-looking as this. No way. Even if she'd overlooked him, someone in her close social circle would have picked him out of the crowds and alerted her to his existence. So, who was he and why was he staring?

The first floor of the library was quiet today, and no one else was opting for a book on sports and games.

Her game was badminton. She knew where it was, having consumed most of the books on that shelf already. The mysterious stranger was researching a sport on the shelf directly opposite.

Before heading down the aisle for this exciting meeting, she needed a quick health check first. She concealed herself behind the end of the aisle and brought her compact mirror into action.

No wayward smudging of make-up. Not a lash out of place.

Perfect.

She turned into the aisle.

Up ahead, the dark-haired stranger had become engrossed in a book and was no longer looking at her. She moved slowly, stroking her hand across the shelved books, willing him to lift his eyes one more time, at least, before she engaged with him.

He must have heard her thoughts. He showed her his eyes again, smiled and winked.

Shit, he's brash!

She looked away. *Expected a smile back? Not so easy now, is it? I'm different from the other girls ... I'll make you work for your supper.*

At her favoured shelf, she chanced a glance at his. Hockey.

She reached up for a book she already owned. *A Brief History of Badminton.* After flicking through to a page on the origin of the shuttlecocks, she leaned against the shelf, side-on, and pretended to read.

She could hear his strong, deep breaths. She could also smell his after-shave. It was stronger than she was accustomed to in partners, but she wasn't offended by it.

After waiting patiently for his move, she took matters into her own hands and dropped the book.

He swooped for the text. Then, he was holding it out to her, and they were looking into each other's eyes.

His eyes were grey with bluish tinges. She looked down at *A Brief History of Badminton.* He had colourful tattoos on the back of his hands, which disappeared up his sleeve and, presumably, up his arm.

She took the book and looked up again, noticing that the same colourful tattoos rose slightly above his buttoned collar.

'Thanks,' she said, 'I like your tattoos. They're colourful.'

'Thank you,' the man said. He had a strong foreign accent. 'Everybody in my family has the same tattoos. From the age of sixteen, our entire bodies are tattooed.'

Vanessa was disappointed. She wasn't a fan of tattoos. And

a full body one *certainly* held no appeal. It was a non-starter. She decided there was time for one more show of politeness, before making a sharp exit. 'Where do you come from?'

'Saint Petersburg. I don't learn here. I am visiting relatives.'

She nodded. 'Well, I hope you have a nice stay ... okay, I have what I need.' She held up the book in front of her. 'A Brief History of Badminton.'

He showed her his book. 'Ice Hockey. There's lots of ice in Russia.'

She stepped to the side. He also stepped to the side, blocking her path. 'Would you like to stay and talk?'

'I'm meeting my boyfriend ...'

'Ah,' the young man said. 'I misunderstood—'

'That's okay, it's—'

'I saw you looking at me.'

Vanessa raised an eyebrow. 'You can't be serious!'

He turned to his side and pointed to the end of the aisle. 'From there. You were staring.'

The cheek! 'Sorry, boyo, but I think you'll find it was the other way round.'

The young man turned to lay his book on the bookshelf beside them. She noticed that he had a red ribbon wound around the knuckles of this hand. 'No, Vanessa, you were ... what's the expression ... making eyes.'

'How do you know my name?' Her stomach suddenly felt like it was full of rocks.

'And *those* eyes, Vanessa. I just love those eyes.'

He reached out and gently took her arm, and with the other hand, let the ribbon fall from his knuckles, until it hung loosely from between his thumb and forefinger.

'What's that?' Her voice was shaking.

'What's this?' He gestured down at the hanging ribbon. 'Just an old bookmark.'

She sidestepped out of his grip and moved forward quickly. He allowed her past. She almost breathed a sigh of relief, but the breath caught in her throat.

Literally.

Her hands flew to her neck, and she clawed at the material wrapped tightly around it.

It had to be that red ribbon.

She wanted to scream but she couldn't get any sound out. Her eyes began to water, and her mouth filled with a sour taste. Her entire head throbbed.

She threw herself backwards, but her assailant was too strong. Her chest started to burn, and the front of her head felt like it was going to explode.

Everything moved away from her; she was shrinking backwards into the ground.

She could no longer feel the sensation of her fingers on the ribbon but knew they were there.

When the blackness shut down her vision, Vanessa wondered, for the briefest moment, if she was still alive.

'POOR ROBIN CRUSOE.... Where have you been?'

Firth smiled over his favourite moment in the book. Crusoe had spent months teaching the parrot to say it back to him, and he'd finally succeeded.

Crusoe, unlike Mr Hyde, in another piece of literature Firth had re-read recently, never lost himself to animal instincts, never became a brute despite his isolation on this island. He remained self-aware at all times. He obsessively recorded all his daily activities in a journal, even when nothing of note actually happened to him. And now, here he was, teaching nature itself to voice his own self-awareness. Through a parrot.

Firth was like Crusoe. He would never lose himself to instinct, and disarray.

He slid the red ribbon bookmark between the two pages and closed the book.

Douglas Firth was, and always would be, very self-aware.

15

*M*ike cared. He truly did. Hold onto that, Jake. *Dammit. Hold onto that.*

Noticing that one of his son's beloved gnomes in the garden had taken a tumble during the heavy rains, Jake went to his rescue. He restored the gnome, an angler, to an upright position, so it could continue to fish in the mud.

He looked down into his plastic bag at the wrapped presents. Sheila may have refused the money the other day, but she'd have to be seriously crabby to knock back these gifts for Frank.

As he knocked on the door, he did recall that his soon-to-be ex-wife spent most of her life in a crabby state, and conceded that, in all likelihood, he'd be hoisting these gifts home again.

Sheila's mother opened the door. Her long white hair had been cut short into a bob, and he almost didn't recognise her, but then she spoke, and his memories of a woman with a tongue dripping with arsenic came flooding back. 'She's not here.'

'Where is she?'

'Out.'

It didn't take a genius to work out from which side of the family Sheila had inherited her abrasive tone.

'I've got some gifts for Frank. There's a train set, a children's tablet, security protected and set up with learning apps, and a couple of DVDs.'

She held out her hand. 'Give them here, then.'

'Maybe I could see Frank myself? I'd like to give him these gifts.'

Jake could see the corners of her lips quiver. She was always so full of anger. 'It's not your day.'

'Sheila wouldn't mind. He's my son—'

'She'd mind.'

Jake put the bag into her hand.

He felt as if a match had been lit in his stomach. 'You never did like me much, did you?'

'Try not to take it personally. There are not many men that would be good enough for my daughter.'

'We were happy ... once ... you forget that.'

'I haven't forgotten Jake. I bit my tongue for a lot of years.'

'Bollocks you did!'

She shrugged. 'Like I said, I bit my tongue. She could've, *should've*, done so much better. And the things you brought into this house ...'

'What do you mean?'

'What do you *think* I mean, Jake?'

Of course, she knew everything.

'The best thing you could do for Sheila, and your son, is just disappear. Leave. Your son is still young. Give him a chance. Take your poison away from him.'

Suddenly feeling light-headed, Jake took a step back. He closed his eyes and saw Lacey prodding Simon Young's corpse with her foot. He saw her mouth moving, and read her lips: *'Your first?'*

'She's finally happy, Jake. Let her be. She's with a good man. A reputable surgeon. Let your son have the father he deserves.'

She closed the door. Jake kneeled, taking deep breaths.

This isn't over, Jake. You have Mike. You have your son. Regardless of what she says, you have him. Hold onto that. Hold onto Mike. Frank.

He stood up, and the fire lit moments before in his stomach, suddenly flared. He marched over to the angling gnome and launched it. It smashed against the garden wall.

As he walked away, he read Lacey's lips again. *'I always knew you had it in you.'*

HE MAY NOT HAVE BEEN his natural son, but Yorke still saw himself in Ewan. They'd grown very close over the years and had far more in common than they'd first realised. For example, both liked to lead situations with calmness and clarity, and desperately tried to find strength in others even on the days when their own resilience felt sorely lacking.

Due to the state of Yorke's ribs, embracing was out of the question, so they touched heads for a moment instead. He then planted a kiss on his son's forehead for good measure.

Yorke looked over at Lexi. 'Thanks for putting up with him.'

To Yorke, she seemed unlike many girls her age. She wore long floral frocks and buttoned-up cardigans. She was stick thin, rather than slim, and Yorke wondered about her eating habits. Add to that, there was the social awkwardness. Many parents probably wouldn't consider her the perfect catch for their bonny blue-eyed boy.

Yorke loved her. As did Patricia. Ewan was more content than he'd been in years. Their debt to this young lady was incalculable.

'It's my pleasure.' She grinned, blushing. She adjusted her glasses. 'He has to put up with me too.'

Patricia came up behind Lexi and put her hands on her bony shoulders. 'Now how could anyone in their right mind, believe that?'

Ewan looked at all three of them in turn. 'Sorry, who here is in their right mind?'

'Good point,' Yorke said. 'And we won't be either until we get out of this place.'

'Mike – keep your voice down,' Patricia said, 'You'll offend them! They've just treated you.'

'Yes, and now I'm better. And grateful. But another day of hospital food and Jeremy Kyle might just have unwound all their hard work. Come on, last one to the car pays for the pizza.'

'Better, eh? Then who is carrying your bags, pray tell?' Patricia said.

Yorke shrugged. 'Well, maybe better was an exaggeration. Slightly better?'

'Don't worry, Auntie Pat,' Ewan said, 'I'll get the heavy one. Uncle Mike has to save his energy to open his wallet.'

'Now there's something I'd love to see,' Patricia said.

After checking out of the hospital, and taking the elevator down to the carpark, Yorke's phone rang. He looked at the screen and saw that it was Willows. 'You go ahead. I have to take this.'

Patricia's fierce facial expression almost catapulted him back into the elevator.

'Three minutes. Maximum.' He offered an apologetic expression and then put the phone to his ear.

'You don't even know where we're parked.' Patricia said.

'Last car on the left,' Ewan said.

Patricia turned the fierce stare onto Ewan.

'Oops. Come on.' Ewan grabbed Lexi's hand, and they went on ahead.

Yorke answered the phone. 'Collette?'

'I don't know if I should be making this phone call.'

'Well, it's too late to wonder now, you've already made it.'

'True ... still ...'

'If I have to use the words *beat* and *bush* in the next sentence, Collette, I think you might just hear a grown man cry. It's been a trying couple of days.'

'Yes sir, sorry sir.'

Patricia was waving for his attention. 'Sorry Collette, one second.'

He covered up the mic on his phone.

'I always give you distance, Mike. Always. I accept who you are. But not today. You're in no state. Don't make me pull rank. Three minutes and then it's over. Okay?'

Yorke smiled and blew her a kiss. 'I'm buying pizza, remember?'

She caught the kiss, turned and walked away. He returned to the conversation with Willows. 'Even though *Operation Tagline* has been immolated, and I've been put out to pasture, you're about to tell me something sensational, aren't you?'

'There's been a murder. In Southampton.'

'Who?'

'A twenty-one-year old student studying English. Strangled. Actually, the forensic pathologist is saying

169

garrotted. Either with wire or strong material of some kind. In a library, sir. Can you believe it? In a *bloody* library.'

Yorke resisted the pull of the crime. Resisted the urge to do what he did best. 'Why are you telling me this, Collette? It's Southampton's issue.'

'Sir, it's *SEROCU*'s issue.'

Yorke felt the pulse in the centre of his head. 'Sorry?'

'The victim, Vanessa, was a Young.'

The pulse became a throb. 'She's a *Young*?'

'Buddy's granddaughter by his only daughter, Bethany.'

The throb became a pounding. 'What else do you know?'

'I've got a close friend at Southampton. She told me that there was skill in this execution. It was a hit, Mike. But he swaggered in and out of the library and has been caught on camera.'

'Borya?'

'No. Much younger. There's no match in the system.'

'Another person who doesn't exist. Another product of *Article SE*.' Yorke took a deep breath, trying to settle the agony building in his skull.

'We have to step away now, sir.' Willows said.

'Why the bloody hell are you phoning to tell me then?'

'I don't know.'

'Jesus, Collette, you usually have an answer for everything!'

'Not this time.'

'Herbert Wheelhouse's niece ends up dead because he was skimming from the Young family. Now, Buddy Young's granddaughter ends up dead. And another ghost. A disappearing killer.'

'Not coincidences, are they?'

'No, they're not, Collette. But this isn't ours anymore,

and I'm sure Robinson will have already reached the same conclusion as we have. He'll be visiting the accountant George Johnson as we speak. Johnson will then give up the fact that Wheelhouse funded the hit on Buddy's granddaughter, Vanessa, and everything will be wrapped up.'

'Sounds about right, sir.'

'Good ... but you don't sound that convinced ...'

'Because I'm not.'

'Bloody hell, Collette. Why?' He clutched his forehead.

'Because of that old expression you always use. If someone tells you it's raining, you should always go out and check.'

Yorke sighed. 'Listen, if I go, Madden and Robinson will flay me alive, and then my wife will disembowel me.'

'Nice images.'

'Statements-of-fact ... okay, Collette .... I want you to go to Johnson now. Interview him. Find out if he knows anything, and if he does, report it back to me and I'll go cap in hand to Robinson to get him on the right trail.'

'I will do, sir.'

'And Collette?'

'Yes, sir?'

'Don't go alone.'

'Of course not. I'll see if Pemberton's free.'

———

THE MACHINES that sustained Buddy Young's life hummed and whirred.

The shrivelled old man was propped up by three pillows; his hair was gone; his head was dotted with liver-spots; and his sallow skin hung from shrunken bones.

Walter Divall, Buddy's most trusted lieutenant, couldn't believe that this used to be Public Enemy number one. Age really was merciless. Far worse than a bullet. Walter was suddenly content with the way he had chosen to live his life. Going early as a result of his profession would be a blessing in disguise.

It'd been over two hours since Walter had broken the news to his bed-ridden boss. His beautiful granddaughter, Vanessa, the only light still shining in his decaying existence, was gone.

And not just gone.

'Plucked from the world like a weed. Exterminated like a pest. Bleached out like a stain.' Buddy had typed these images into a tiny keyboard sitting beneath his right hand. Despite being withered, this hand could still type. Just. The other hand was already an arthritic claw. Speakers alongside the life-support machines threw out the robotic voice.

'I'm sorry, sir. It will be dealt with,' Walter had replied.

Now, these two hours later, Walter returned with a little drawstring bag which was damp with blood.

Buddy Young's eyes narrowed. Apart from the fingers on the hand that prodded the keyboard, his eyes were the only way you could ever really tell he was still alive. They were the same eyes that his late son, Simon, had inherited. Stony eyes. Eyes that seemed to bore through any person held by them.

In this instance, that person was Walter. And he had to admit to quite enjoying it. It made him feel alive. He inwardly smiled.

'It was as we thought,' Walter said.

A flickering passed over Buddy's eyes, and he stared at the drawstring bag in Walter's hand.

He wants to see ... the sick old puppy wants to look at his trophy!

Walter obliged and opened the sodden bag beneath Buddy's face. The old man's eyes widened, and his breathing mask fogged over. The monitor also showed his heartbeat accelerating.

Buddy continued to type as he investigated the bag. 'Such precision. You took away his connection to the world.'

Walter nodded. 'As you asked.'

The typing was slow, and the tension of waiting for the robotic voice was palpable. 'It is a fate worse than death. To sever that connection.'

'I agree.'

'Close the bag.'

Walter obeyed.

While Buddy typed out his message, Walter looked around his boss's bedroom. It wasn't really the room in which you expect a very wealthy man to while away his final hours. Floral wallpaper and bulky furniture from the 60s and 70s. It was certainly very traditional, and probably kept the old man at ease. It was the world in which he'd grown up. If Walter was ever in Buddy's position, he certainly wouldn't be opting for traditional. He would spend that cash. And spend it hard. He would rather be suffocated by flamboyance than drown in the ordinary.

'You know what to do next.' Buddy's surrogate voice came out with a burst of static. Walter flinched.

Buy you a new speaker, he thought.

'Of course, sir.'

Walter waited while Buddy typed out the next message. He moved at the speed of the second hand on a clock. He resisted the urge to tap his foot, and stood rigid, hoping that the message was a farewell, so he could break free of the monotony.

It wasn't.

'You must use the best again.'

'At such short notice, sir? I don't think—'

Buddy didn't need to interrupt with sound. He just needed his eyes.

Walter waited patiently for his employer's impatient message. 'Pay double then.'

Walter wanted to call that option into doubt but settled for a nod instead. He didn't want to wind his boss up, and neither did he want to sit through another series of messages.

'I'll let you know when it's done, sir.'

Walter was about to turn to leave when Buddy hit the palm of his hand on the keyboard. It wasn't hard, but it was enough to stop Walter turning. He typed his message out and then gestured at the drawstring bag in Walter's hand.

'This time, that won't be enough. This time, you bring me everything.'

No children. *His number one rule.*

From his car, parked on the other side of the road, Jake photographed the elderly Russian man coming out of his home with his visiting daughter. She was in her twenties, so his no-child policy was under no threat, and he would still be able to get *some* sleep at night.

His photographs would be time and date stamped, but he decided to be extra cautious. He checked his watch and scribbled in a small notebook. His employers valued precision above everything else. Their subsequent movements would be fuelled by Jake's accuracy. Mistakes cost lives.

Luke Parkinson had learned this the hard way.

The frail Russian man struggled to walk, so his daughter, who had been born and raised in England following her father's escape from Russia, held him upright.

Jake took some more photographs of the daughter helping him into her car and again, dutifully, wrote down the timings. He then flicked back through his notebook.

This had happened at the same time every week for the previous two months. Not to the second, of course. Or even to the minute. But most definitely within a fifteen-minute window.

It wasn't the most exciting way to spend the afternoon of your day off, but it paid very well.

However, during the past hour of sitting in the car awaiting this reoccurring event, Jake had reached some conclusions.

He wasn't built to be a police officer.

He *certainly* wasn't built to be a father, or a husband.

And he *still* believed - although evidence was building up to the contrary – that he wasn't built to be a criminal.

After delivering these photographs today, he would be returning to his bedsit to retrieve the money he'd saved so far. Most of it he would push through Sheila's letterbox. A small percentage he would take with him. It was time to start again.

He tailed the Russian family to their favourite bistro in town. Unfortunately for them, they were people of routine. This made it all the easier for his employers in their next step. Jake didn't know what was planned for them, but he suspected that it wasn't good. What had this man done so wrong in his past life to warrant such dangerous scrutiny?

Jake parked opposite the bistro and took photographs of them entering the restaurant. He wrote in his logbook again and looked back at the previous week. He could be waiting over two hours. He most certainly could slip away, and return nearer the time, but those weren't his instructions. To deviate from what he'd been asked to do was dangerous.

So, he hunkered down, pulled out his mobile phone, went through to his personal photographs, and scrolled through his images of Frank.

Jake paused, every now and again, to wipe tears from his eyes.

16

I N A SHAKING hand, Firth held the framed photograph of his boy.

Banging the window ... the trail of blood on the road ... his fist through the glass ... Patricia beside him ... her hand still open ... the hand she'd been holding his with only moments before ...

Firth put the photograph back on the desk.

Was that when I lost you too, Patricia? When I pulled my hand away? Did I sever the connection?

He sat beside his reading desk and ran his hand over the cover of *Robinson Crusoe.*

Self-awareness was important. It got Crusoe through his twenty-eight-year ordeal. Being *aware* helped you change and adapt. Potentially for the better. Crusoe had abandoned atheism to become a pious Christian. Throughout his entire life, his entire ordeal, Firth, too, had changed and adapted.

He stood up and walked over to Wheelhouse's bed. He was currently sleeping. There was a moment, earlier in the library, when emotion had overwhelmed Wheelhouse, and the guards had given him permission to return to his bunk and take a prescription hypnotic.

Firth sat on the edge of the bed, stroking Wheelhouse's hair, considering all these ways he'd changed and adapted.

The most important thing that he'd learned since the death of his only boy was that the scales had to balance. That you couldn't have one thing without the other. The good came with the bad. To take you had to give. To love you had to hate.

The world was balanced and to tip it in one direction was a futile endeavour.

He leaned over and kissed Wheelhouse's forehead. This old man had not learned this yet. This *poor, sweet* old man who the world had condemned.

'Am I interrupting something?' Harris said from behind him.

Wheelhouse turned to look at the guard. 'Only something you could never understand.'

'Oh, I understood alright.' Harris said and smiled. 'Anyway, good news ... it's done.'

Firth looked back at Wheelhouse. *You got what you wanted, Herb. I hope it makes you happy. But balance must, and will, be restored.*

'You also have a visitor.'

Firth stood up. 'That didn't take long.'

Harris smiled again. 'It never really does, does it?'

ANOTHER GUARD ESCORTED Firth to see his visitor. Harris chose to linger behind in his cell.

Wheelhouse snored gently from the bottom bunk as

Harris worked his way around the confines, touching and prodding.

Books ... photographs ... letters ... pens ... notepaper ... clothes ...

It always fascinated Harris to see a life enclosed in such a small place. Minimalism in the extreme. Some of the happiest people he knew were convicts. He wondered if there really was truth to the philosophy that the less you owned, the happier you were.

He sat on the edge of Wheelhouse's bed. In the same spot, Firth had been sitting moments ago.

Unlike Firth though, he opted not to pet Wheelhouse. Instead, he took his chewing gum out of his mouth, rolled it in a ball and pressed it into Wheelhouse's wrinkled forehead. It didn't really stick, but because the old man was on his back, it stayed in place.

Harris smiled, stood back up and looked down at the old man. 'You've been a bad, bad boy, *Reaper*. You really have.'

Patricia unlocked their front door. Yorke came up alongside her and slipped an arm around her waist. 'I'd carry you over the threshold, but I'm worried my final rib might give out.'

'Never mind your rib,' Ewan said from behind them both, 'if you two carry on like this, my stomach is going to give out.'

Yorke heard Lexi whisper to Ewan, 'Go easy. They're just happy to see each other.'

'This is Ewan taking it easy,' Yorke said. 'There's a level of banter in this household that often soars way beyond acceptable levels.'

Patricia and Ewan helped Yorke to the couch. He settled into it with a groan. Patricia went to the kitchen to make a cup of tea.

'Would you like anything on the television, Mr Yorke?' Lexi said.

'Mike, please. And, no. I've had enough television in hospital to last me a lifetime. I'm just going to fiddle on my phone and surf the net. Maybe have a nap.'

'We're off upstairs. Enjoy your surf!' Ewan made quotation marks around the word *surf* with his fingers.

'What's your point?'

'Just not heard *surf* in a while.'

'Okay, smartarse, if that's so archaic, what term do you use?'

Ewan shrugged. 'Browsing? Using?'

Yorke smiled. 'Yawn. I *definitely* win points for trying to sound more interesting then.'

'Whatever!'

'Come on,' Lexi said, taking his hand. 'Let Mr ... sorry ... Mike rest.'

Yorke smiled again. 'The child I never had.'

Ewan shook his head. 'Everybody in this house is always telling you to rest and you never listen!'

'True,' Yorke said. 'But I don't think it's ever been said with such sincerity. I thank you Lexi.'

She blushed.

As Ewan and Lexi wandered off upstairs, Yorke thought about his conversation with Patricia several days ago.

Don't worry Mike, they're not having sex ... mother's intuition.

Now, why did father's intuition suggest otherwise?

There was probably a strong argument that father's

intuition was just paranoia, but it continued to bug him regardless.

His mobile buzzed in his jacket pocket.

Willows.

He went for his phone so quickly that his ribs sent a sharp reminder of their fragility. He groaned, and almost swore out-loud when he saw it was just a reminder from his bank that he'd just slipped into his overdraft again.

He sighed, closed his eyes, wondered if Willows was alright, and decided to phone her, but fell asleep before he had chance.

IN YORKE'S DREAM, he was able to see his sister Danielle again, and apologise for the time it had taken him to discover the truth. 'It just never seemed there to find. I searched so hard, and for so long.'

'It's what they do best. They lie ... and they conceal.'

'I know that ... but I've always been so good at breaking down the wall. But not this time ... not the time it mattered the most for me ... and for you.'

Danielle stood in the shadows, so he couldn't see her face. She often did this in his dreams. The last time he'd ever seen her had been in the morgue with half her face burnt away.

It was hard enough to imagine her now without that damage, so the shadows were good. They helped him to remember the way she once was.

'You've lost so much, Mike. A sister, a best friend. Even the people closest to you manoeuvred behind your back. But now you have the answers. Accept this peace. *Move on.*'

Despite this being a dream, Yorke felt the blow in his kidney. It knocked the wind out of him and propelled him forward into the shadows.

Thankfully, Danielle was gone before he could crash into her, and behold, yet again, her terrible injuries.

He swung to see who had kidney-punched him.

It was the giant.

Borya.

'Time to move on, policeman?' Borya smiled the same smile he'd used just before he'd split an innocent man in two. 'Or time for one last dance?' He extended the boxcutter.

Despite his monstrous size, he came fast, and gracefully, like a gazelle. Yorke closed his eyes, and felt his same cheek being slashed again. The pain was excruciating, but he stood his ground. If Borya wanted to dance again then he wouldn't be doing it from a horizontal position this time.

He opened his eyes. The Russian was gone. Instead, Janice Edwards stood there. Her eyes and skin were grey, and part of her forehead was missing where the bullet had torn free. 'They will forget about me.'

'They won't.'

'I don't matter. Just like Danielle didn't matter. Just like you don't matter.'

'They'll get Borya. They'll get you justice.'

'With what he knows, Michael? With everything he's seen, and done for *Article SE*? You think they want him in prison or dead? A man like that is already gone. And under the ground, he offers nothing to *SEROCU* in the way of justice. There is no justice for any of us, Michael.'

'It's the same old story, Michael,' Alfie said.

Yorke looked over at the old man's kind face. He tried not to move his eyes downwards. He knew what was there.

He knew that Alfie had been carved open like a pumpkin. It was one of the worst things that he'd ever seen. 'Believe me, both of you, it will end. Everything ends. And when it does, you will have your justice.'

'We don't believe you, Michael,' Janice said.

'Well, you should do, because unlike some of my colleagues, I don't lie. Never really have done.'

Yorke awoke sweating and clutching his ribs. His mouth was dry, so he reached over to the table where Patricia had left him a cup of tea. It was cold, but he drank it down anyway. It made him feel better.

Then he phoned Willows because, yes, everything did end, but Yorke really wanted to make sure it ended well.

WHEELHOUSE WAS awake when Firth returned.

'Where have you been?' He looked and sounded groggy.

'The library,' he lied, 'To finish the job you started. Are you sure you only took one of those tablets, Herb?'

'Yes, why do you ask?'

'Several reasons. One of which is that both of your eyes seem to be pointing in different directions.'

'Very funny. Sorry, Doug, for having another meltdown. Didn't sleep last night. I feel better after that nap.'

'Well, you could've fooled me, looking at the state of you,' Firth said, sitting on the edge of the bed. 'Listen Herb ...'

'It's done, isn't it?'

Firth sighed and nodded.

Wheelhouse looked away, chewing his lip, deep in

thought. 'Now that bastard will feel how I feel. He'll understand what it's like.'

Firth stood up and wandered over to the photograph of his late son. 'I'm glad it's given you some peace, Herb.' He recalled the moment he pinned Geoff Stirling to the back of a stall with his father's bayonet. *It never gave me any peace.*

'She didn't suffer, did she?'

Firth turned to look at Wheelhouse. The excitement on his old friend's face was already waning.

'I think so,' Firth said. 'If they did what I asked.'

'Ahh.' Herb said and looked down. 'Closure, eh?'

Firth smiled at him. How little the poor man knew. 'And then another door opens.'

'Indeed,' Wheelhouse said, lay back, put his hands behind his head and closed his eyes.

Wearing gloves, Jake crammed the envelope containing the USB drive full of photographs and scanned logs through the letterbox of the derelict house in Tidworth.

The dereliction was a ruse. This place was very much in action.

Feeling sullied, but knowing now, without a shadow of a doubt, that this would be his last time, he breathed a sigh of relief.

There was still one thing he'd like to know though.

He drove around the block several times, and then returned to the same street. He parked three cars back from the front door of the derelict house. It was ajar. Someone had already watched him leave, and then entered the house to collect the drop.

He didn't expect to recognise the person collecting

these drops, and when they emerged, he wished he'd just let sleeping dogs lie.

Curiosity had led him to one hell of a shock.

'Better out *than* fucking in,' Jake said to himself, starting his car. 'Time to take the money and *run*.'

17

F AMILY LIAISON OFFICER Bryan Kelly stood in DCI Yorke's lounge with a worried expression on his face. 'I wanted to see if you needed anything.'

'Well, Bryan, I *need* you to knock *that* expression off your face for a start. I thought you'd come offering support, not paranoia.'

Bryan's big cheeks flushed. 'I'm sorry, sir, but you do look in a bad way.'

Yorke felt guilty. He didn't usually bite people's heads off. It didn't suit him. 'I look worse than I am, buddy. Thanks for calling by, but you don't need to stay.'

Bryan, who meant well, but whose career to date was a curate's egg, reached into his inside pocket. He pulled out a card. 'I'll get out your hair if you make me two promises.'

Wow, Yorke thought, *those blemishes on your career really have strengthened your backbone.*

'Because you made the effort to see if I was alright, I'll make you one of your promises.'

'Two would be better, sir ...'

'Don't push it, Bryan. One promise where you wouldn't

normally have any is actually a fantastic position to find yourself in.'

'Okay ... well, here it goes ... a while ago I suffered from stress. After I buggered up on the Sarah Ray case. Do you remember?'

Yorke nodded. 'She drugged you and ran.'

'Yep. I thought she wouldn't come back alive. When she did, I thought the anxiety would lift. It didn't.' He waved the card in his hand. 'Michelle ... my psychiatrist helped me accept the mistake I made. She helped me with the PTSD. What happened to you, sir ... well, to be attacked in such a manner ... to see what you saw ...'

'Yes, Bryan I get the picture.'

'Well, please promise me that you'll call her.'

Yorke reflected on the dream he'd had earlier where Borya had attacked him again, just before he exchanged pleasantries with the Russian's two victims. Bryan was probably right. There could be some form of PTSD on the cards. Still ...

'And the other promise, Bryan?'

'Let me come and check on you this evening. I've been here before ... with victims who have experienced similar trauma. You may not want to talk to me now, sir, but by the evening, the picture may be different.'

'I doubt this particular picture of me will be changing much,' Yorke said, stretching himself out on the sofa with a grimace.

'You said you'd make one of the two promises ...'

'Okay ... okay ... I'll make the second promise. I'd love to see you for a cup of tea this evening Bryan.'

'Great, sir.' Bryan held the card in the air. 'And this? Michelle? Please think about it ...'

Yorke smiled. 'Pop it on the mantelpiece, Bryan, you

never know. No doubt Pat will be badgering me into something similar over the next couple of weeks.'

'It's because we care, sir.'

'I know you do, Bryan, and I'm grateful.'

THEY HELD HANDS, and Willows was grateful because she'd never seen anything like this before. Then, the mutilated accountant lurched forward, and Pemberton started to drag her away.

It seemed a lifetime since Mrs Johnson had opened the front door to Willows and Pemberton, and there'd been nothing in the elderly widow's manner to suggest that this atrocity was awaiting them upstairs. Mrs Johnson was deaf. Fortunately, Pemberton had a sibling with hearing problems, so she was able to sign with George's mum. Mrs Johnson revealed that he'd had had two visitors an hour before. 'Clients,' she signed. 'I read their lips. They were very polite.'

In this instance, being deaf was a blessing. Mrs Johnson must have sat in ignorance throughout her son's entire ordeal. Willows imagined her nonchalantly nursing a cup of tea while her middle-aged son was being 'worked' on upstairs.

Right now, Willows was thankful that Pemberton had signed to Mrs Johnson not to trouble herself, that there was no need to make them both a drink, and there was certainly no need to wear herself out escorting them up the stairs.

Because then she would have seen her son with his eyes cut out.

Hours of lifting weights had given Borya Turgenev an energy boost. Rather than drain him, punishing exercise always fuelled him. One of his fellow dancers, back in a life based around the frivolity of friendship, had said Borya was like a self-charging battery; the harder he danced, the more extreme his movements became, until he didn't just outclass those around him, but defied reason in the patterns he wove together.

He was now in need of release.

He checked his watch and saw that his visitor would not be here for another forty-five minutes. Then, he took the glass jar which contained his parents' eyes floating in formaldehyde from the safe behind the leather sofa. He placed it onto the coffee table and pushed the sofa back.

As he sat back on the wooded chair, he felt his erection jamming hard against the front of his shorts. High from the endorphins of his workout, this wasn't surprising. He pulled his shorts down to free himself. He reached over to the remote control and pumped the lights up to 100%.

He looked up at the eyeballs floating in the sallow liquid. The optic nerves still trailed behind them. He recalled using his thumb and forefinger to pull them from his parents' heads and remembered the feel of the scalpel he'd used to slice them loose. His hand closed around himself and he sighed.

Realising he'd forgotten to pump the music up, he reached for the stereo controls on the table. They didn't work. Batteries must have died. He threw the remote back down. He didn't want to stop now that he'd found rhythm so would do without *Cannibal Corpse* just this once.

He prodded his bottom lip with his tongue and continued.

There was a knock at the door—

You're early. You shouldn't be here yet.

He increased speed.

She knocked again.

Nothing can distract me. Nothing can beat me.

The third knock was louder.

She cannot see inside ... the curtains are closed ... her efforts to end my pleasure are in vain ...

His parents' eyes turned in the yellowing liquid. He followed the movement towards climax. His heart rate increased. Sweat loosened from his shoulders and dampened his shirt.

Another knock. *Heavy ...*

The weight started to push down on his erection.

Continuous knocking. *Desperate. Incessant...*

His erection was waning.

He withdrew his hand; he was flaccid.

He threw his head back and roared. Outside on his doorstep, she wouldn't hear it, not through his soundproofed walls.

Not that he cared. He wanted her to hear his frustration ...

Who was she to demand his presence like this?

He was on his feet now. He gritted his teeth.

Forty minutes early.

With a distraction that had beaten him.

He hoisted up his jeans, fastened them and marched out of the lounge to the front door. He turned the key and steadied his hand on the handle.

You may have been beaten ... but a true warrior gets right back up ... and takes control ...

He opened the front door.

His visitor was already walking away. When she heard him, she turned back and brushed her long black hair behind her ears, revealing jagged cheekbones.

He began to feel his erection again. 'Why are you so early, Superintendent Madden?'

She walked to him, holding her hand open to catch the first droplets of rain. 'Some of us are busy, Borya, and it's about to rain like a bastard. I saw your light was on—'

She didn't finish the sentence because he'd already grabbed her hair, dragged her in through the front door, and slammed it shut.

Time to take back control.

───────

FROM THE FLOOR, George Johnson reached out. The blood-stained palm glistened. He moaned, and his hollow eye-sockets seemed to widen. He pitched forward. Willows flinched, and then flinched a second time when Johnson landed face first on his parquet floor with a thump.

Instinctively, Willows moved to assist him, but Pemberton was how holding her hand between both of hers, and she went nowhere.

Johnson rolled over onto his back. 'My eyes. They took my *fucking* eyes!'

He clawed at his empty sockets.

Willows looked back at Pemberton. '*Let go!*'

'He's dangerous—'

'*Look at him!*' Willows managed to pull her arm free.

'I'll phone it in,' Pemberton said.

Willows ran over to Johnson, knelt beside him, and saw that the extent of damage stretched further than just his eyes. Ear lobes and teeth were missing. His fingers were twisted and bent. Most of his fingernails had been torn loose; some still hung from their roots beneath the cuticles. He groaned as Willows drew him to his chest.

'Help me, *please* help me.' His face was swollen from an excessive beating, and his words were muffled.

She brushed his blood-stained hair away from his eyes and stroked his forehead. He shook. It could have been blood loss, or it could have been terror; more than likely a combination of both. She shushed him gently. 'Imagine the most beautiful place you can.'

'I can't ... the pain ... it's too much.'

'Try George. Try to imagine somewhere you've been. Somewhere you loved. Somewhere beautiful.'

There was a pause. Willows continued to stroke his head and encourage him with gentle hushing sounds.

'The beach,' he said.

'Good, now walk down that beach, and tell me what you see.'

'The sea. So calm. Barely a wave.'

'Can you feel the sand between your toes?'

'Yes.'

'Do you want to continue walking?'

'I want to go into the sea. It'd be cooler. Everything hurts so much.'

'Go in then, George.'

'Can I take my mother? She's here with me. We go together every year.'

'Of course.'

Willows waited for George to play out the scenario in his head.

She'd once been told that you could still cry with no eyes. That tear ducts were a separate structure in your face. She'd struggled to believe that at the time.

She was having no problems believing it now.

George Robinson cried a river of blood.

BORYA HAD the lower part of Madden's bony face between his thumb and forefinger. He knew he could burst her jaw like a balloon. He pushed her head against a mirror by the front door and pressed his whole body against her to prevent being kicked. He could see his face in the mirror.

'You disturbed me.' In the reflection, Borya watched his mouth move, saw the savagery in his eyes and felt capable of so very much.

He dragged his eyes away from himself and back onto her. He bared his teeth.

'I can feel your hard cock on me, animal,' Madden said.

Borya snarled. Keeping one hand on her face, he closed his other hand into a fist and raised it.

'Remember, *animal*, not the face, not the—'

He lowered his fist and swung. He felt the muscles in her taut abdomen slacken. He moved back and let her collapse to her knees, gasping for air. *Harder than last time, wasn't it? Did that surprise you?*

He looked up at his reflection and curled his lip up into another snarl. He sensed her movement, her attempt to strike back, and without breaking eye contact with himself, he dropped his hand to catch her tiny fist. Her pebble in his ocean.

He pressed her hand against his erection. *Now, another surprise.*

'Next time.' He watched his lips move in his reflection. 'You.' He punched her in the face. 'Come.' *Punch.* 'On.' *Punch.* 'Time.'

He was curious about her reaction. *How surprised was*

she that he'd broken the golden rule? He looked down. She was looking up at him. Her eye was puffy, her nose crooked, possibly dislocated, and her lip split. Yet, she smiled.

He released her fist and allowed her to undo the zipper on his jeans. He moaned as she pulled him out. She leaned forward and let the blood dribble from her mouth onto his erection, using it to lubricate him; then, she thrust her hand swiftly and forcefully along the shaft.

He looked at his reflection again. His top lip trembled. He took a deep breath and prepared for climax—

She stopped.

He glared down. '*Continue.*'

Madden looked up at him with a chin covered in blood and spit. 'I told you. Not the face.'

He reached down and closed his hand around her neck. He lifted her from the floor and pinned her to the mirror again. Her face glowed, and she clawed at his hands. His eyes moved to his reflection. His lips were pursed, and his forehead creased. Determination. He looked back at her and saw her tongue protruding.

He didn't want to kill her, but he wasn't able to release her. It just felt too right.

He looked in the mirror again and addressed himself. *Are you going to lose control again tonight? Or are you going to learn from earlier?*

He looked back at her and saw the bluish tinge in her face.

He took a deep breath and felt the moment.

Everything was quiet. Still.

Peace.

He released her, and she slumped to the floor, gasping for air.

Sucking in a deep breath, he clutched her hair. He dragged her down the hallway as she spluttered and gagged.

When they reached the lounge, he flung her in, so she landed face first beside the chair and the table. She lifted her head, and Borya heard her cry out when she saw his parents' eyes in the jar.

Before she had chance to turn over, and delay again what needed to happen, Borja had torn her trousers down, and clambered onto her.

Borya watched the eyes as he thrust, and the eyes watched Borya as he came.

18

YORKE COULD BARELY understand what Willows was saying.

Someone had been murdered, he'd gathered that much. And violently so. But who it was, and why it'd happened remained lost in translation.

Despite this, he was incredibly patient. She'd experienced severe trauma. He let her splutter out her experiences and then found a moment of silence. 'Who are you with, Collette?'

'Pemberton. Outside Johnson's house.'

'Okay, so it's Johnson?'

'Have you not been listening, sir?'

Trying to. Yes. 'Just clarifying, Collette.'

He was glad Willows was with Pemberton. He'd never heard her like this before. If she'd been alone, Yorke would already have been in his car despite his injuries.

'Collette, do you have a drink in your car?'

A pause. 'Yes ... I think so. A bottle of water.'

'Good. I'd like you to hand the phone to Pemberton, go to the car, sit down and have a drink.'

'I'm fine, sir.'

Clearly not. 'I'm not being patronising, Collette. Just two minutes, please, and we will pick up where we left off ... okay?'

'Yes, sir.'

He heard the rustle of the phone being handed over. He glanced up at the psychiatrist's card Bryan Kelly had left on his mantlepiece.

We'll all be needing that before the week is out.

'Sir?'

'Pemberton. Are you okay?'

'As well as can be, sir.'

She sounded calmer than Willows. Good.

'Has Collette gone to her car?'

'Yes, sir.'

'Good. She needs to calm down. Pemberton, please talk me through what happened.'

She filled in the blanks left by Willows. Of which they were many.

Afterwards, Yorke sank back into the sofa. He didn't need a mirror to see how pale he suddenly was.

'I'm *so* sorry, Lorraine ...'

'I'm okay, sir, a little bit shaken—'

'*No,* I'm sorry for sending you there.'

'You weren't to know.'

'That's not the point.' He felt his lips tremble. 'The investigation is over, and I put you and Collette in danger. *Needlessly.*'

'Not true. We were doing our jobs.'

That wasn't the case though, was it? The job they'd been given by SEROCU was clear ...

Stay out of it.

He leaned forward, felt the pain in his ribs, welcomed

it, saw it as a form of penance, and massaged his forehead with his thumb and forefinger. 'If you'd arrived earlier ... Jesus ... I can't even think about it ...'

'We'd have stopped it,' Pemberton said. 'Which is why I still believe it was the right thing to do - we were just unfortunate with timing.'

Or fortunate, Yorke thought. *You could have ended up like Johnson ...*

'Who is there?' Yorke said.

'Everyone. Major Incidents. SEROCU. No sign of the Super though. Her phone is off, apparently. Uncharacteristic.'

'Is Johnson alive?'

'Barely. He went into shock when the ambulance arrived. I haven't had an update. Collette is back. Do you want to talk to her?'

'Yes, please. I'm so sorry—'

'Sir.' It was Willows on the other end again. 'I'm feeling better now. I apologise. What I saw in there—'

'No, Collette, you've done nothing wrong. This is on me.'

'How's this your fault?'

'I was incompetent. This is SEROCU's gig now.'

'Yes, you can tell. They're everywhere.'

'I want you and Lorraine to give your statement and come away.'

'If that's what you want, sir.'

'Yes, it is. I also don't want you at work tomorrow. There's nothing you can do regarding this anyway. It will be going home with Robinson and his people. In fact, come here tomorrow, for breakfast. I want to check you're okay.'

'That won't be necessary, sir.'

'I insist Collette and tell Lorraine I would like to see her in the afternoon. You both deserve an apology face-to-face.'

Despite Willows' continued protestations, Yorke finally got her consent. As soon as the call ended, he received another from Bryan Kelly. When he saw the name on the phone, he immediately felt overwhelmed with guilt. For years, he'd admonished Kelly for his failures. Yet, here he was, sitting on a mistake that was almost catastrophic. He'd sent two of his best officers into a lion's den, and if he'd done it any earlier, they might have ended up as the animal's food.

'Bryan?'

'Sir, I'm so sorry, something has come up. My wife has been called away by work. Emergency organ transplant. Happens often to her, I'm afraid.'

'You don't have to be sorry for standing me up because a life has to be saved, Bryan.'

'Thanks sir, I knew you'd understand. I'll pop in tomorrow.'

'I'd like that, Bryan.'

After the call ended, Yorke felt tears in his eyes. He looked forward to seeing all these people tomorrow.

He planned to apologise to them all, profusely.

NAKED, Borya meditated on the sofa. He hovered with his parents' eyes in the jar. It was a pleasant experience. The only other time he'd felt this weightless when he'd danced.

He didn't miss it. That was another life. A rather meaningless life. A life as a show pony. What he had become, *evolved into*, was of far greater significance. The people around him were now part of *his* show. They were here for *his* entertainment. *He* was what mattered.

'I'm going now,' Madden said from the lounge door.

He didn't break his trance but responded. 'While you were gone, I emailed the information that you gave me. I've already been informed that the information was good. Your money will be deposited today.'

'Of course, my information is good. It is *always* good.'

'Yes,' Borya said, 'it seems so. Must be the resources at your disposal.'

'And the father and daughter on the photographs my man provided?'

'What about them?'

'What will become of them?'

'Not your concern.'

'True. And you? Are you concerned for your fellow countrymen?'

Borya smiled. 'It's been a long time since someone asked me a question like that.'

'Maybe you're glad? After all, they fled your country. *Betrayed* your country.'

'Everyone betrays everyone in my country. A retreating GRU officer is not something that interests me.'

'Just the people you work for.'

Borya nodded slowly, still partially lost in the dance of the eyes.

'Are you capable of any feelings, Borya?'

'I enjoyed *fucking* you, so I must be capable of feeling something.'

'You enjoyed the control, Borya. That's different. What you were doing, and who it was with were irrelevant to you.'

Borya broke his trance to turn and smile again. 'In the

same way you enjoyed *being* controlled. Don't pretend that who and what were relevant to you.'

Madden smiled. She winced. Her eye and lips were puffing up nicely. 'True, but we did have an agreement.'

Borya turned back to the jar. 'I remember. Not the face.'

'Yes ... so?'

'So? I'm just saying I remember ...'

'Are we all just nothing to you?'

'*Everything* is nothing.'

'Goodbye, Borya. I won't be back.'

You will, he thought as she slammed the lounge door. *You always come back.*

———————

YORKE WAS in the bathroom trying to peek under the bandage on his face when Robinson called him.

'Before you say anything, sir, I made a mistake. I'm sorry.'

'It's not me you should be apologising to, Mike. It's your two officers—'

'*I know!*' Yorke cut him off rather abruptly, but it was clearly a sore point. He then took a deep breath and apologised for his tone. 'But my gut instinct told me that Wheelhouse was behind the murder of Buddy's granddaughter. The fact that Johnson has been tortured, nearly to death, suggests I was probably right.'

'I'm sure we'd have arrived at the same lead, Mike.'

'I've no doubt, sir, but I thought you'd have your hands full, and would appreciate the support.'

'Despite the fact that I told you to completely remove yourself from the investigation?'

'I've had a rough time, sir, my judgement was clouded. I apologise again. Has Johnson woken?'

'Rough time or not, Mike, I'm not answering that question until I have your cast-iron guarantee that you're completely hands off.'

'Cast-iron.'

Robinson sighed. 'No, he hasn't woken and until he does, *if* he even does, we're working on guesswork, but one thing is probably sure ...'

'Go on.'

'Buddy had the same hunch as you. Whoever tortured Johnson works for Buddy alright.'

'How do you know?'

'Years back, before *Article SE*, when Buddy was ruling the roost instead of simply existing on machines, he used to take souvenirs.'

'The eyes?' Yorke said, recalling the grisly details from Pemberton.

'Yes. It looks like someone has done this on his orders.'

'Unless, someone has made it look like he's responsible?'

'Another possibility.'

Despite the fatigue, and pain in his ribs, Yorke paced the bathroom. His adrenaline was up. He so badly wanted to be part of this investigation.

'You must have grilled Wheelhouse and Firth by now?'

'We tried. Firth is very adept at pleading ignorant. He's an experienced man.'

'Yes, I noticed.'

'When we saw Wheelhouse, he was out of it on a sedative too, which didn't help matters. He says he's dealing with loss.'

'Seems he dealt with it,' Yorke said, 'An eye for an eye.'

'Possibly, Mike, but listen, you've given me that

guarantee now. I like you. You're a fantastic copper with instincts as sharp as a razor, but next time this won't be as pleasant. Next time, I'll push Joan to discipline you.'

'Fair enough, sir ... could I at least get updates?'

'You're unstoppable ... when I can, and if appropriate, Mike, but right now you need to rest.'

After the phone call, Yorke returned to the mirror. He was just about to sneak a long-awaited peek at his split cheek when the bathroom door flew open. It was Ewan.

'Shit ... bollocks ... sorry, Mike.'

'Since when have profanities made up fifty percent of your vocabulary?'

'Since I walked in on you in the bathroom.'

'Don't worry, my fault, forgot to lock it; pain medication has sent me a bit sideways.'

'I was going to ask you later, but now is as good a time as any. Is it okay if Lexi stays over?'

Yorke reeled and the question came out before he'd even thought it through. 'Are you two having sex?'

Ewan blushed.

So did Yorke. 'Sorry, I just blurted that out. What I meant—'

'No ... we're not. I was going to suggest she sleeps in the spare room anyway.'

'Of course. Sorry ... it's these medicines. Yes, that's fine. Spare room.'

'Thanks Mike.' Glowing, he turned away.

'Oh ... Ewan,' Yorke said.

He turned back.

'If you ever ... you know ... want to chat about things, just let me know, okay?'

Ewan nodded and left him in the bathroom.

Yorke had led many incident rooms in his time. Some

pretty unforgiving ones at that. But never, ever, had he felt as lost for words as he did right now.

He closed the door, locked it, and sat down before his jelly legs gave out on him.

WHEN BORYA HEARD the ping of his email, he wondered if his next target was the ex-GRU officer and his daughter. It made sense. Russians often liked to use their own to clean up.

Borya wouldn't mind being assigned Alexander Antonovich. He'd easily be his most high-profile target to date, and further testament to his ascension to greatness.

Antonovich was famous for writing books about Josef Stalin. Books that stripped away the propaganda. Books that riled his motherland.

Carrying a soviet court conviction, Antonovich had originally been smuggled over from Switzerland, and the UK government was in no rush to extradite him back. He had been a useful informant over the years, and anyone that riled Russia with bestselling books was welcome to stay.

Yes, Borya thought, *I would like that job very much.*

Borya was surprised to find another email from *'Power Protein.'* They often changed the company name in subsequent emails. This suggested one of two things. They were growing complacent. Unlikely. It was most likely the second option: they were in a rush.

They didn't usually rush, which implied that whoever had requested the contract had offered more money.

Interesting ... maybe it isn't the Russian spy, after all ...

He clicked the email. He opened a pad in front of him, picked up a pen, and starting with the words, 'Exclusive offer.' He counted twenty letters. T. Then, another fifteen. H ...

He followed his usual process until he'd written: THE HOBBIT, BEVOIS VALLEY ROAD. It was a famous Tolkien-inspired public house in Southampton.

He then counted the testimonials from the fictional Power Protein junkies which would indicate the time of the meeting. There were thirty-three, which did not work against any clock Borya had ever come across.

Fortunately, he knew what it meant.

Many years ago, he'd been warned that this could happen in the future. It never had. Until now.

The difference between thirty-three and twenty-four was nine. His meeting was at nine o'clock this evening.

He looked at his watch. Less than an hour to go.

Borya rarely felt excited, but this felt very different.

———

Jake lay awake. The rain pounded his bedsit. White noise usually calmed him. Not tonight.

Instead of counting sheep, he counted all the ways his life had gone wrong. He smirked. It should keep him going most of the night. And, at least if he didn't sleep, then he might have the definitive reason for the state he was in.

Where did he start? The return of Lacey Ray? The sociopathic ex-girlfriend who took offense at being called *emotionally stunted*. Bringing that up had given birth to a vendetta which had lasted for years. A vendetta that had led to his pregnant wife being threatened; him being chained to a chair and threatened with secateurs; and the execution of a devious plot which had led Jake to violent murder in order to protect those he loved.

He was lying to himself. *She* wasn't the only reason.

Prior to the return of Lacey, his relationship with Sheila had been crumbling for years. He'd written off the advice that you should always look at your potential mother-in-law before you took a wife. For the second time in this melancholy sheep-counting exercise, he smirked.

There were moments of happiness amongst the wreckage of their marriage. Frank being the best of these. He brought short periods of clarity and happiness to their time together because it was something they could share away from the job and the mother-in-law. But he'd also made a mockery of that by embarking on an affair.

He'd like to return to Lacey, and blame the malignant narcissist, but she was out of his life now. She'd been institutionalised and was unlikely to see the light of day anytime soon. Yet, he'd continued walking this path of self-destruction. *Running* rather than *walking.* Shaking down people for money on behalf of organised crime; following and tracking the movement of potential hits; incorrectly logging, and sometimes damaging, evidence; and, giving out protected data, such as addresses and phone numbers.

No, the buck really had to stop with him. He had to own this. Had to admit that his life, as he had known it, was well and truly over. He was dangerous and destructive. His mother-in-law had been right. Time to disappear. Exactly how Mark Topham, his good friend, had disappeared.

He vowed that tomorrow would be the beginning of his future. He would miss his son, dreadfully. The possibility of never knowing how Frank's life evolved sawed through his entire being, but how could he continue? Even Yorke knew now. Really? How long could his noble colleague allow this to continue? He smiled over the thought of his closest friend. They'd had some good times. Yorke had always been a rock for him. He'd miss him.

But before leaving, he had one good deed to complete. It wouldn't make up for everything, but it was a start. He could walk away knowing he had made a significant difference to someone else's life. And he could also walk away knowing that he'd never broken his golden rule. Because not a single child had ever been hurt as a result of his actions. Not like Herbert Wheelhouse, not like Lacey Ray, not like Simon Young ...

He wasn't like any of *them*. At least he would see out the rest of his life, knowing that.

Eventually, he slept with a single thought on his mind: it's time for a new beginning.

FROM HIS JAIL CELL, Firth couldn't hear the heavy rain that was forecast, but he tried to imagine it.

He recalled a time, long ago, when the rain would help him sleep, especially after the loss of his son.

But try as he might, the sleep just wouldn't come. And when his mind started to drift to the events of tomorrow, he became even more agitated.

He climbed down from the top bunk and switched his desk lamp on. It was lights out, but this was one of his 'special privileges.' Not that he exercised it often. He never wanted to keep Wheelhouse awake. However, tonight, his friend was out for the count on another hypnotic, so there was no rousing him.

Firth had already composed his weekly letter to Patricia and Jeanette, but he wanted to write another one to Patricia. One with a slightly different tone, one that matched tomorrow, and the sense of finality which was looming. He wanted Patricia to know her importance in his existence despite their estrangement.

Dear Patricia,

It may not seem like it to you, my darling, but it still feels like yesterday when I walked you to school, when I read to you in bed, when I helped you to ride your bicycle. All those times. All those experiences. Priceless moments. They're so vivid that when I close my eyes, I can still hear you breathing beside me, and feel your tiny hand in mine.

These are moments I can't lose, no matter what happens. Day by day, I live through them, and if the day comes in which I can't find them again, then I'll be no more.

I like to believe, want to believe, Pat, that these are the moments that define me. Not what has happened since. Those moments with you, and Ian. And your mother. All of us together. Happy. Before Geoff Stirling and his Ford Capri.

But I know that life isn't that kind. And I certainly don't expect you to overlook everything that happened those years after we lost Ian. The choices I made to support you and your mother were unacceptable. I know that now. All I did was drive an even thicker wedge between us all.

I have my priceless moments, but I also have those other moments. The moments I want to forget but must face every night when I lie down, and every morning when I first look at myself in the mirror. You know of the times I'm referring to. One of those moments physically damaged you, scarred my poor baby's back. I know that no matter how many times I apologise, I can never get it right. Know this though, Patricia, my darling, it wasn't your father asleep, drunk, in that car. The true man, your true father was gone long before that.

You remember when you held my hand? The day I watched your brother die?

I pulled my hand away from you. Not because I didn't want to support you, because I did, and still desperately do, but because I felt myself dying inside, and I didn't want to contaminate you. Death had taken Ian, and it was taking me too, and I was not letting it get its bony hands on you.

Patricia, when all is said and done, and one day it will be, probably sooner than you realise, I want you to remember me for the man I was before that day, and not the man I became.

I know it's such a long time ago for you, and your memory will be hazy, but whatever you have, please hold onto. Those priceless moments. Drops of rain. Frozen forever. Don't let them melt. Hold them close. And if you ever want to know more about me, who I was, before, ask your mother. She will speak fondly of me because we were happy then. Genuinely. There is a treasure chest of precious moments right there for you to open, and I pray to God, every single night now, that one day you'll open it.

I love you, more than you could ever believe.

If this was to be my last letter to you, I know that it's a fitting farewell.

Yours truly,

Daddy.

After sealing the envelope, writing on the address, wiping tears away, Firth turned off the lamp. He climbed the steps to his bunk. He lay there and thought of all those precious moments that had made his life so full, and all those *other* moments that had eventually ruined it.

Eventually, he slept with a single thought on his mind: it's time for a new beginning.

19

TODAY FELT LIKE a new beginning to Borya Turgenev.

And not simply because the ash cloud was predicted to clear today, but rather because of the assignment he'd been given.

It hadn't been the Russian defector as he'd first suspected. That had already been assigned. He didn't regret this. *That* was an easy task. The most challenging task had been reserved for the best.

The rain had taken a break this morning, but it was due back at some point today, so he carried an umbrella.

When in his car, he switched on the lights. Despite it being day, the world was still dark.

After Borya had been asked to kill his entire family, he'd never expected to be tasked with so ambitious a challenge again. He'd been wrong.

And he thanked his lucky stars.

JAKE WAS UP EARLY for his new beginning.

There wasn't much to pack, so he had a couple of cups of coffee instead and thought of where he should go. He hadn't given his actual exit plan too much thought so far. Most of his focus had gone into the good deed he was planning.

Using the internet on his phone, he scheduled himself onto an overnight ferry from Portsmouth to St Malo in France. Having visited the port city in Brittany in the past with Sheila, he knew it well enough to lie low there for a few days before deciding on his next move.

The mast-filled port city of St Malo was walled, and Jake recalled standing with Sheila at the highest point, looking down at the waves lashing the ramparts. The sky, like the skies here now, had been black and swollen, and the air was moist with sea spray and the beginning of rain. It had been untamed and wild and was one of Jake's favourite memories.

It was also a time of happiness for them both. They'd both been young, and very much in love.

He looked inside the black holdall. He brushed aside his clothing and double-checked the first bundle of cash was there. This one was for Frank and Sheila. In the other holdall, there was an inside zipper pocket. Last night, he'd slit the inside of this pocket, so he was able to stuff his cash into the lining of the bag rather than the main compartment.

If he was stopped by customs on his journey out of the UK, they hopefully wouldn't find it. He'd be able to convert it into Euros in small increments when he reached St Malo. It was a risk, he knew that, but he'd never had a rigorous customs check when travelling, and leaving his life behind with no money was unthinkable.

He looked at his watch. It was time to make a move.

He checked around the bedsit one last time. He'd left a few provisions in the freezer and two bottles of *Summer Lightning* in the fridge for the next unlucky sod who reached a bump in the road and decided to hunker down in this squalor.

When certain he'd not left anything important, he left the bedsit, closed another chapter in his unhappy life, and went off to do his one good deed of the year.

'WHILE YOU WERE asleep last night, I called to tell Alice that I needed some time,' Pemberton ran her fingertips up and down Willows' exposed back. 'Told her I was staying with my mother.'

'Did she believe you?' Willows said.

'Your guess is as good as mine. She never really seems to believe me about anything.'

'Why's that?'

'Dunno. She thinks I'm too sarcastic.'

'You are ... but you're not a liar.'

'How do you know?'

'Good point.'

'She says I use sarcasm to mask my feelings which is the same as lying.'

Willows rolled over in bed to face her. Pemberton was glad; she could now run her fingertips down over her breasts and stomach.

Willows smiled. 'I guess you kept your feelings *masked* from me for a while.'

'I think we both played that game.'

'Who's to say I had feelings for you to start with?'

'Now, who's lying?'

They paused to stare at each other for a time. Willows looked quite tearful.

'I'm proud of you, Collette,' Pemberton said.

'Why?'

'You know why. You went to Johnson. You held him while—'

'*No,*' Willows said. 'We have today off for a reason. Let's not relive it again and again.'

'I held you back. I'm sorry.'

'Really Lorraine ... let's not discuss it. You were just trying to protect me. But, please, no more. This instead ...' Willows moved in and they kissed.

Pemberton started to move her fingertips further down her stomach. Willows took the wandering hand and broke away from the kiss. 'Do you love her?'

Pemberton rolled onto her back, looked up at the ceiling and sighed. 'I guess so.'

'Great.' Willows also rolled onto her back.

'At least I'm telling you the truth. Regardless of what Alice thinks, I'm not a liar. But loving and being with someone are two totally different things. There are so many problems in our relationship – trust issues only scratch the surface.'

'This is starting to feel very much about you.' Willows sat up. 'And no one else.'

'That's not fair, Collette. This is a long-term relationship, not some student fling. We own a house together. I can't just set fire to everything.'

Willows glared at her. 'That's patronising. Do you think that I don't understand?'

'You told me that your longest relationship was nine months, and that was with a man, so forgive me if I'm ...'

'Being a bitch?' Willows said, swinging her legs out of the bed.

'Woah ... extreme!'

'So was your patronising tone.' Willows got out of bed and started to get dressed.

'Fine. Be like that. I've got a lot to think about.'

'Whereas I don't?' Willows widened her eyes. 'Because I'm single, this is easy for me? Not only am I having to come to terms with my sexuality, but I'm in danger of becoming a homewrecker ... yet, it's all about you and your anxieties.'

Pemberton looked down as Willows finished getting dressed.

By the time, Willows was dressed, Pemberton was on her feet, ready to apologise. 'Look ... I'm sorry, that was on me. I get carried away with the self-pity sometimes.'

Willows rose her eyebrows. 'You're telling me.'

'Back to bed?' Pemberton said, raising her eyebrows too. 'Please?'

Willows sighed. 'I just need a bit of space today, Lorraine, okay? You're right. Last night was tough. I'll ring you later, promise. I'm going to Mike's for breakfast now.'

'Yes, and I'm due there for afternoon tea! What does he want?'

'I guess he feels guilty. Possibly, he's stressed, and probably wants some friendly faces. We've been through a lot together over the years. Some truly horrible things to be honest. He's lost a lot of people close to him in that time.'

'Isn't it best we just go together now?'

'It's not what he asked for. He probably wouldn't mind but, to be honest, I'd appreciate the headspace for a couple of hours.'

'Have I fucked this up, Collette?'

Willows shrugged. 'I don't know. I think you just have to decide what you want ... and fast.'

'I'm going to need more time,' Pemberton said.

'I know,' Willows sighed. 'But I really don't know if I'm the person that can give you that ... you can see yourself out. Just post the key back though.'

Pemberton watched Willows leave the bedroom and then climbed back into bed.

She lay down and stared at the ceiling for ten minutes.

'*Shit!*'

She rolled onto her side and closed her eyes.

'BREAKFAST IN BED? In prison? You've got to be fucking kidding me!' Wheelhouse brought the tray closer to him and ran his nose over the bacon and sausages. He looked at Firth, who was sitting in his desk chair, and winked. 'And it's not even my birthday, honey!'

Firth winked. 'Enjoy Herb, you've had a tough deal of late.' He looked up at Harris. 'You can go now.'

The guard smirked. 'Am I not invited to breakfast club?'

'We'll be using big words,' Firth said.

'Funny. How about some gratitude for bringing your boyfriend his bacon and eggs?'

'You forgot the HP Sauce.'

'Good job it paid well. Although, how long's that going to last now that reliable George is in intensive care missing his eyes?'

Firth heard Wheelhouse drop his fork onto his plate.

'Dickhead,' Firth said.

Harris put his hand to his mouth. 'Oops! Did I spoil his breakfast?' He sniggered and left.

Firth sighed and looked at Wheelhouse who was staring over at him with wide eyes. 'I was going to get to it. I just wanted you to enjoy your breakfast first. And I didn't order room service to butter you up either. I only found out about George an hour ago.'

'What the fuck does this mean?'

'It means that Buddy sent some men to torture George.'

'Because of Vanessa?'

'Why else?'

'How did he know who it was? How *could* he have known?'

'He didn't, or at least he didn't *before*. I don't know what George said to them before they put his lights out.'

Wheelhouse pushed his tray away. 'With that kind of torture going on, *everything,* I imagine. How careful were you?'

Firth widened his eyes. 'I'll ignore that question, Herb. You're shocked ... as was I earlier.'

Wheelhouse hit the metal ladder attached to the bunk. 'He always was a canny fucker that Buddy. He's got more enemies than pounds in the bank, and yet he immediately suspects the jailbird.'

'We were stupid, Herb. I warned you over the costs of vengeance. Granted, I never thought these costs would be so swift, and so brutal.'

'Now what?'

'We wait, Herb. If George talked, if Buddy knows, it won't be long until we hear from him.'

'Are we safe in here?'

'We couldn't be safer. While we continue to pay Harris and his lackeys, he'll struggle to get to us. But this won't go away. He'll want payment for his loss, but I've no idea what he's charging.'

'Our lives, perhaps?'

'More than likely. Hopefully, he'll be patient enough to wait until we're released. We might outlive him.'

'Buddy Young is not a patient man.'

'No, he is not. One of his men will be in that visitor's room sooner rather than later. Until then, we are going to have to be vigilant.'

'And our money?'

'Most of it be okay,' Firth said. 'George only holds twenty percent of the money in our main accounts. He keeps the records for these on his work computer, and in his paper documents in his office. He holds no records of the other eighty percent hidden away in separate accounts. Worse comes to worse, George will have given up the existence of the smaller accounts under torture, but I doubt Buddy's men will have felt the need to press further. These accounts will have looked rosy enough; they wouldn't have suspected the existence of more.'

'So, you reckon only twenty percent of our money is compromised?'

Firth nodded. 'And I'm hoping that when Buddy does calm down and makes his play for compensation, he accepts that twenty percent.'

'And if he doesn't?'

Firth sighed. 'Well then, we don't want to make parole while he's still breathing ... but I'm confident he will do. Like I said, he's not patient. Potentially, he may have to wait over ten years for revenge. He knows he won't live that long. Seeing us broke and destitute might be the best he can hope for.'

'He could still take our money, and then have us murdered in ten years anyway.'

'Buddy Young is old-school. He's a vicious, ruthless

man, but he isn't a backstabber and a cheat. Everybody knows that Buddy can be taken for his word. He prides himself on his integrity. If he takes the twenty, we'll live to enjoy the eighty.'

'Still, twenty is a lot—'

Firth was on his feet before Wheelhouse could finish his sentence. 'Aren't you getting this, Herb? I warned you of the costs, and you still wanted to move forward. And now, I offer you the best-case scenario, which is survival, and you're turning your nose up at it?'

Wheelhouse glowered and looked away. 'Not turning my nose up at it. I'm just pointing out the fact that it's a lot of money.'

'Do you have a better solution?'

Wheelhouse sighed. 'When did you set all this up with George anyway?'

'I didn't. He did. Standard practise for our bent accountant. He only told me about it when I approached him to pay for the hit. I told him I was worried about repercussions, and he told me this was how he helped protect most of his clients' wealth. A separate invisible account. He told me that if anyone came looking, they would be duped into thinking this was the client's total wealth. He did it mainly to evade the law, but it would come in handy if anyone more sinister came sniffing.'

'I'm not sure I like it. What if he snuffs it? How am I going to access this invisible account?'

'Easy. There're three of them. There's a silent partnership at play here. They all have their own clients, but they share their profits. Any of them kick the bucket, the clients' details are immediately picked up by one of the other two.'

'Sounds like a lot of trust is required here.'

'Come on, Herb. Look at their typical clientele ... they wouldn't still be here if they were in the business of ripping people off.'

'True,' Wheelhouse said, nodding.

'So, pull that tray back over, try and relax a little, and enjoy the breakfast I spent a fortune on.'

'Yes, you're right. I wouldn't take it back. Whatever to the money. If he cared even a smidgeon for his granddaughter as I cared for Janice, it will have been worth every penny. And I'll pay you back your twenty percent, Doug, you know I will.'

'That's up to you. I'd pay anything to see you happy. You've always been a good friend to me.'

As Wheelhouse continued to eat, Firth looked at the letter to Patricia on his desk. He'd forgotten to give it to Harris to put in the mail but would do when he returned.

He stroked the envelope and then looked back at Wheelhouse, who was attacking a rasher of bacon.

To new beginnings. Firth though. *Enjoy your breakfast, Herb. It's the least I could do today.*

'AND AS YOU CAN SEE, BRYAN,' Yorke said from the other side of the dining room table, 'I'm feeling ten times better. I slept well, and I'm off the sofa. At least for breakfast.'

'That's great news, sir.' Bryan took a mouthful of tea. 'Sir ... I know you don't hold me in the highest regard, but I've been here before, and I hope you listen to me ... things change quickly when you've experienced trauma. It can be manic. One minute you can be high as a kite, but the next minute ...'

Yorke jolted. Bryan's acknowledgement that Yorke was

not his greatest fan was shocking. Yes, there was truth in it, but Yorke's own failings over the last day, and the growing evidence that he was also far from infallible, caused a wave of guilt to wash over him. It hadn't been a mistake to be critical of Bryan – that was necessary; the mistake had been not to counterbalance criticism with compliment. 'I apologise for not being kinder to you Bryan. During your career, there've been moments when you've supported families through the unspeakable.'

Bryan blushed again. 'Thanks sir ... I never knew you thought like that. In the past, you've been quite vocal over some of my screw-ups.'

'There's a big difference between holding someone to account, and considering them a failure, Bryan. You've made mistakes and I ensured you were held to account. I'd do the same with any member of my team.' He paused and looked away.

In his dream, he'd told Alfie and Janice that he wasn't a liar.

But hadn't he just lied?

He wasn't holding Jake to account, was he?

'Are you okay, sir?'

'Yes, just came over all funny for a second there, Bryan. It's the pain medication. As I was saying, I should have told you long ago how much I respected what you did for Iain following the murder of his wife, and how much supported Holly and Ryan Mitchell when they lost their son. You're a good person and a *necessary* person. Don't think I'm pushing your support away. I'm not. I just don't like people fussing over me, never really have.'

'Thanks sir. I appreciate—'

The doorbell interrupted them.

'You want me to go, sir?'

'No, let me. I need the exercise.'

Yorke left the kitchen, and saw Patricia coming down the stairs to his left. 'I've got it.'

Patricia stopped half-way down. 'Okay, I'll go back to rousing Ewan and his visitor.'

'Separate rooms?'

Patricia smiled. 'After your conversation with him, I don't think they'd have dared to try any different.'

'It wasn't *that* bad.'

Patricia raised her eyebrows and walked back upstairs.

Yorke answered the front door. It was Willows. 'How're you feeling, sir?'

'Well everything is a milestone and answering the door to you is an important one.' He backed away to allow her in.

Willows held up a paper bag as she passed him. 'Croissants. Freshly baked from around the corner.'

Yorke smiled. 'Make that the *most important* milestone yet.'

After Ewan opted out of breakfast by running down and grabbing a handful of toast for Lexi and him, Yorke, Willows, Bryan and Patricia enjoyed the croissants. Beatrice was asleep in Patricia's arms.

It was clear to everyone that Yorke was struggling to eat. The cut on his face burned every time he put something into his mouth, and his ribcage felt like it was going to burst every time he swallowed. One by one, they continually asked him if he was okay.

'The next time someone asks me that question,' Yorke said, 'I'm going to say *no*.'

Awkward looks passed between them all.

'Okay, point taken,' Patricia said, stroking Beatrice's hair, 'no more sympathy.'

'Sympathy is unsettling,' Yorke said with a smile, 'I'm not used to it.'

Patricia played an imaginary violin. 'I promise to bring you breakfast in bed next time you are ravaged by man-flu.'

Yorke wanted to offer her a sardonic smile but knew that would hurt his cheek too much. He opted for 'Ha-ha' instead.

Willows smiled. 'Anyway, on a more important note than sir's feelings, I've read the ash cloud's days are numbered.'

They all looked out the lounge window. The sky was swollen, and another torrential downpour couldn't be long away.

'Well I, for one, can't wait,' Patricia said, 'Some daylight would be fantastic.'

'Life back to normal again,' Bryan said, 'Sounds like bliss.'

Yorke kept his opinions to himself. Obviously, he wasn't opposed to normality, but the end of *Operation Tagline* still rankled him; it had been a long time since he'd failed to see out an operation and restore justice.

He felt his blood boil when he thought of Borja Turgenev still walking free. He killed an innocent woman, and elderly man, and almost imposed extreme loss on his family. It wasn't about Yorke himself bringing Borya to justice, he'd never been that conceited. It was just that he was now forced to trust others to do this.

And considering recent revelations, trust was in short supply.

'To be honest, the world is a chaotic place,' Willows said. 'These days, I just see chaos as normal.'

Bryan and Patricia were silent.

Yorke smiled. There was Collette Willows. She'd come back from her recent experiences just fine.

FROM HIS CAR, on the other side of the road, Jake watched Nina Livingstone stroll down her father's drive. Until Nina's arrival, he'd been watching two kids in the adjacent driveway playing badminton, making the most of the fresh air before the sky burst open again.

As always, Nina ran her fingers down the side of her father's red Porsche Boxster. She was a creature of habit, and Jake now knew those habits well. They were habits he wanted to preserve; so, he was here to warn her, and her father, that they'd been located. His one good deed. His moment of redemption before leaving.

Peter Livingstone, formally known as Alexander Antonovich, the ex- soviet military intelligence officer, opened the door to his daughter.

Jake watched Nina go into her father's house. Saturday's routine was slightly different to the weekly one. She'd stop for a drink first before driving them both somewhere for brunch. Jake planned to follow them, stop alongside them outside the café, and warn them. He didn't want to risk doing it here. Being sighted outside their house would be a disaster. The less reason to make himself a target for *Article SE*, the better. Jake wanted to disappear an irrelevant man.

To be honest, he couldn't believe Alexander Antonovich had lasted this long. The Russians were usually resourceful when locating their traitors. Alexander had also thrown major clues their way in the form of popular books on Josef Stalin, albeit under his British name, Peter

Livingstone. The UK government had been very generous with Antonovich's new identity. They'd given him a degree in history from Oxford University, a PHD, and he'd scored a lucrative job reporting for the *National Geographic*.

This was all about to come to an end for Antonovich. He would have to run, but at least he would survive.

One of the kids won a point against his brother and whooped in celebration. Jake thought of Frank and felt a hollowness inside.

He phoned Superintendent Joan Madden. She answered on her fourth ring.

'It's DS Jake Pettman. I won't be coming in today.'

'What are you contacting me for, officer? You have a line manager.'

'In fact, I won't be coming in again, ma'am. *Ever.* I'm done.'

'Are you feeling alright? You're not making any—'

'*I know.*'

She didn't respond.

'I said I know about you, Superintendent Joan Madden.'

Jake felt a burst of adrenaline when one of the young boys burst out onto the street chasing a shuttlecock. He breathed a sigh of relief when he looked in the rear-view mirror and saw there was no traffic coming.

'And what is it you think you know exactly, DS Pettman?'

'I watched you pick up the USB stick from the squat in Tidworth.'

'Did you now? Clever boy ... I guess that puts a whole different perspective on our current conversation.'

'I guess it does.'

'And what do you intend to do with that information, Jake?'

He'd never heard her address him by his first name before; it was unnerving. '*Nothing*. I just told you - I'm done.'

She laughed.

He held in his anger, and instead watched the two boys lamping the shuttlecock back and forth.

'You're not done, Jake.'

'We'll see about that—'

'Do you know who we work for?'

'I'm irrelevant. They'll forget about me soon enough.'

Madden laughed again. 'Do you really believe that? No one is irrelevant, Jake. *No one*. You are dealing with the most careful organisation that ever existed. There isn't a single *T* that isn't crossed, or a single *I* that isn't dotted.'

'I'll take my chances.'

'You'll fail, Jake. The best thing you could do, right now, is come to HQ and talk to me directly. We're on the same side.'

It was Jake's turn to laugh. 'No, we're not. And if Mark Topham can disappear, I can too.'

'Mark Topham is dead, Jake.'

'Prove it.'

'I don't have to. Isn't it obvious? No one can disappear. Not in today's world. He *must* be dead, or he'd have been found.'

'You'll be saying the same thing about me in a couple of weeks.'

'And you'll be dead too.'

'This is not the life I want for myself. Goodbye ma'am.'

'Jake—'

He hung up and switched his phone off in case she decided to call back.

The boys smashed the shuttlecock back and forth; they had found a steady rhythm now.

The front door of Alexander Antonovich's opened and Nina stepped out first. She turned to offer her arm to her frail father who promptly took it. She escorted him to the passenger side of his Boxster, opened the door and helped him in.

The smallest of the two boys missed the shuttlecock. It looped over the fence and into Alexander Antonovich's drive.

Nina climbed into the driver's side. The boy ran around the fence and into the drive for his shuttlecock. Fortunately, it'd landed in the shrubbery by the fence rather than behind the Boxster which Nina would be nonchalantly reversing out the drive any second—

The car exploded.

Jake shielded his eyes from the sudden glare. He felt his insides melting. 'No ... no ...'

The car was an inferno. Fire streaked out of every smashed window and licked the air hungrily. The young boy lay twisted in the shrubbery.

Jake threw himself from his car and started to run. Neighbours were pouring out onto their lawns. His ears were ringing, but he could make out some gasps and screams.

'GET AN AMBULANCE!' Jake shouted. He could barely hear his own voice through his stunned ears.

The heat coming off the twisted metal carcass was intense; it burned Jake's face and hands as he neared. He went in as close to the shrubbery as he could, fighting the pain all the way. He had no choice but to scoop the boy up without checking him; they were too close to the carnage to delay.

Running from the blaze with the boy clutched to his chest, his eyes streamed from the smoke, or was it from emotion? He wasn't sure.

Away from the heat, he fell to his knees in the centre of the road and shouted again. 'GET AN AMBULANCE.'

He looked down into the eyes of the broken boy in his arms. He was beyond repair.

Then the sky burst open and the rain came.

20

THEY'D MOVED INTO the lounge to enjoy post-breakfast coffee when Yorke pointed out of the window at a young woman running past his garden wall, braving the elements by holding a plastic bag over her hair.

'That's not going to cut it,' Yorke said.

There was a moment of laughter followed by the sharp silence of surprise when the young woman opted to turn down Yorke's drive.

'Is that who I think it is?' Yorke said. 'Pemberton?'

Willows was already on her feet. 'Yes, it bloody well is.'

'She's early.'

'No. She's here to see me,' Willows said.

'The more the merrier,' Patricia said. 'But she could have saved herself a drenching by just phoning you.'

Yorke looked up at Willows. 'Is everything alright?'

Willows smiled. 'Not really.' She looked between Patricia and Bryan, blushing.

'You're among friends,' Bryan said. Patricia nodded.

'We've gotten close recently ... we had a bit of a disagreement earlier. I told her I needed some space.'

'Would you like me to answer the door, darling?' Patricia said. 'I could tell her you've left.'

'Speaking of the door,' Bryan said, 'Have you actually heard the doorbell?'

'Probably on the blink again,' Yorke said. 'Although you'd expect her to be pounding the door down to get out of that weather.'

'She's probably thinking up excuses for being here,' Willows said. 'I'll go. This is my issue. Not yours.'

Patricia rubbed her back. 'Okay, honey. Offer's there though.'

'I'll be fine,' Willows said.

Willows exited the lounge by the door beside the sofa straight into the hallway. She closed the door behind her to keep the impending conversation as private as possible.

The front door was opposite the foot of the stairs. Knowing that Ewan and his girlfriend were upstairs, she glanced up to check they weren't looking over the balcony.

After appeasing her paranoia, she turned, took a deep breath and opened the door.

No one was there.

WHEELHOUSE FINISHED STACKING the new shelf before standing back and admiring his handywork.

Firth came and stood beside him. He ran his finger over the fifty red hardback spines and then looked at his fingertip.

'Clean?' Wheelhouse said.

'Not a speck.'

'Gets your approval then?'

'Of course, although I did prefer them when they

arrived covered in dust. There's something about turning the page of a classic and having to blow the build-up of dead skin particles off the page.'

'You bring romanticism to every situation.'

'Why thank you, sir.' Firth put his hand on Wheelhouse's shoulder. 'There's more where these came from too. The hospital library is clearing out another two shelves over the next month.'

'Wait until the clientele hear about this.'

'Yes, I do believe there is potential to grow our customer base from seven to eight—'

'*Ladies,* you're supposed to be working.'

Harris came down the centre of the aisle, he was dragging his baton across the spines of the books. He was not alone.

Harris was a short man, but the man beside him was shorter. In a suit and tie, he was far smarter though. His hair was neatly clipped, and his skin was tanned.

Wheelhouse suspected he was a lawyer.

His eyes moved back to Harris' baton which was bumping off each book's spine. He'd never seen the guard with a weapon before. In fact, he didn't think he'd ever seen a weapon in this prison. Subdued HMP Hancock wasn't known for its riots. He felt his stomach tighten, and tasted acid in his mouth.

He looked at Firth. His friend didn't look overly anxious, so he took this as some encouragement, but still, he'd be stupid to think that everything was alright here.

Harris and the lawyer stopped less than a metre from them.

'Hello again, Douglas,' the lawyer said. He had a deep, calming voice. He held out his hand, and Firth shook it.

Wheelhouse's stomach eased, and the acid slipped back

down his throat. Firth knew him, and the relationship seemed genial.

Harris smiled. 'Take a step back, Douglas.'

Firth didn't move.

Harris brought the baton to his chest and ran his hand up and down the shaft. 'Take ... a .... step ... back.'

'Fuck you,' Firth said.

'What's going on?' Wheelhouse said to Firth, suddenly tasting the acid in his stomach again.

'Douglas ... please do as he says,' the lawyer said.

Wheelhouse grabbed Firth's arm. 'Doug, what the hell is going on?'

His friend did not look at him. Instead, he took a step back, pulling free of Wheelhouse's grip.

'I've been wanting to do this for so long,' Harris said.

Wheelhouse continued to look at Firth, but his friend wouldn't meet his stare. From the corner of his eye, he saw Harris swinging the baton. His aging knee shattered, and he collapsed to the floor.

WILLOWS STEPPED out onto the covered porch and immediately recognised the dark eyes and the red mouth. *The Dancer*, Borya Turgenev, stood off to her left, about two metres away. With his left arm, he had Pemberton crushed against his chest in a headlock, while still managing to keep the umbrella above them both with his gloved left hand. He was a giant, and Pemberton looked tiny and frail in comparison. He could break her in two. Not that he needed to because, with his right hand, he had a pistol pinned to the side of her head.

Willows gasped, and then for fear of startling him and

his trigger finger, she quickly put her hand over her mouth. She knew such concerns were probably pointless. The monster looked unflappable.

Pemberton's eyes were wide. She seemed to be quivering, but it was hard to ascertain whether this was just a visual effect caused by the shimmering stream of rainwater that tore down from the umbrella's edge.

Borya stared at Willows. He seemed content to wait for her move. *But did she really have a move to make?* Without a weapon, Willows was as defenceless as her lover was. Like most people in this world, she'd be no physical match for this enormous Russian. But time was running out. If Borya didn't shoot her soon, the muscles wrapped around her neck would surely do the job anyway.

Think, Collette … for fuck's sake, think!

She considered darting back into the house to get to Yorke and call reinforcements, but she knew, deep down, that it'd mean certain death for Pemberton.

So, she did all she could. She held the palms of her hands out to show Borja she was unarmed, hoping that this would be enough to relax his trigger finger and the iron grip around her neck.

Surprisingly, it seemed to work. Borya slipped his arm away from Pemberton's neck and, keeping his umbrella upright, took a large step back, away from her.

Pemberton was already wet from her journey here, but without Borya's umbrella, the rain made quick work of her. Her hair was immediately plastered to her face, and she struggled to open her eyes fully.

Willows waved Pemberton towards her. 'Come.'

Pemberton brushed hair from her eyes and started forward.

Willows saw Borya raise his pistol. '*It's a trick! Get down! GET DOWN!*'

Pemberton jerked, her left arm lifted in the air and spasmed. She forced herself on.

'*GET DOWN, PEMBERTON!*'

She jolted a second time. Her upper body seemed to twist at an impossible angle to the lower part; unbelievably, she straightened out and resumed her gait.

To meet her, Willows dived from the covered porch into the rain. Pemberton thudded into her with such force that it was clear she'd taken another bullet.

Willows was immediately drenched. As both her arms were now around Pemberton, she was forced to snap her head back to flick the wet hair from her eyes.

Pemberton was heavy. She wouldn't stay upright without support. 'Please, Lorraine, hold on ...' She looked into the half-closed eyes and realised that it was almost over for her. 'Lorraine ...'

Her head lolled forward.

Willows looked up. Borya watched her with dark eyes. He still held his umbrella above his head. He had dropped the gun to his side.

She noticed that both of his hands were gloved, and he wore plastic blue overshoes.

He was here to kill them all.

Keeping hold of Pemberton, Willows edged backwards. Not only was she heavy, but the rain had made her slippery. She had to keep hold of her though. The thought of using her as a shield sickened her to the core, but she was out of options.

Borya saw her intention. He raised his pistol again. Although she couldn't see the gunfire, Willows felt it in

Pemberton's jolting body. She stumbled backwards, managing to keep upright.

Borya came quickly, firing at will. Willows was pummelled by Pemberton's convulsing body. She stepped under the covered porch; she was inches from the open front door, and could shortly make a dive for it ... Pemberton's head thrashed back and forth, bashing Willows' face ...

The air was smacked from her body and there was a crushing pain in her chest. Pemberton slipped from her grasp and fell flat on the floor.

She knew what she was going to see but looked anyway. Blood oozing from just under her collar bone. A bullet had made it through.

She looked up to see Borya barely a metre away, pointing the pistol at her.

'Fuck you,' she said.

DRENCHED, with a dead boy in his arms, Jake struggled to find the willpower to move, but he had no choice. Within minutes, emergency services would be here, and he would be standing at the centre of it all.

What would be his excuse for being there? What hope would there be for him avoiding arresting, never mind making it to St Malo on this evening's ferry?

Residents, holding umbrellas, were gathering. Some attempted to get nearer to the blazing car but quickly steered away when they felt the flesh-eating heat licking their faces. No-one was alive in that car, and no one else needed to die to confirm the obvious.

A scream pulled Jake back to awareness. He looked up

at a soaking woman. He laid the boy down, rose and stumbled back, allowing the distressed mother to fall onto her child.

'I'm sorry,' Jake said. 'I'm so very, very sorry.'

He turned to see a man running towards them. The boy's father, presumably. The other child was sitting in the driveway, still clutching his badminton racket, crying.

Jake backed away, across the street, and climbed into his open vehicle. No one seemed to notice. Panic was swelling with the numbers of people.

Now what? Jake thought, starting the engine. *I told them.* He punched the wheel. *No children.*

He started the car. He didn't bother wiping the rainwater away, he let it streak down his face.

Lacey had been right. *It's inside me. It took root and is growing like a cancer.*

With his wipers on full blast, he eased the car away from the curb, weaving around some people in the expanding crowd.

I'm no different from the rest of them. And like them, I don't deserve to live.

He found space on the road and drove to God knows where.

WHEELHOUSE WAS SITTING on the floor, moaning as he clutched his shattered kneecap.

Firth looked down at his suffering friend. Laughing, Harris pushed the baton into his hands.

Walter spoke slowly and deeply. 'Mr Firth. Quickly now. He's making too much noise.'

Firth gripped the baton. Wheelhouse looked up at him.

His eyes were wide, and there was spittle frothing at the corners of his mouth. 'Doug? What's happening? What does he mean?'

Walter stepped behind Wheelhouse and placed his hands on the injured man's shoulders. He stared at Firth with a ghost of a smile on his face. He raised a perfectly trimmed eyebrow. 'Answer his questions. He deserves that much.'

Firth glared at Walter, and then looked back at Wheelhouse. 'I'm sorry, Herb ... I really am. But I warned you. I told you that actions would have consequences.'

'I don't understand, Doug ...'

Walter tightened his grip on his shoulders, massaging him. 'I think he said he warned you, Mr Wheelhouse, or is it *the Reaper*, which do you prefer?'

'Don't you fucking call me that, *you ponce* ...' The spittle sprayed from Wheelhouse's mouth.

'Now, Mr Firth,' Walter removed his hands from Wheelhouse's shoulders. 'Now.'

Inevitability squeezed his eyes shut. There was no getting away from it. 'I'm sorry, Herb.' He opened his eyes and swung the baton.

Wheelhouse remained upright, but the blow silenced the moaning. His eyes remained fixed on Firth while blood ran into them from his forehead.

Don't look at me, please ... don't look at me.

'Again,' Walter said.

Firth swung. Wheelhouse's head snapped back. He hoped that his friend would slump to his side with his eyes closed. That this would be enough.

It wasn't.

Wheelhouse stared up at Firth with even more blood streaming down his face.

'You're not strong enough, old man,' Harris said. 'Better going for here.' He leaned over and touched the top of Wheelhouse's head. 'The crown.'

Wheelhouse was swaying but keeping himself upright. '*Doug ...*'

'*Again,*' Walter said.

Firth brought the baton down like a hammer.

Wheelhouse's head lolled forward.

Keep your head down, have mercy, don't look at me ...

'*Again.*'

Firth slammed the baton down.

'*Again.*'

This time his friend's skull gave way.

'Did you hear that?' Harris said. 'His head fucking popping?'

'*Again,*' Walter said.

Firth swung ... and swung.

In his head, he heard Walter's calls for 'again' over and over, but whether the man was *actually* chanting, he couldn't be sure.

Trapped in this loop, he closed his eyes. Again ... swing ... again ... swing ... again ... swing ...

Silence.

'Mr Firth?' Walter said.

Again ... swing ... swing ...

Firth felt a hand on his back.

'*Mr Firth?*'

Swing ... swing.

'*Mr Firth?*'

Firth opened his eyes. At some point, he'd fallen to his knees. He was still swinging but was now just hitting the floor. Wheelhouse was curled up. It was Harris who had his hand on his back. 'It's done ... Firth ... *it's done!*'

Firth threw the baton to one side. He was panting and sweat was running into his eyes.

Harris knelt beside Firth and looked at the pulpy mess on the floor. He looked at Firth, smiling. 'Fuck me, Firth. You've almost taken his head clean off.' He patted him on the back. 'Good job. Did you really like this man? I don't think I've ever seen someone enjoy themselves so—'

Firth clambered on top of Harris. He was exhausted, and had very little left in him, but he managed to strike the smarmy bastard, just once, in the face, before he was hoisted back by Walter.

21

'SHALL I JUST check that she's okay?' Bryan said.

Patricia raised her eyebrow. 'Would you want interrupting if you were having a deep and meaningful?'

Bryan smiled. 'If you met my wife, you would know that I'd welcome the interruption.'

'Actually, it's been a while ... maybe I'll just check they're okay?' Yorke said, nodding out the window at a world distorted by blackness and rain. 'Get them both in for a cup of tea. We can sit in stony silence if necessary. They've both had a tough time.' *Because of me.*

Patricia stood up. 'I'll go. Bryan you make the tea.'

'Shall I just keep my lazy arse on the sofa then?' Yorke said.

Patricia smiled again. 'I have a whole list of words to describe you, Mike, but lazy is not one of them. More's the pity.'

Patricia headed to the door. She'd just grabbed the handle when Bryan stood to block her off. 'Let me go. Believe it or not, I'm good in these sensitive situations.' He smiled.

'Unless it involves your wife?' Patricia said.

Bryan smiled. 'Spot on.'

'I'm not sure, maybe it's best—'

'Trust me, Pat. Sensitivity is my strong point.'

Patricia stepped back and sighed. 'My world is so full of sensitive men.'

Bryan went through the door into the hallway.

'Guess I'll make the tea then,' Patricia said, heading out the other door to the kitchen.

Yorke thought he'd used the quiet moment to check up on his work emails. Although it wasn't expected when absent due to illness, work plagued his thoughts most of the time. Living in ignorance would be both painful and impossible. He reached over for his mobile on the living room table, wincing when his ribs clearly didn't appreciate the manoeuvre—

'*SIR!*' It was Bryan, and it was clearly a cry for help.

Trying to ignore the damage in his body, Yorke rose quickly to his feet. Patricia was already back at the kitchen door. He held his palm out to stop her, and then moved at pace to the other door.

He stepped out into the hallway, fighting the stiffness in his body.

The front door was ajar, but not enough so he could see outside. There was no sign of Bryan, Willows or Pemberton. A familiar coldness flared up at the bottom of his neck.

He put his hand there, but he was wearing a T-shirt, and so the option to button-up and protect wasn't available.

You're being paranoid, Mike. No one is dead.

Despite his efforts to reassure himself, he felt the cold sensation spreading over his entire body. An even stranger feeling when your heart was beating full blast and your body temperature should be boiling over.

'Mike?'

Patricia. Behind him. He glanced back over his shoulder. 'Go to the children.'

Patricia nodded, slipped past him and disappeared up the stairs.

Yorke continued to the front door. He had no idea what he was going to see out there. The only thing he was certain of now was the ice in his veins. He knew he should go back for a weapon of some kind, just in case, but it seemed like a lifetime now since Bryan had called out for help. He opened the front door.

Willows lay on the covered porch, sheltered from the rain, but still drenched. There was a pool of blood around her. She had her eyes closed but was breathing. Bryan was on his knees beside her, holding her hand tightly between both of his.

Yorke stepped forward. His hand flew to his mouth when he saw the prone figure of Pemberton off to his left. She lay on her front. The back of her jacket was ripped and frayed. *Bullets*. Blood flowed away from her with the rushing rainwater.

Bryan looked up at Yorke. '*It's bad.*'

'*I'll get an ambulance—*'

'Run.' It was Willows. Her eyes were open now, and blood snaked down her cheek from the corner of her mouth. 'Run. *He's here.*'

Yorke saw Borya Turgenev, armed with an umbrella and a pistol, emerge from around the side of his house.

Feeling again Borya's debilitating first punch from several nights ago, and seeing that devastating flash, Yorke suddenly felt unsteady on his feet. Momentarily, he lost control, and had to steady himself against the door frame. He felt the burn of the boxcutter as it tore open his cheek—

'*Run!*' Willows cried again.

'I'm not leaving you,' Bryan said.

Yorke took a deep breath. Borya was coming, and he had his pistol raised. Ignoring the cries of his damaged ribcage, Yorke leaned over and grabbed Willows' arm. 'Bryan, help me get her in, *quickly!*'

Bryan gritted his teeth and pushed. Yorke pulled. Willows moaned in pain. The blood and rainwater helped her slide. She started to cross the threshold into the house.

'*Harder!*' Yorke said.

Sliding on the blood himself, Bryan managed to thrust as hard as he could. For a second, Yorke thought the liaison officer would slip to his side, leaving him vulnerable to the approaching Russian.

But he didn't, and Willows made it inside the house.

Yorke fell to his backside, and hurried backwards, dragging her further inside.

But Bryan was taking too long to follow them in. He obviously didn't fancy his chances of getting to his feet in all the slippery fluid, so he was still on his knees, practically crawling in.

'Bryan, *hurry up!*'

His head snapped sideways. There was a cloud of blood. His eyes rolled up as if he was somehow looking for the bullet that had entered his skull. He slumped face down.

Yorke scurried forward like a crab and closed the front door with his feet. It caught against the top of Bryan's head and remained ajar.

Borja wouldn't be more than a metre away, moving slowly, and confidently. There was no rush when you were this good at killing.

Yorke lay on his back, pulled his legs back and jabbed at

the door with his feet. He could feel the resistance of Bryan's head, and the door wasn't catching.

'Sorry Bryan.' Yorke yanked his feet back again and thrust with all his might. He felt Bryan's body give way, and the door clunked shut.

He flipped around to slide the deadbolt at the bottom of the door, and then jumped to his feet to slam home the one at the top. He also lifted the handle to engage the locking mechanism, turned the key, pulled it loose, and thrust it into his pocket.

Suspecting what was coming next, Yorke hit the deck again.

Thud. A hole appeared midway up the front door.

Despite knowing there was little danger of Willows getting up with her injuries, he hissed a warning anyway. '*Stay down!*'

Thud-thud.

Two more holes appeared in the oak door. One bullet hit the bannister post and splinters of wood sprayed into the air.

Yorke looked at Willows. Unbelievably, she managed to roll onto her front, moaning as she did so. She didn't look in the best shape. He was in awe of her determination, but now was not the time to tell her so.

'*Crawl forwards,*' he hissed.

She managed to lift herself slightly on her hands, lope about half-a-metre, before folding back to the ground. He heard her gasping for air. *Yes, she was struggling, but she was doing it.*

There hadn't been a bullet for a short time. He expected Borya would be backing away to circle the house and look for another way in. A deathly silence crept into the house. Now was the time for his move—

Patricia stood at the top of the stairs looking down. 'Are you okay?'

Adrenaline whipped through him. He lifted himself up on his left arm and waved her away with his right hand. 'Get out through the window—'

Thud.

Yorke dropped back down. He felt splinters pepper the back of his head.

When he looked back up, he was relieved to see Patricia was gone. If she hadn't realised there was an almighty problem here, she certainly would do now. His family's best option was to go out of the window of the back bedroom, drop down into the back garden, and make a run for it through the back gate. He hoped to God they were currently taking it.

He also hoped to God that she was already calling for back-up.

He tasted bile. *Would help get here in time for him and Willows?*

This was *The Dancer*. In the house, his movements would be swift. He would come and go in the blink of an eye, and no one would live.

He crawled up alongside Willows and whispered in her ear. 'Where're you hurt?'

'Below the collar bone.'

'Straight ahead, there's a small door underneath the stairs. You'll be able to reach up to the handle. Crawl inside and wait. Help is coming.'

She looked tearful. 'Pemberton.'

'Not now ... later.'

There was so much blood; it was smeared all over his parquet floor from the front door to where she'd crawled to.

Yorke pulled off the unbuttoned shirt he had over his T-shirt and handed it to her.

'It'll hurt but apply pressure with this. You could do with keeping hold of your blood.'

'Thanks.' A tear rolled down her face. 'Your family?'

'I'm hoping they've run. I need to check. Go and hide.' Yorke felt dreadful that he couldn't take her with him. She'd never get up the stairs in this state, and they'd be sitting ducks on the journey.

Yorke looked back at front door. Light glowed in through the bullet holes, except one. But then the dark hole brightened, and another blackened. Borya was moving his eye between them. Watching them.

Yorke could hear Willows shuffling towards sanctuary; he could also hear his own quick, ragged breaths. He needed to get to the top of the stairs. To check his family had fled before Borya found his way in.

The holes stopped flickering. Hoping that Borya had given up shooting at them to go off and locate another entry point, Yorke started to rise to his feet.

Crash.

The front door shook. *Shit! He wasn't going to find another way in. Why scour the house and sneak in, when you were strong enough to just take out the front door?*

Crash. Crack.

The wood splintered.

As Yorke rose to his feet, he felt every muscle and bone in his body burn.

He took a quick glance back to the crawling Willows, prayed that she made it, and then made for the stairs.

Crash ... crash ...

He almost hit the stairs face-first rather than feet-first,

but managed to right himself at the last second, and get a solid grip on the first step.

Crash … crack …

He was half-way up the stairs when the mouldy daylight entered the house. He didn't need to look back to know that the front door was no longer his only barricade to death.

Expecting the bullet, and the blackness at any second, he forced himself onwards—

Thwap.

If the bullet had hit him, he didn't feel it.

Thwap … thud.

He's still here … God knows how. He reached the top step with such force that he collapsed to his knees.

Thwap … thud.

He felt plaster sprinkling the top of his neck.

Gritting his teeth against the pain which seemed to start at his throbbing cheek and radiate through his entire being, Yorke rolled clear of the top of the stairs.

Thwap.

Flat on his back, Yorke watched as another bullet hole opened in the wall at the top of the stairs.

A wasted shot. Was the Russian toying with him?

Yorke looked right. Patricia was peering around the bathroom door.

Shit. She shouldn't still be in the house! She crawled out of the bathroom, and towards him, dragging something along with her.

'The kids?' Yorke whispered.

She gestured at the room behind Yorke. 'Through the window. They're safe. I watched them go.'

Thank God. 'You phoned the police?'

She nodded.

'Why are you still here?'

'I'm not leaving without you—'

Yorke heard a creak on the fourth step. He knew it was the fourth step, because they'd be planning to have it looked at for months. *The Dancer* may have been light on his feet, despite his great size, but that creak was unavoidable.

'*He's coming,*' Yorke said. His heart thrashed so hard against his battered ribs that his breathing became laboured. 'Get back in the bathroom .... and lock the door.'

Patricia reached out with a hollow metal bar. She'd unscrewed it from the towel rack.

He closed his hand around it and was surprised he was able to grip it with the sweat running from his palms. He smiled at her. 'We'll get through this. I love you. Now ... on three, the bathroom. One ... two ... *three.*'

Yorke rose to his feet as Patricia scurried back to the bathroom. He saw the hairless head of Borya, which was almost level with the balcony Yorke stood on. The giant swerved his pistol. His intention was clear, he was going to shoot Yorke though the railings of the bannister. Yorke had other ideas. He swung the metal bar like a golf club. There was the clank of metal on metal. Borya's gun sailed off down the stairs. Yorke pulled back and swung a second time.

Borya caught the bar mid-flight and snatched it from Yorke. *The Dancer's* reflexes were impressive, but Yorke wanted to showcase his own. He leaned forward and threw a punch with his left hand before Borya could swing the bar back at him.

With his other hand, Borya caught Yorke's fist, applied pressure to make him cry out and then yanked him over the balcony. Despite the rush of air, and the terror of heading face first towards the steps, Yorke found the inspiration to throw out his right arm. He managed to drive it in the side of the beast's thick neck. On any other occasion, Borya wouldn't have flinched, but perched on a step, gripping a heavy man by the hand, it would be difficult for even this, the most dextrous and strong human being Yorke had ever encountered, to remain upright.

He didn't.

As they were tumbling together down the stairs, Yorke was repeatedly bashed by Borya's incredible weight. He was going to come off a lot worse ...

When everything went still, Yorke struggled to open his eyes. He felt crushed.

He thought of Patricia in the bathroom, willing her to leave the same way the children had, but knowing that she wouldn't.

I'm not leaving you.

Yorke managed to open his eyes and saw that all good fortune was abandoning him.

Borya was kneeling on top of him, smiling. 'Here we are again.'

'Someone will kill you one day,' Yorke said.

'It won't be you.' He watched Borya raise his fist. It felt horribly familiar. Yorke wasn't sure which came first. The punch or the darkness.

But they both came.

FIRTH WAS HOISTED OFF HARRIS.

For such a diminutive man, Walter Divall was certainly strong. Firth himself was no small man, but he was lifted and sat to one side like a naughty toddler. He leaned back against a shelf, gasping for air.

'I'm a big believer in *calm* and *control*, Mr Firth, and

that was one of the reasons I liked you, and gave you this chance, but right now you don't seem to be displaying any of these good qualities.' Walter stooped to bring his eyes level with the aging prisoner. 'So, *calm* down, and show some *control.*'

Firth nodded and then flinched when he caught a glimpse of Wheelhouse. Harris had not been exaggerating. He'd practically decapitated him.

His best friend.

Behind the body, Harris was dusting himself off following Firth's ambush. He was no longer smiling. The man's shame was at least one positive in this horrendous shitstorm.

'And because I like you,' Walter continued, 'I will offer you some reassurance. But I only offer this once; after that, if I don't see the composure that I saw in you yesterday when I visited, then I will have to rethink our arrangement.'

Harris cracked his knuckles. He was obviously happy to forgo any future paydays just to see Walter come good on his threat.

'You didn't have a choice. *Never* had a choice. As soon as Mr Wheelhouse made that decision to move against Mr Young, he was finished. *You* knew that, but you allowed him to continue anyway. I asked you yesterday why you allowed this. Do you remember the answer you gave me?'

Firth nodded. 'Because he had the right to that decision.'

'And you would have made the same decision, would you not?'

'Yes.'

'Precisely. So now we arrive at *exactly* the same conclusion that we did yesterday. This is inevitability. When Mr Turgenev ended Ms Edward's life, he started a chain of events that couldn't be broken. Mr Wheelhouse's death was the natural end. Yet, there was still one variable, wasn't there? Do you remember what that was?'

Firth nodded. 'How it finished for me.'

'Yes. And how does it finish for you?'

Firth didn't like the sound of this. This was a done deal, wasn't it? He narrowed his eyes. 'With me working for you ... I've done what you asked.'

'Yes, you've certainly fulfilled your end of the agreement. You've proven yourself to me.' He looked behind him at the body. 'Above and beyond, but we still have a problem ...'

Firth started to rise to his feet. His breathing had levelled out, and he did feel more in *control*. But *calmer*? He didn't think he'd ever felt *less* calm. 'This sounds like I've been lied to.'

'You've not been lied to. Anything but. You're a man of talent and you've just demonstrated this. There has never been any reason for you to come to a sad end because of someone else's mistakes but, alas, this *one* problem still remains.'

Firth saw Harris smiling now. The problem was obviously bad. He was tempted to charge over there and pummel that arrogant prick's head in too. If he had to die after that, so be it. At least he'd be going down with some satisfaction.

'The problem is my employer, Mr Young. Truth be told, he's my ex-employer but, of course, he doesn't know this yet.'

'I don't understand ...' Firth shook his head. He was genuinely confused. 'We're all standing here because of what happened to Buddy's granddaughter, Vanessa. If you don't work for him anymore then why are we all here?'

'Pretence. My *real* boss, *our* boss, Mr Firth, is of far greater significance than Mr Young. In fact, he is the most significant man that you'll ever meet, if you're lucky enough to ever meet him. He no longer sees the use for Mr Young and, having worked for him for many years, I tend to agree. He is obsessive, impulsive, archaic and, above all else, at death's door. The problem is the stubborn man is holding on.'

'And preventing you from ascending to the throne in Southampton?'

Walter smirked. 'Everything that Southampton is right now is down to me, and me alone.'

'I don't disagree,' Firth said, 'But surely vanity and pride are traits best avoided in someone as professional as you?'

'I avoid them when necessary and enjoy them when I have time.'

'So, just kill Buddy then? It's been a long time coming ...'

'And that there's the problem, Mr Firth. Not only are his properties part of Southampton, but he himself is also part of it.'

'Every king dies.'

'True, but it's the manner of a king's death that is significant. My boss wants to seamlessly assimilate everything the Young family have built. If people suspect Mr Young has been forcibly removed by a bigger enterprise, we'll struggle to gain the trust of everyone still involved.'

'Will people care that much? He's been a mean and vicious bastard for as long as anyone can remember.'

'I don't know, but my employer is more professional than you could ever imagine, and he will not take the risk.'

'Okay, so where do I fit in?'

'I need you to kill Mr Young.'

Firth smiled. 'You're joking. How the hell do you expect me to do that? Have you noticed where I am?'

'As I've said, you've proven yourself. Parole will be granted.'

'You have that much power?'

Walter nodded. 'Yes.'

'Why does me killing him make any difference? Why don't you just do it?'

'Because if you kill him it's not a business killing, it's a revenge killing. It won't be attached to me, or my employer.'

'Revenge for what exactly?'

Walter took a deep breath.

'*For what?*'

'This is where you need that calm and that control, Mr Firth. In fact, you'll need it more than you've ever needed it before. You cannot stop what is about to happen, and for you to die now would be unfortunate, and unnecessary.'

'*Revenge for what?*' Firth shook as he spoke because he already suspected the answer.

And it was unfathomable.

Walter widened his eyes. 'Revenge for the murder of your daughter, Patricia.'

Firth closed his eyes, and saw the blood on the road, saw himself snatching his hand away from his daughter, and saw him putting his fist through the glass.

It was happening all over again.

BORYA STARED down at the prone figure of the detective. For the second time in three days, he was the victor. He remained unbeaten.

The policeman was alive. Not for long. Borya had

retrieved his pistol which had been knocked from his hand moments before and had it pointed down at the meddling detective's head.

He sighed. He preferred his quarry conscious. He took satisfaction from the look in their eyes before he closed them down, but he'd no more time for games.

He took a deep breath and began to tighten his trigger finger—

His shoulder burned, the shot was thrown off and the bullet fractured the floor beside the target's head.

Borya spun and saw the detective's wife at the bottom of the stairs wielding a bloody pair of scissors. *My clever dancer.*

She slammed the scissors into his chest.

With his free hand, he gripped the weapon and her hand simultaneously. She squealed. He then delivered a blow with the pistol. Her head snapped back, and her body quickly followed. She landed on the stairs.

He glanced down at the scissors and, in a rare moment of ungainliness, moved backwards and stumbled over the detective.

While on the floor, he examined the sharp instrument in his chest. Not too deep. It'd had to travel through a lot of muscle; internally, he should be fine. He pulled them out. There was a short spurt of blood, but nothing significant.

He watched her fleeing up the stairs.

You move well, my agile dancer, but now it's my turn …

He picked up the pistol, aimed at her and fired.

Click.

Empty. And he'd used his spare clip already. He slipped the pistol in his inside jacket pocket, took the scissors and rose to his feet. He bolted for the stairs. Normally, he liked to take his time, but so far, he'd only executed two people in a reasonably busy house, and neither of them had been a target. They'd been collateral damage. Or bonuses. Depending on how you looked at it. The police, probably armed, wouldn't be long away. Time was not a luxury he could enjoy right now. He took three steps at a time. She'd only just made it to the top, when he was just over half-way. He felt the warmth of her ankle on his palm, but it slipped free and his hand closed on empty air. *My nimble dancer.* She continued to impress him.

She rounded the bannister post at the top of the stairs. He thrust his arm through the railings. She vaulted his hand. *My spritely dancer.*

At the top of the stairs, he turned around the bannister post in time to watch her disappear into a room. He got there as the door slammed. He listened to the click of a lock being engaged.

He wanted to tell her that this was useless, but why bother telling her, when he could just show her? He stepped backwards, so he was against the bannister, and then charged shoulder first.

Crash.

He could feel her pushing back on the door with everything she had. It wouldn't be enough.

Crash.

There was splintering sound. *Are you ready, my elegant dancer?*

Crash.

The door frame broke rendering the lock and handle useless. She remained behind the door though, so it still wasn't open.

He was still holding the scissors that had been buried in his body twice. He barely acknowledged the pain. They felt like nettle stings. With his other hand, he pushed the door. It started to open.

You move well, but strength is a totally different animal.

She accepted her disadvantage, let go of the door and darted backwards. She was going for the small bathroom window. There was no point. No one could get through a window that size. Not unless you were in pieces.

He grabbed her by the shoulder and spun her around. She spat in his face and kicked him in the shin. Another nettle-sting. He grabbed her by the hair and threw her in the bathtub.

'Where is your family?'

She rolled onto her back in the bathtub. 'They've gone, dickhead. Out of the window.'

Borya took a deep breath. He'd taken too long to get into the house. Their guests – the extra police officers had been his undoing. He'd not anticipated them. They'd delayed him outside. Saved the life of this woman's family. Never mind. Here was the true target. This is who they desperately wanted dead.

He leaned over and grabbed his graceful dancer by the throat, just like he'd done to Joan Madden the previous evening.

Except this time, he wouldn't be stopping.

She clawed at his hand as her face began to glow.

FIRTH ROARED. Let the warden come. Let *them* all come. He'd tell them everything. It was Patricia's only chance now.

Walter and Harris didn't try to restrain him. They just

watched him as if he were a caged animal. A fascinating wild beast that posed no threat to them.

'*This was never discussed! Call it off – I'll do anything!*'

'It's too late, Mr Firth. It was due to happen ten minutes ago. Mr Young paid for efficiency. He opted for Mr Turgenev.'

'*The Dancer? The prick who killed Herb's niece?*'

Walter nodded. 'So, you see, there's nothing that can be done. It's over. I'm sorry for your loss. And now, Mr Firth, it's time to take the only option available—'

Firth spun and tore the books off the shelves. The classics that Wheelhouse had just stacked came crashing down. He grabbed the unit at either side and shook, letting loose the agony bubbling deep inside himself. The remaining books clattered to the floor. He shoved the unit, which smashed down onto the next one along. The next one wobbled, threatening a domino effect, but then stabilised, holding up the first unit at a tilt.

'Finished?' Walter said.

Firth spun back. 'I'll tell you when I've *fucking* finished.'

'Okay.' He looked at his watch. 'You have three minutes, and then my deal is off the table.'

'What? After you made me murder my best friend, and had my daughter killed?'

'Let's be clear on one thing. Mr Young had your daughter killed for arranging the murder of his granddaughter. I had nothing to do with that decision.'

'Yes, but you knew, you arranged it, you could have stopped it, or warned me.'

Walter nodded again. 'Indeed, I could've done any of these things.' He sighed. 'But I didn't.' He looked at his watch. 'Two minutes.'

'That was a fast minute,' Firth said.

'I'm in a rush.'

Firth felt the tears in his eyes. He wiped them away with the back of his hand.

'If it's any consolation, I don't have any family either,' Walter said.

'Why would that be of any consolation?'

'Kindred spirits, perhaps? Maybe I could be the person you'd like to work for?'

Harris leaned over. 'The Cleaner will be here any minute, Mr Divall.' He gestured down at Wheelhouse's body. 'He only works in silence, and alone—'

Walter silenced Harris with a raised finger. 'You can explain any delays to The Cleaner yourself, Mr Harris. I have given Mr Firth one last chance, and three minutes, to consider his options. You will afford him the respect he deserves in this final minute.'

Firth wiped tears away again. 'Another fast minute.'

'I believe you've made your decision already.'

Firth paced back and forth in front of the fallen shelf. 'And what decision is that?'

Walter smiled. 'Thirty seconds.'

'Fuck you.'

'Twenty seconds.'

'Where the fuck did you get your watch anyway?'

'Ten seconds.'

'*I'm going to tear Buddy Young's heart out.*'

Walter clapped and looked at Harris. 'And that, my friend, is why you always give someone thinking time.' He looked back at Firth. 'Let the old world of chaos and irrationality crumble ... welcome to a time of order and control. Welcome to the future.'

Firth took a deep breath and closed his eyes.

His TARGET's eyes bulged and watered. Borya could have crushed her neck with relative ease. But she was special, this one. She'd been elegant, graceful and offered a challenge. Every competitor was entitled to *feel* their defeat. Every second of it. So, he starved her of oxygen, but didn't grind her spinal column to dust.

When he'd done this before, to his own mother, she'd pleaded with her eyes. She'd tried to influence the outcome by begging for his mercy. That was part of the reason he'd cut her eyes out when he'd finished with her.

There was no pleading here. Neither was there acceptance. He was looking for hate, but not really seeing that either. As his target's face began to take on a bluish tinge, he saw the real emotion in her eyes.

Sympathy.

Was he mistaken? He stared harder into those bloodshot eyes.

No, there it was. Pity.

He rarely felt anger, but he felt it now. He forced it back. Controlling his fragmented emotions, when they seldom appeared, was one of his specialities.

He lied with a smile instead. His lie, like everything else about him, was perfect.

'Don't pity me,' Borya said, 'I've lived through things you couldn't even imagine. I'm more full than you could ever believe. It's you who shall die empty.'

He felt something hitting his back. Hard. It stunned him. Which was surprising. He wasn't often fazed by the blows of others.

'Get the *fuck* off her.'

He felt a second blow. It was hard enough to wind him and force him to release his target.

He was dealing with someone of significant strength here. He smiled as he turned.

Although the man wielding the same pathetic bar that the detective had only minutes ago wasn't as big as Borya, he was bigger than any adversary he was yet to face. His back stung from where the bar had struck him twice. He enjoyed the challenge. He licked his lips in anticipation.

Borya tore the bar from his challenger's hand and threw it to the side and over the bannister.

Game on.

JAKE DIDN'T QUITE UNDERSTAND how he'd arrived at this moment. Everything had moved so quickly. It started with a panic attack behind the wheel of his car. A quick journey into sheer hell as he relived again and again the explosion, and a little boy's death.

He'd considered many options at that point. Confront Madden at HQ, turn himself in, go gung-ho and lay siege to the gangsters who had initiated this sorry affair, or just continue his retreat to St Malo in France.

None of these options had appealed, and he went instead for the default option. Michael Yorke. Confidante. Best friend. The closest thing to a brother he'd ever had. It was time to come clean about everything, open himself up to the greatest detective, and his greatest friend. Time to put himself at his mercy.

It hadn't quite worked out that way.

Instead, he'd encountered the bloodbath on Yorke's

doorstep. Pemberton had been riddled with bullets. No pulse. Bryan had taken a head wound. No pulse.

Then, Jake had gone in through the front door without a weapon. Caution wouldn't stop him. Not when some of the people he loved the most were inside that house. Inside, Yorke was lying on the floor. Feeling his heart in his mouth, he fell to his knees beside his motionless friend ...

A pulse.

No time to cry with relief though. There was blood all over the floor, but no visible bullet holes on his friend. The blood trailed off alongside the stairs. *Who else had paid the ultimate price in this house?*

Before he had chance to follow the trail, he was distracted by muffled voices from the next floor. After swooping for a metal bar, which was light and hollow, but in the least, *something*, he took the stairs as quietly as he could.

The fourth stair creaked loudly. He paused for a deep breath, praying he'd not blown his cover, desperate not to see a gunman leaning over ...

Nothing.

He continued his journey and, when he saw between the bannister railings a massive man hunched over a bath in the bathroom, he felt adrenaline surge through his body. *He was holding someone down in the bath.* He took the last steps quickly.

As he rounded the bannister post, he could hear the man talking. He had a heavy Russian accent. *Borya Turgenev?* 'Don't pity me, I've lived through things you couldn't even imagine.'

Jake charged down the corridor.

'I'm more full than you could ever believe.'

Jake turned into the bathroom, bar ready.

'It's you who shall die empty.'

Jake hit the large bastard's back. Hard. He drew back for a second blow, fearing that the first had not even fazed him. 'Get the *fuck* off her.'

He swung again. *Clunk.* The vibrating bar stung his hands. He worried that it was doing him more harm than Borya.

Borya turned, smiling.

At six foot seven, Jake rarely had to look up to people. He suddenly felt very disorientated. To be told someone was this big was one thing, to behold someone *this* big was another thing entirely.

Borya licked his lips, tore the hollow bar from his hand and threw it over his head like a matchstick.

Jake had taken a lot of punches in his time, the big guy usually did, but never anything like this. Borya caught the side of his head, and the world seemed to disappear momentarily.

Recovering his senses, he swooped backwards out the door, and Borya's next strike splintered the doorframe. Jake was no stranger to an old-fashioned street-fight. Misspent teenage years impressing others with his size and strength could come in handy now. To fool Borya into thinking he'd lost his footing, he let his legs buckle, before delivering a crushing uppercut.

Borya's head snapped backwards.

Jake sprang upwards, using the momentum to deliver a devastating left hook.

Jake felt a rush of adrenaline. He had Borya on the ropes. Stooping now, Jake darted in with some body blows. He kept his forehead against the giant's solid chest, so he was able to deliver some rapid, fierce jabs.

Jake thought of the little boy lying on the road. He felt the rage burn. He ached for release.

Jab-jab-jab.

Jake moved backwards, both to catch his breath and survey the damage done. Borya didn't sway, but he stood motionless with his head lowered, and his monstrous arms hanging at his side.

Fucking knuckle-dragger—

From the corner of his eye, Jake saw Patricia rising from the bath. He held out the palm of his hand in her direction. '*Stay there!*'

I need this time with him.

He closed his palm into a fist. 'Come on, fucker.'

Jake slammed his fist hard into the side of Borya's head. His knuckles burned, but it was the most pleasurable pain he'd ever felt. Borya stumbled backwards.

'That's for Pemberton.'

To give the knuckles on his right hand a break, he used his weaker left hand. With the adrenaline coursing through his veins, it was no less crushing.

'That one is for Bryan.'

Borya stumbled further back. He heard the police sirens.

No, Jake thought. *No. This is mine.* 'Lift up your head, fucker.'

He didn't.

'Fine. This is going to be a long list, prick. Buckle up. This one is for Janice.' He darted in and swung.

His fist came to a sudden halt. It felt as if his hand had sunk into glue. How he wished that was the truth. Borya had caught his fist in a giant paw.

Borya raised his head; his face was puffy, the corner of one eye bled and his lips were ruptured. He smiled and showed blood-stained teeth. 'You lead well.'

The pain in Jake's hand was excruciating. He forced

back the scream. And he forced himself to stay standing, despite his shaking legs. He would not let the Russian send him to his knees.

'Now it's my turn,' Borya said. Keeping tight hold of his fist, he placed the palm of his hand against the side of Jake's head.

'No—' Jake felt the sudden thrust, felt the explosion in the side of his skull where it collided with the wall, and his vision disintegrated into an incomprehensible mess.

'Get off him, you fucker.'

No ... Patricia .... Jake forced his vision into a whole, but he was still reeling too much to speak. He saw Patricia shove Borya, but the killer was an immovable object. Borya released Jake's fist, and delivered a backhand. She flew back across the bathroom, struck the toilet and crumpled to the floor.

Patricia ...

Jake reached out for Borya, but he was completely disorientated now. His hand flailed uselessly in the air. The sirens of the emergency services grew louder in the background. *Hope ...*

He saw Borya leaning over and clutch the front of his jacket. He bashed his fists off the assassin's arms, but they were like columns of stone.

Then he was being swung into the wooden banister.

Crash.

He couldn't believe that, merely seconds ago, he'd been winning this battle.

Crash.

Dream on, Jake, you've been played.

Crash. Crack.

Was that the bannister cracking, or his bones?

Crash. Crack.

His entire body burned. He squeezed his eyes closed. He didn't bother trying to see. That ship had long sailed.

Crash. Crack

Then he was falling, and when he opened his eyes, in a brief moment of clarity, he saw Borya smiling down at him from the balcony.

Jake lay mid-way down the stairs among the debris of the bannister.

The sirens were seconds away. *Surely now, Borya would make a run for it?*

Borya smiled and reached his foot through the hole in the bannister. He was coming down to Jake.

BORYA HEARD the sirens clear enough, but to leave before tearing his opponent's throat out would be the true crime here.

His vision clouded from the blood running into it. This policeman had been a worthy opponent. The best he'd ever faced. He deserved to *feel* the defeat.

He stepped through the broken bannister. His legs were long enough that he'd be able to get within two steps of his opponent. It would then be a simple matter to lean over and offer him a brief nod of approval for his attempt on his life before ending him.

Even now, his enemy was rustling in the debris for a weapon. *Such a worthy adversary*. He nodded. The policeman selected a sharp, broken post from the bannister. *A good choice,* Borya thought, *if you'd any strength left to use it.*

Borya took a deep breath and felt the moment.

Everything was quiet. Still.

Peace.

His foot found the step.

Perfectly—

The shove in his back wasn't hard. Didn't need to be. He was standing in an awkward position with one foot on the balcony and the other on the step.

He thought he'd hit the detective's wife hard enough to put her down for the foreseeable. *My elegant dancer.*

As he fell through the air, chest first, he felt no fear. A short fall like this would not harm him. The worst it'd do would crush the life out of his opponent, relieving him of the final pleasure of killing him with his bare hands.

A cold pain gripped Borya's stomach, and then spread its claws up into his chest.

He rolled free of his opponent and slid down the stairs on his back.

Something was sucking the energy out of him.

At the bottom of the stairs, flat on his back, he looked down at his body.

The broken post was pointing out of his stomach, away from him, at a diagonal angle.

He reached down to it. It had entered the top of his abdomen and had most certainly slid under his rib cage. The fact that he was still breathing might indicate that it hadn't yet made it to his heart.

He reached down to it, but another pair of hands arrived there too.

He looked up into the face of his opponent.

'For Janice, remember?'

Borya smiled.

He felt the shove of the post, and the coldness bit deep into his chest.

Beaten.

At first, Yorke was confused.

His whole body ached, and his vision was like a broken autofocus on a camera, erratically moving back and forth between distortion and clarity.

It was the face, close to his own, that eventually stilled the chaos. 'Jake ...'

'Ambulance is about to arrive. Your family is safe. *All of them.*'

'Borya?'

'Dead.'

'Did you ...?'

Jake nodded.

The relief was as overpowering as the disorientation. He closed his eyes, wondered if it was best just to rest, when a memory bit into him and tugged. His eyes bolted open. 'Collette?'

'Patricia is with her. She'll be fine.'

'Thanks Jake.'

He heard Jake apologising, but before he could hear the reason why, he'd already closed his eyes and returned to the warm blackness.

EPILOGUE

SUPERINTENDENT JOAN MADDEN pushed Jake deep into the hospital grounds.

The wheelchair squeaked under Jake's weight.

Madden found a nice flowerbed. The skies had cleared under the colossal rainfall two days ago. It had not been this blue for a while.

'Now, we can finally start Spring,' Madden said, parking Jake alongside a wooden bench, and then taking a seat.

'You look worse than me,' Jake said. 'Should we get you a wheelchair too?'

Madden's facial expression didn't change. He wasn't surprised. Her face was that bruised it would be sheer agony to attempt it.

'Borya Turgenev was evil. I suspect you enjoyed staking the vampire's heart.'

'Yes, immensely,' Jake said with a smirk. 'Just look at me.'

He paused to stare at the array of flowers, threatening to burst into life. He sighed. He could cover it up with sarcasm, but the truth was he'd enjoyed that final moment when he drove that post deeper into the bastard's chest.

'Well, make no mistakes, there'll be others. Others just as evil ... if not more so. Which is why you can't run. You limited your choices when you opted in, I'm afraid. If you don't want to listen to this from a boss, listen to it from a friend. Jake.'

Jake snorted. 'You're no one's friend, ma'am.'

'I hope, for your sake, Jake, that you're wrong. You need me ... and, believe it or not, I need you.'

'Symbiotic?' Jake said with another smirk.

Madden nodded. 'That is where we are.'

'I held a dead boy in my arms.'

'I can't imagine—'

'Do you have any children?'

'You know I don't.'

'A dead boy, ma'am. *A dead child.*'

'The world is merciless, Jake. I made my choices when I was younger. Far younger than you are right now. I'd regret them if regret had an outcome. It doesn't. I advise you to start thinking the same way. There're not many certainties left in the life we've chosen, Jake, but there're some. If you run, you die.'

Jake took a deep breath.

'You can still do good.'

Jake raised his eyebrows. '*What?*'

'You saved three lives, Jake. *You.*'

Jake reflected. 'I got lucky. It has nothing to do with what I've become.'

'*Nonsense.* It has everything to do with it. How many people would have taken on Borya, let alone killed him?'

Jake sighed. She had a point. He looked at his hands.

They looked no different. And he *felt* no different being a killer. But he was.

Nothing was more certain now.

She handed him an envelope.

'Another Russian target?'

Madden nodded. 'Another agent who fled years ago.'

'Will he die horrifically too?'

'More discreetly this time. *Quietly*. They've gotten access to Porton Down.'

'The chemical factory? It's military run!'

Madden shrugged. 'The next time will be silent. You have my word.'

'And do I have your word on the children?' Jake said, staring at a bumblebee settling onto a sunflower.

'Yes, Jake, you have my word.'

ALL OF US TOGETHER. *Happy. Before Geoff Stirling and his Ford Capri.*

Patricia froze. She placed her father's letter down beside her on the sofa. She just needed a moment to collect herself.

Geoff Stirling and his Ford Capri.

Despite her early age, it was an event in her memory that still burned. A moment like that seared any possibility of true contentment.

She picked up the letter and continued.

You remember when you held my hand? The day I watched your brother die?

She looked down at her shaking hand clutching the letter. 'Of course, Dad. I needed you and you pulled your hand away.'

I didn't want to contaminate you.

Patricia felt the first tear run down her face. 'It's not an excuse, Dad, it's just not an excuse.'

Patricia, when all is said and done, and one day it will be, probably sooner than you realise, I want you to remember me for the man I was before that day, and not the man I became.

'There isn't a day that goes past Dad when I don't long for who you were before.'

Those priceless moments. Drops of rain. Frozen forever. Don't let them melt. Hold them close.

She cried as quietly as she could. Her family were in the kitchen, and she didn't want to spoil their time together. Their priceless moments.

Her father signed off with the suggestion that this may be his last letter to her.

She'd had this letter for two months now, ever since he was released on parole. She'd not received another one since.

She didn't even know if he was alive or dead.

Crying quietly, she tried, but failed, to identify how she truly felt about this.

Firth had met Buddy Young twice before.

The only thing he recognised about the fading kingpin were his eyes.

Back in the day, when things were good, both he and Wheelhouse used to joke about these eyes. *The Devil's eyes.* They could root around in your body, find the truth, and then incinerate your soul if need be.

Firth wondered if these eyes could see the truth in him right now. The reason he was here.

He certainly wouldn't recognise him. They were both old men now and had been much younger when they'd last met. To Buddy, he would be nothing more than an aging nurse, here to check up on the machinery that kept him functioning.

But, for Buddy Young, sensing someone's intent was the name of the game, not facial recognition.

Firth made a show of checking the wires around the back of the machine while Buddy's fingers tapped a keyboard.

'Get on with it.' The robotic voice cackled.

The perfect gentleman, as always.

Walter Divall stood near. Firth could feel his eyes burning into him. The purpose for this vicious stare, Firth reasoned, was to maintain the pretence. Walter was Buddy's most trusted man, so he needed to continue the façade that the old man was well and truly protected.

The other reason would be to warn Firth that he must finish what they'd started.

Borya had not succeeded with Patricia. Firth's relief had been indescribable. Despite what he'd done to his best friend earlier, he'd felt a moment of happiness.

Yet, they were still here. The fact that Buddy had *tried* to have Patricia killed was still motive enough. Firth still had his task to complete. And it was no small task either. Killing a crime lord.

Firth looked at Walter and saw the frustration in his eyes. He wanted him to get on with it. He must have been desperate to nod his command, but to do so, would be dangerous for him.

'Almost done, sir,' Firth said to Buddy.

There was another bodyguard standing just behind Firth. He, like all the rest, looked deadly serious.

Firth moved around Buddy's bed and looked up at the bodyguard. 'Young man, could I trouble you for a moment? Could you hold Mr Young forward while I fluff his pillows?'

The bodyguard nodded his reply and came over to the bed. He put one hand on the old gangster's chest, another on his back and tilted him forward. Already withered and frail, Buddy looked even more like a baby in those large hands.

The bodyguard was so preoccupied with handling his dangerous boss carefully, he failed to notice Firth take out his silenced gun from inside his gown. When he did finally acknowledge the gun, it was too late, and Firth blew his brains out.

Buddy slumped back. The bodyguard hit the floor. The humming machines were covered in blood and started to crackle.

'Don't worry, Buddy, you won't be needing them,' Firth said, pulling off Buddy's oxygen mask.

Buddy's stony eyes widened. Firth wondered if this was the only time the cold-hearted bastard had ever felt truly vulnerable.

Buddy's trembling hand moved over the keyboard. 'Walter?' The robotic voice hissed out through a speaker covered with the contents of the bodyguard's head.

'It's over, sir,' Walter said from behind Firth.

Firth allowed Buddy to type one more message. 'Who are you?'

Firth smiled. 'Does it matter? I could be anyone. I have come on behalf of anyone you have caused misery in your malignant life. But I dedicate this one to my good friend, Herb. Goodbye Buddy.'

He shot Buddy in the neck, so he could gag and splutter on his own blood for a time before dying.

He then turned to Walter, who had moved closer.

'In the shoulder, Mr Firth, as we planned.'

Firth raised the gun. 'Yes, Mr Divall. In the shoulder as we planned.'

He fired.

WHEN EX-DETECTIVE EMMA GARDNER had Yorke over for lunch, he was stunned, and not just by the quality of the tuna niçoise salad. 'I know mentioning a woman's weight is a no-no ... but that's some serious weight loss.'

'A stone and a half in two months.'

'Is that how long it's been since I last saw you?'

'It's three months actually. It was just after Christmas.'

'Shit ... sorry.'

'It's no use apologising to me. It's your goddaughter you should be apologising too. She was starting to take a real shine to you.'

'Takes after her mother then,' Yorke said with a smile.

'Hmm ... yes, there were times when working with you meant a lot, Mike, but my life has been a whole lot better without you in it as much.'

Yorke put his fork down and laughed. 'I really don't know how to take that.'

Gardner shrugged. 'Two ways. You are an impressive man in that you led us down paths no one else could. The problem is that I never felt comfortable with what we found down them.'

'I always tried to support you, and everyone else, as much as was possible.'

'I know, Mike, but in the heart of darkness, there is only so much support you can actually give. Sometimes the darkness just takes back. Anyway, Mike, the job wasn't for me anymore ... and I'm positive it still isn't.'

'We're re-treading familiar ground here, Emma, let's rewind. The weight loss?'

'Well, I had to get into this.' She stood and twirled to show her black security officer outfit.

'Yes, but how did you lose it?'

She smiled and pointed at his salad. 'It's in front of you.'

'Yes, delicious, but you can't sustain life on it ...'

'Well, you can sustain *less* life which is kind of the point.'

Yorke smiled. 'But is it a life worth living? Anyway, I bet you still guzzle back those Tic tacs.'

She rolled her eyes. 'They're one calorie each, Mike!'

'Yes, but if you multiply that by a thousand a day, then I guess you're still racking up the count.'

They both laughed.

Towards the end of their reunion, which had been pleasant, and a timely reminder to Yorke that he had many good people in his life, he probed her further on her new life. 'What's it like working a nine to five. Really?'

'Consistent, safe, calm.'

Yorke nodded. 'Sounds appealing.'

'Sometimes boring,' Gardner said and smiled. 'But my life isn't just about me anymore. I can handle being a little bored if it means I can be home for Anabelle, safe and calm.'

'I understand. Those things that happened to you. Terrence Lock ... the stabbing ... there isn't a day that goes by that I don't think—'

'Stop it, Mike, none of those things were your fault.'

'I was in charge. I led you down those paths, remember?'

'You didn't lead me anywhere I didn't want to go.'

Yorke nodded. 'I think I've had enough too now, Emma. I think I've become like you—'

'*Bollocks!*'

'I did it again. Collette almost died.'

'Collette followed you for the same reason I followed you. It's in her blood, like it's in mine, and it's in yours. I've made a choice, a sacrifice for my family, but you're not going to make the same choice.'

'Oh,' Yorke said, raising an eyebrow, 'And why not?'

'Because Michael Yorke, you are the best, and despite the fact that you always lead your team into that black heart, you always come back out the other side and, when you do, the world is a better and safer place for it.'

LATER, after Yorke had left, Gardner prepared the evening meal. Now she was a security guard, it was essential she worked one weekend day, so she'd managed to secure Thursday as a regular day off. After chopping the vegetables, she heaped them into the slow cooker.

Her phone rang. She looked at the number. It was Robert Brislane. Her private investigator.

'Hi Robert,' Gardner said. 'If it's about this month's expenses, I'll get onto it later—'

'*Emma.*' His voice shook.

'Robert, is everything okay?'

'I'm in Leeds ... *I found him.*'

Gardner steadied herself against the work surface. 'Sorry, Robert, did you—'

'I found Mark.'

Topham.

After the phone call ended, she went to the bathroom and stared into the mirror.

Ex-detective Emma Gardner didn't need Michael Yorke to travel into the heart of darkness, she was more than capable of doing that all by herself.

YOUR FREE DCI YORKE QUICK READ

To receive your FREE and EXCLUSIVE DCI Michael Yorke quick read, *A Lesson in Crime*, scan the QR code.

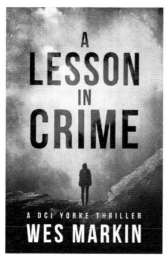

Scan the QR to
READ NOW!

CONTINUE YORKE'S STORY IN CHRISTMAS WITH THE CONDUIT

DCI Michael Yorke and Emma Gardner are still plagued by guilt over their failure to catch the murderous psychiatrist known as the Conduit, and the loss of their former colleague to insanity.

On Christmas Day, following a brutal massacre in Leeds, Yorke and Gardner find themselves once again chasing the ruthless puppeteer, believing that they have the initiative.

But as the two investigators draw closer to the Conduit, they quickly discover that they were never truly in control, and completely vulnerable to what comes next.

A rising tide of psychological warfare.

And the horrendous truth behind the fate of their former colleague.

Scan the QR to READ NOW!

START THE JAKE PETTMAN SERIES TODAY WITH THE KILLING PIT

A broken ex-detective. A corrupt chief of police. A merciless drug lord.

And a missing child.

Running from a world which wants him dead, ex-detective Sergeant Jake Pettman journeys to the isolated town of Blue Falls, Maine, home of his infamous murderous ancestors.

But Jake struggles to hide from who he is, and when a child disappears, he finds himself drawn into an investigation that shares no parallels to anything he has ever seen before.

Held back by a chief of police plagued and tormented by his own secrets, Jake fights for the truth. All the way to the door of Jotham MacLeoid. An insidious megalomaniac who feeds his victims to a Killing Pit.

And the terrifying secrets that lie within.

Scan the QR to READ NOW!

Still grieving from the tragic death of her colleague, DCI Emma Gardner continues to blame herself and is struggling to focus. So, when she is seconded to the wilds of Yorkshire, Emma hopes she'll be able to get her mind back on the job, doing what she does best - putting killers behind bars.

But when she is immediately thrown into another violent murder, Emma has no time to rest. Desperate to get answers and find the killer, Emma needs all the help she can. But her new partner, DI Paul Riddick, has demons and issues of his own.

And when this new murder reveals links to an old case Riddick was involved with, Emma fears that history might be about to repeat itself...

Don't miss the brand-new gripping crime series by bestselling British crime author Wes Markin!

What people are saying about Wes Markin…

'Cracking start to an exciting new series. Twist and turns, thrills and kills. I loved it.'

Bestselling author **Ross Greenwood**

'Markin stuns with his latest offering… Mind-bendingly dark and deep, you know it's not for the faint hearted from page one. Intricate plotting, devious twists and excellent characterisation take this tale to a whole new level. Any serious crime fan will love it!'

Bestselling author **Owen Mullen**

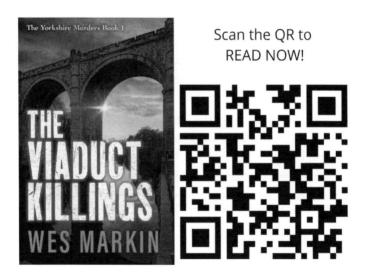

Scan the QR to READ NOW!

ACKNOWLEDGMENTS

Before I get to the individual mentions, I just wanted to pause a moment and tell you how genuine these thankyous are. Due to your continued support, I am now fortunate enough to be able to divide my time between both writing and teaching, my two greatest passions. When I began writing about DCI Yorke and his adventures (or rather, ordeals), it was as a hobby. To make this part of my career really is a dream come true, so please believe me when I tell you how grateful I am.

Firstly, my family, Jo, Janet, Peter, Douglas, Ian and Eileen for supporting me during the many moments I disappear into my own world. Not forgetting the comedy duo, Hugo and Beatrice, who make sure my mornings are early.

Thanks, as always, to Jake, who helped me start this adventure, and helps me keep the pace. Huge appreciation again to Cherie Foxley, who continues to work magic with colour on the front covers. Thank you to Aubrey Parsons who continues to practise his West-Country accent on Audible.

Thank you to Jay Arscott, Kath Middleton, Jo Fletcher, Karen Ashman and Jenny Cook for getting their teeth into those earlier drafts. Thank you to all my Beta Readers who took the time to help put Yorke on track – Keith, Carly,

Cathy, Donna, Yvonne, Holly and Alex. Thank you to the bloggers who remain behind me – Shell, Susan, Dee, Caroline and Jason.

I hope you enjoyed Yorke's latest dance, and I hope you all join me and Yorke at Christmas when an old foe returns to spoil his festivities ...

STAY IN TOUCH

To keep up to date with new publications, tours, and promotions, or if you would like the opportunity to view pre-release novels, please contact me:

Website: www.wesmarkinauthor.com

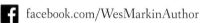 facebook.com/WesMarkinAuthor

instagram.com/wesmarkinauthor

twitter.com/markinwes

amazon.com/Wes-Markin/e/B07MJP4FXP

REVIEW

If you enjoyed reading **Dance with the Reaper**, please take a few moments to leave a review on Amazon, Goodreads or BookBub.

Printed in Great Britain
by Amazon

32297547R00173